SUDDENLY
A
MURDER

SUDDENLY
A
MURDER

LAUREN MUÑOZ

HOT
KEY
BOOKS

First published in Great Britain in 2023 by
HOT KEY BOOKS
4th Floor, Victoria House, Bloomsbury Square
London WC1B 4DA
Owned by Bonnier Books
Sveavägen 56, Stockholm, Sweden
bonnierbooks.co.uk/HotKeyBooks

A CIP catalogue record for this book is available from the British Library.

ISBN: 978-1-4714-1423-7
Also available as an ebook and in audio

2

Typeset by Eileen Savage
Printed and bound in Great Britain by Clays Ltd, Elcograf S.p.A.

Hot Key Books is an imprint of Bonnier Books UK
bonnierbooks.co.uk

For Rixie

PROLOGUE

◈

The knife burns cold in my trembling hand.

I lock Blaine's door with a soft click so no one can follow me into his bedroom. The others are busy getting dressed for cocktail hour, but it would be unforgivable to take any risks now that I've come this far.

The antique shower plumbing whistles and bangs as loudly as the rusty boiler in Marian Academy's basement. Even so, I hold my breath as I creep toward the bathroom. I hide behind the cracked door and peer through the gap. Blaine is standing in the canary-yellow tub, a sheer shower curtain drawn around him, his head and chest barely visible through the swirling steam. The vintage wool bathing suit he'd worn to the beach is in a heap on the mosaic tile.

Each bathroom in Ashwood Manor has been meticulously preserved, and Blaine's is decorated with golden art deco mirrors.

I look at the gold blade of my knife.

They match.

If I were the kind of person who believed in signs, I might think the universe approved of the crime I was about to commit.

But I'm not that kind of person. That person would have spilled their secret to Kassidy weeks ago, hoping the universe would repay their good deed. I'm more of a don't-fuck-with-my-future-if-you-don't-want-to-meet-my-knife kind of girl. At least I want to be. My shaking hands tell a different story.

Blaine's eyes are closed, his head tipped up to the water as it cascades down with the delicate patter typical of old houses, a quiet contrast to the thumping plumbing in the walls. It's a soothing sound, like spring rain, and I briefly flash back to the day before prom, when Blaine danced in my apartment building's courtyard during a storm while my family and I laughed from the sidewalk.

He looked vulnerable and young then, just as he does now, standing naked and defenseless in the shower. I've been waiting for this moment. Obsessing over the details in my head for days. But as Blaine runs his hands through his ginger hair, slowly pushing a stream of water off his forehead and down his freckled back, a burning guilt spreads through my arms, almost making me drop the knife.

Blaine doesn't deserve this—not really. But neither do I. And I can't sit back and let him destroy my life.

I grip the knife tighter and step through the doorway.

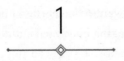

1

A glass shatters. Someone screams below deck as the *Blood Rose* hits a patch of choppy sea. Kassidy ignores the noise and keeps talking. "Chloe may be super smart or whatever, but even Dean Halliwell nodded off during her valedictorian speech, and he's the most boring person I've ever met."

Kassidy doesn't seem to care that Chloe could climb the stairs at any minute and hear us talking about her. I adjust my seasickness wristbands and take a steadying breath. The loungers on Kassidy's yacht are plush, but I can't get comfortable. Maybe I'm uneasy because of the rocking waves. Or maybe because I know what's buried inside the backpack resting at my feet. Either way, I keep hoping to see Sparrow Island on the horizon.

It's a cool day for June, but the sun shines brightly above the dark water. Seabirds coo and caw overhead, occasionally dipping their bills into the cold sea for fish. Kassidy has pulled her graduation dress above her thighs so her long legs don't get tan lines. If she were less wealthy, her skin would be ivory from living through winters in Maine. But when you spend your school breaks in places like Seychelles, you end up with a honey glow year-round. I don't need to travel to look tan—my last name's Morales.

The telltale pop of a cork reaches our ears.

"They've opened the champagne!" says Kassidy, jumping off her lounger and running to the metal railing. The *Blood Rose* has tiered levels, so from each deck you can see the edge of the next. "Bring me a glass, babe," she calls to Blaine, leaning so far over the railing her head disappears from view. "And one for Izzy too."

I reluctantly slide off my lounger and join Kassidy. Blaine is no longer wearing his cap and gown, or even his shirt. His broad back is bent over a table where he's filling glasses from a magnum bottle of something that probably costs more than I've made at Pegasus Books all semester.

The smile he flashes at Kassidy falters when he sees me. I hurry away from the railing and return to my lounger.

Kassidy pops back up and ties her glossy blond waves into a messy bun. "Anyway," she says obliviously, "I think students should vote for the valedictorian. Otherwise, you end up with drippy geniuses reciting tortured clichés about their hopes and dreams."

I nod, only half listening. *Stupid Blaine,* I think. *He's going to ruin everything if he keeps looking at me with those guilty eyes.*

I respond a few beats too late. "At least you didn't have to watch the other parents treat your mom like a pariah at the reception."

Kassidy rolls her eyes sympathetically. "Like, how dare she give their precious babies tough math grades." She flops onto her lounger and smiles. "My parents couldn't believe she gave me a C in calculus. They thought I'd get the best-friend grade boost."

A stiff breeze lifts my curls into the air. The cool spray of water and the buzzing hum of the engine make me feel a million miles away from my family's apartment in Harker.

I wonder what my mom and sister are doing at home without

me. It's hard to believe only three hours ago we were stuck in a stuffy auditorium listening to Chloe's address: *Though our time at Marian Academy is over, the lessons we've learned here will never fade. As you go into the world and confront its challenges, always remember the school motto: Fortis Fortuna adiuvat!*

Fortune favors the bold.

I think about my backpack again. I felt like a budding sociopath when I packed the knife, wrapping it carefully in a pair of jeans and shoving it to the bottom of my bag. Now I wonder: Will I have the strength to be bold?

Footsteps sound on the stairs. "Your butler has arrived," says a sarcastic voice. I turn to see Fergus balancing three glasses of champagne between his fingers. He's dressed in what he calls Euro chic but his critics at school have deemed Euro geek: snug olive slacks, brown loafers, and a button-down shirt with sleeves rolled up to his pasty elbows. His dirty-blond hair is styled with a swirl, like a 1950s greaser, and his small brown eyes are scrunched with his ever-present smirk.

He nods at Kassidy, who flashes him a tight-lipped smile. Fergus is Blaine's best friend from childhood, and he and Kassidy have been locked in a battle for Blaine's attention for years.

"Blaine's too busy to serve you," says Fergus. "He's begging Ellison for details about next year's Olympic rowing trials."

Kassidy and I each grab a glass. Fergus clinks his against ours. "To never setting foot in that prison full of backstabbing prima donnas again," he says.

"Gus, what are you talking about?" I laugh. "You loved Marian."

"And you're the *top* backstabbing prima donna," adds Kassidy. "Prince of the theater."

Fergus's face turns sour. "I suppose you think Blaine is the king."

"More like a god." Kassidy playfully fans her face as she says it, but I know she's not joking. It was Blaine's performance in *Almost, Maine* that brought them together. When she saw him onstage our freshman year, she fell into his blue-eyed smolder and never returned.

"Gross," says Fergus. "The only reason so many students came to our productions is that Ms. Kepler invited all the Hollywood B-listers her dad works with. And if I *occasionally* dropped hints about gossip to include in the school paper," he says, turning to me, "that doesn't make me a backstabber."

I laugh again. "Never change, Gus."

My friends had bloomed like flowers at Marian Academy; I'd been more like an invasive weed. Kassidy cried when we walked out of Marian for the last time, but I felt only relief. Relief that I'd never again have to wave at my mom in the halls, or see the other students smirk at my faded uniform, or stand by Kassidy's side looking like a short, curvy letter S next to her perfect T. Relief and hope that things might be different in college.

"I want in on the toast," says a deep voice from the staircase.

A few seconds later, Ellison finishes the climb from middeck and slams his glass against ours with such enthusiasm I can't believe they don't break.

"Sorry." He laughs. "Guess I don't know my own strength."

Fergus rolls his eyes so hard they look like boiled eggs.

Ellison props himself against the railing, which comes only to the top of his thighs. The stubble usually dotting his dark-brown skin has been shaved for the graduation ceremony.

Every inch of him looks like a future Olympic athlete. I'm half-surprised he didn't row himself to Sparrow Island.

Ellison yells to the deck below. "Blaine, you coming?"

Heavy footsteps bang up the stairs. Blaine barrels into sight, still holding the magnum of champagne. The black T-shirt he's put on over his dark jeans contrasts sharply with the big white sneakers hugging his feet. Blaine's always decked out in the kind of hypercasual look popular among the rich kids who can spend thousands of dollars on the latest kicks.

"Looks like I found the party," he says. He puts down the champagne and connects his phone to a little Bluetooth speaker he pulls out of his back pocket. When he presses PLAY, loud rap drowns out the jet-engine sound of the wind. Blaine's giant watch sparkles in the sun as he grabs the champagne again and chugs straight from the bottle.

"Your girlfriend is worshipping your godlike feats of acting," says Fergus, his voice dripping with derision. "Might want to take advantage of her good mood."

Blaine squeezes himself onto Kassidy's lounger and pulls her into his lap with his free hand. "My girl's always in a good mood," he says, earning a laugh from the rest of us, who have all been on the receiving end of one of Kassidy's sulks. She leans against him, and they indulge in the kind of kiss most of us would hide behind closed doors.

"I wondered where you went," says the lilting voice of Marian's valedictorian.

Kassidy and Blaine tense and break apart. Ellison stands a little straighter and runs a smoothing palm over his short brown hair.

Chloe Li mounts the final stair and walks hesitantly over to the group with a still-full glass of champagne. Like Blaine, she's dressed casually: high-waisted jeans, a sporty crop top, and red trainers. She recently chopped her straight black hair to her chin, and some evil stylist cut her bangs too short, like a sadistic child might do to a Bratz doll. It's not a good look.

Kassidy scowls at Chloe, then rolls off Blaine and walks to the other side of the deck. Blaine sets down the champagne bottle and follows her with a barely audible groan. Chloe frowns at them, not used to their fireworks.

Ellison breaks the awkward silence. "Loved the gradua-tion issue of the school paper," he says to me, smiling warmly. "Especially the retrospective you did on old Calloway."

"Kassidy helped me on that one," I say. "Dr. Calloway used to work as a model in New York. She loves Kassidy's fashion column."

"I can't believe she's taught at Marian for fifty years," adds Chloe, clearly relieved to have something to say. "It's weird to think I might never have met any of you if she hadn't pushed the administration to let girls apply."

Ellison holds his glass out to her. "That would be a loss for all of us," he says.

Chloe flushes pink as she clinks his glass. I turn away to hide my grin. Although it's been a while since Ellison set off butter-flies in my stomach, I remember how pleasant the sensation is. It's a good thing Nestor couldn't come on the trip; he wouldn't like watching Chloe get swept up in a new flirtation so soon after dumping her.

Fergus, who's been watching Ellison and Chloe with stormy eyes, interrupts their conversation. "Where's Marlowe?" he asks.

"Inside, on one of the couches," says Chloe. "He told me he'd rather finish his book than get slapped by the wind."

"Typical," mutters Fergus. "He probably gets seasick and doesn't want to admit it."

"Or maybe he's not used to being on a yacht this small," jokes Ellison.

Kassidy and Blaine return arm in arm a few minutes later, smiling happily. Whatever she was pissed about, she's over it. That's one of the best things about Kassidy: She doesn't hold a grudge.

Just as I start to debate joining Marlowe, Kassidy squeals and begins to dance on her tiptoes. "There's Sparrow Island!" she says, pointing at a fast-approaching rock covered with wild grasses and thick pine groves. It looks like someone dropped a crescent of forest into the middle of the ocean. "You can't see Ashwood Manor because it's on the other side of the hill."

"I told you I should have sent my Jag over on the ferry," grumbles Blaine. "You packed like ten suitcases. We'll never be able to lug them up that hill."

"Relax," says Kassidy. "We have drivers waiting for us." I can tell she's trying not to look too pleased with herself, which makes me suspicious. She'd told me about the surprise graduation trip to Ashwood Manor only a few days before. And she hadn't said anything about cars.

After what feels like another queasy hour but is really only ten minutes, the yacht pulls into port. Crewmen jump off the boat and use lines to maneuver us close to a long dock surrounded by bright-green ferns. Once we're tied up, they attach a ladder to the side so we can climb off without falling. A crew member tries to shoo away the gulls scavenging crumbs on the dock, but they scurry around him like he's part of the scenery.

I grab my backpack and strap it on firmly. It's no mystery why the nerves rolling through my stomach won't settle: It's how I always feel when I'm about to talk to Marlowe.

Before I can not-so-secretly rush to meet him as we disembark, Kassidy grabs my arm and holds me back while the others clamber down the stairs to collect their bags. She's bouncing on her feet as if she might dive overboard.

For a minute, I forget about Marlowe. "I've seen this look," I say. "You have another surprise."

She smiles. "You know me too well."

"Please tell me it's not strippers again."

She laughs so loudly the gulls screech with displeasure and launch themselves into the sky. "Not strippers," she assures me. Then her face turns serious. "My surprise involves everyone, but I want you to know that everything I did, I did for the two of us." She drags me toward the staircase. "I can't wait to see your face. This is going to be the best week ever."

2

KASSIDY'S HOUSE
Three Days Ago

Kassidy and Izzy sat in their usual spot: the teal leather recliners in the front row of Kassidy's home theater. The room was tucked in the corner of the east wing, so Kassidy's parents couldn't hear the piercing music of the old movies Kassidy and Izzy screened every Wednesday after school.

This evening, Kassidy couldn't sit still. Every few minutes, she jumped up, ball gown trailing behind her, and twirled like a ballerina.

Izzy mindlessly stuffed buttered popcorn into her mouth. No matter how hard she tried to focus, her thoughts were far away from the movie. It wasn't until Kassidy hopped up for the fifth time that Izzy finally noticed her.

"Did you pop a pill or something?" asked Izzy as Kassidy almost fell over from spinning so fast. *The Secret of the Ruby Dagger* played on in the background. "You're not allowed to be bored during our favorite movie."

Kassidy stopped whirling. "I have two words for you, Izzy."

Izzy waited, distracted by Marla Nevercross, the silent-screen siren famous for her wide-eyed pout and her obsession with cheetahs. Izzy and Kassidy were at the part of the movie where she catches her husband seducing Cara Ashwood in the rose garden. "Well?" asked Izzy. "What are they?"

"I want you to guess," said Kassidy, tucking her hair behind her ears.

"You want me to guess two words out of the whole English language?"

"It's about your graduation surprise."

Izzy groaned. "Please tell me it's not something that will get us arrested. Or killed."

"Get a grip," said Kassidy. "When have I ever planned anything dangerous?"

"How about two years ago when we built a canoe by watching YouTube videos and nearly capsized in the river?" said Izzy. "Or last summer, when we stole your dad's motorcycles and rode them up to that folk festival in Canada?"

Kassidy laughed. "The people at those biker bars were super nice."

"I can't believe they didn't check our IDs."

"And you spent all that time making them in Photoshop." Kassidy paused. "This plan is different. It's . . . sophisticated."

"Sophisticated how?"

"It involves an island."

Izzy's mind scrolled through the possibilities. "Let me guess," she said. "Diving with sharks? Hang gliding off bluffs into the ocean?" She swept a piece of popcorn off the recliner. "Maybe we should skip the hard part and go straight to drowning ourselves."

Kassidy sighed louder than the music in the movie. "I'll give you a hint if you promise to keep an open mind."

"Fine," said Izzy. "But I will *not* be doing anything that involves sharks."

"You won't regret this," called Kassidy as she darted out of the theater. Izzy could hear the tread of her bare feet on the creaking staircase that led to the staff kitchen.

Izzy slid off the leather recliner and paced around the home theater while Marla Nevercross slapped her screen husband across the face. The room was dark and cool, and Izzy shivered in the delicate flapper dress she'd borrowed from Mrs. Logan's warehouse-sized closet.

Ever since Kassidy's mom had discovered, midspeech at the Marian Academy holiday ball, that one of her priceless Vionnet dresses had butter stains on the hem, she'd banned Kassidy and Izzy from wearing any of her vintage pieces. Kassidy grudgingly wore replicas in the months that followed, but she insisted that their last after-school screening deserved the best her mom's closet had to offer.

Kassidy shuffled back into the room balancing two tumblers clinking with ice. Her wavy hair fell into her face, giving her the tousled, bohemian look dozens of girls at school had tried to copy without success. She handed Izzy one of the drinks.

"Here's your clue," she said. "They're virgin. I know your mom would freak if you came home toasted on a school night."

Izzy took a sip, then another. She was used to drinking the fancy alcohol the Logans stocked in their cabinets. When Kassidy's parents went out of town, her parties never involved kegs or red Solo cups; she was strictly an upscale-drinks-in-a-real-glass kind of girl.

"Any guesses?" asked Kassidy.

Izzy wasn't in the mood for guessing games. She should have lied and told Kassidy she was too sick to come over. If Kassidy knew the secret Izzy was keeping from her, she wouldn't have wanted her there anyway.

"I give up," said Izzy.

Kassidy frowned. "You clearly woke up on the wrong side of the bed, so I'll give you another hint. Well, not a hint. More like a gift."

Izzy rubbed her temples. "A cocktail with real alcohol?"

Kassidy laughed. "No, but it is something sweet. I invited Marlowe to Ashwood Manor."

For the first time all evening, Kassidy had Izzy's full attention. "Marlowe?" asked Izzy. "Wait . . . *That* Ashwood Manor?" She pointed to the screen, where Marla Nevercross stood sobbing over her husband's body, which was sprawled across a flagstone terrace on the grounds of Theodore Ashwood's estate.

"I wasn't planning to tell you yet, but you know I can't stand moping."

"I thought you said the museum doesn't open until fall," said Izzy.

Kassidy smiled. "My parents have donated enough money to the restoration to ask for a special favor."

Izzy clapped her hands to her face. "We get to be the first ones to tour the house?"

"Not tour. Stay. For a week."

"A *week* at Ashwood Manor," repeated Izzy in a daze. Then she remembered the other part of Kassidy's surprise. "With Marlowe? I told you I was over him."

"And I'm your best friend, so I knew you were lying."

She was right. Izzy had tried so hard to ignore her crush on Marlowe. But it hadn't worked. Every time she saw him, it felt like the world narrowed until they were in a bubble universe no one else could enter.

"He has a girlfriend," said Izzy.

Kassidy rolled her eyes. "He told you that months ago," she said. "Plus, she lives in Rome. No way they last."

"You don't even like Marlowe," said Izzy. "Won't a week with just the three of us be awkward?"

"God, yes," said Kassidy with a shiver. "Which is why I also invited Blaine, Chloe, Fergus, and Ellison. I asked Nestor, but his parents are whisking him away to Monaco after graduation to see his grandparents. The owner agreed to rent the house exclusively, so it'll just be the seven of us and some staff. Your mom said she can take care of Caye while you're gone."

Excitement broke through Izzy's malaise. A whole week on the island where her favorite movie of all time was filmed. And not only that. A whole week unsupervised with Marlowe.

So far, her relationship with Marlowe didn't add up to much. Nods in the hallways at Marian. A few awkward conversations at Pegasus Books. But that hadn't stopped her from daydreaming about eating lunch with him in the courtyard or kissing him in the stockroom.

That last fantasy played on repeat during duller work shifts.

"What does a cocktail have to do with Ashwood Manor?" asked Izzy, remembering the clue.

Kassidy's shrug was casual when she answered. Too casual. "Theodore Ashwood built the house in the 1920s, and that's when French 75s were popular." Izzy opened her mouth to press her for whatever she still wasn't saying, but Kassidy cut her off. "Shush, we'll miss the last scene."

They watched the silent actors mime their final, tearful good-bye. As the shock of Kassidy's surprise wore off, a tiny glimmer of hope sparkled in Izzy's thoughts: Blaine was coming to Ashwood Manor too.

In an estate that big and on an island that remote, it wouldn't be hard to find a way to isolate him from the others. It might finally be the perfect opportunity. She would just have to be ready.

After the movie ended, Izzy followed Kassidy back to her bedroom, where they changed into normal clothes. "I can't believe you're bailing on Paris," said Izzy, flopping onto a bubblegum-pink pouf. Spending time in Kassidy's room was like being trapped in a child's dollhouse. Pastels and lacy ruffles and cutesy stuffed animals reached into every corner. "Ashwood Manor is amazing, but it's not the Louvre."

Kassidy stared out her picture windows at the sun setting behind the hills. She was the kind of beautiful that made art students want to paint her, and in the dying light she looked like a Thayer angel. "This might be the last time we're all together," she said. "Everything's going to change when we go to college."

"You and I will always be best friends, Kass."

Kassidy shot Izzy a crooked smile. "I know. But Blaine will be a thousand miles away. And everyone keeps telling me long-distance relationships are doomed to—"

Screaming interrupted Kassidy's train of thought, and stomping rattled the fan. Izzy looked at the ceiling in alarm. "Since when do your parents yell at each other?"

"It's nothing," said Kassidy. "Just drama at my dad's work."

She hurried away from the windows. "I'll ask Miguel to get the Bentley."

KASSIDY'S DRIVER DROPPED Izzy off at her apartment building on the outskirts of town. It was a three-story brick complex with uneven sidewalks and burglar bars over the windows. Izzy's mom sat at a round table in their cramped kitchen, grading exams.

"¿Tienes tarea?" she asked.

Izzy shook her head and responded in English. "There are two days of class left. You're the only teacher still assigning seniors work."

"There are no breaks in the real world."

Izzy grabbed an orange soda from the fridge. "My friends will never have to face the real world."

Her mom blew out air like a bull. "Money doesn't protect you from everything," she said, splashing red X's across the papers.

Her mom had taught at Marian Academy since Izzy's freshman year of high school. She heard the whispers about how she was hired only because she was Latina, but criticisms rolled off her like water off wax paper. Izzy sometimes thought the other teachers envied her mom's youth. She'd fallen pregnant with Izzy in high school and hadn't gotten her degree until after Caye was born. Izzy stared at her long curly hair and smooth skin and wondered if she'd be as pretty at that age. Then her thoughts turned dark: Beauty wasn't always a blessing.

"Isadora, are you listening?"

When the room came into focus around Izzy, she realized her mom had called her name multiple times. "Caye's waiting for you. You should say good night so she can go to sleep."

Izzy swigged her final sip of soda and headed down the narrow hallway to her sister's bedroom, scooting around the wheelchair collapsed against the wall.

Caye lay in bed wearing patterned pajamas that were much too young for her and clutching an old stuffed cat. "You're home!" she shrieked.

Izzy quickly hushed her.

"Sorry," said Caye with wide eyes. "I forgot not to make noise."

"It's fine," soothed Izzy. "We just don't want the neighbors to complain again."

Caye smooshed a bent finger against her mouth. "You weren't here," she whispered.

"I was at Kassidy's," said Izzy. She could tell Caye wasn't sure who she was talking about, even though she'd met Kassidy a hundred times over the past four years. "Do you need anything before I turn off the light?"

"Mommy helped me shower."

"That's good, Caye. Anything else?"

"She brushed my teeth."

"Sounds like you're all set, then."

Caye held out a clenched hand. "Sing the moon song."

Izzy always felt stupid singing aloud, but "Querida Luna" was Caye's favorite song, and disappointing Caye was like kicking a puppy. She sang the verses her dad had taught them, all the way to the end. When she finished, Caye's eyes were closed, and her lips were parted over her teeth. A bolt of protective fury shot through Izzy's temples. She wanted to wrap her arms around Caye like someone taking the impact of a grenade, but she tamed the urge and went to the living room.

Izzy's mom appeared from the hallway. She'd changed into

a sleep tank and shorts and was carrying a glass of water. "Did you have a good time at Kassidy's?" There was a knowing arch in her voice that hinted at what she was really asking.

"Kass told me about the trip to Ashwood Manor," said Izzy. "Thanks for letting me go."

A faint flush spread across her mom's high cheekbones. She and Izzy hadn't spoken much in the past month. Caye and school and work kept them so busy they could go entire days without exchanging more than a few functional words.

"You're welcome," she said. "I don't want you to worry about me and Caye. It'll be good practice for when you leave for college."

Her mom went to bed, and Izzy transitioned the living room from day to night. Caye needed at least ten hours of uninterrupted sleep, and the apartment had only two bedrooms, so Izzy slept on the pullout couch. She yanked the thin mattress from under the cushions and piled pillows on top. Then she closed the privacy curtain that divided the living room and kitchen and lay down.

Her scholarship to Brown University included a private room. The intensity of the ache for her own space was almost scary. Every night, she imagined herself in a real bed, gazing out a window that overlooked something green, where garbage trucks didn't wake her up at the break of dawn.

Some people counted sheep; Izzy counted days until fall semester started.

Then she thought of Caye, and bitterness rose in her throat. Izzy had worked her ass off to go Ivy League, but unless she acted soon, there would be no private room, no courtyard view, and no college. She'd be stuck in her family's apartment forever.

The week at Ashwood Manor was the solution—if she had enough daring to pull it off. As she lay in the living room listening to screams from the parking lot and sinking through the pillows onto the metal bars under her mattress, she decided that to get away from this life, she would dare anything.

3

Marlowe is already down the ladder when Kassidy and I leave the yacht. A small ferry station dwarfed by birch trees sits at the end of the dock. I can just make out Marlowe's head of dark curls entering the sliding glass doors. Chloe and Ellison stand about halfway up the dock, looking at something through a pair of binoculars. Blaine is nowhere to be seen.

Beyond the ferry station, a narrow road snakes up the hill to a craggy peak. Sheer bluffs fall into waves that crash over rocks poking out of the water like clutches of black dinosaur eggs.

"People think Sparrow Island looks like a giant's tooth," says Kassidy.

I try to picture a giant with his mouth open under the ocean. "If giants' teeth were covered with bushy trees and wildflowers, maybe."

Suddenly, someone behind me yanks my backpack hard, then releases it.

"Boomerang!" shouts a familiar voice.

The rebound of my overstuffed backpack tilts me forward, and I fall onto the dock with a shrill scream.

"That wasn't funny, Blaine!" yells Kassidy, helping me up. "Sorry, Izzy. He's being a jerk because his dad was too busy scouting basketball players in Europe to attend graduation."

Blaine scowls, his cheeks turning almost as red as his hair. "Like I care about that. I was just messing around."

"I'm fine," I say, checking my hands for splinters. "Let's catch up with the others." I hurry ahead of Kassidy and Blaine, but I'm close enough to hear her arguing with him in a hissing whisper. He's been acting out in small ways since our fight, which is one reason I've been avoiding him. If Kassidy has noticed, she hasn't said anything.

When I'm nearly at the ferry station, Kassidy runs up and loops my arm through hers. "Ready?" she says, an excited smile on her face.

"Why is there a ferry station for a single house?" I ask.

"Theodore Ashwood insisted the ferry bring him groceries and mail from the mainland every day," says Kassidy. "When he died, his niece moved in and used the money from the Ashwood Manor Trust to maintain the station. My mom says it's a good thing she did—when the museum opens, they'll have to run several boats a day from Bar Harbor."

The station's amenities are basic: restrooms, ticket counter, a few scratched-up benches that look like old church pews. A single bored security guard sits behind the counter reading a battered paperback. He must be expecting us, because he barely glances up before returning to his book. The sliding glass doors on the opposite end of the station open with an oily squeal as we approach. When I see what's parked outside, I stop dead.

In front of us are two open-air Rolls-Royce Silver Ghosts— exact replicas of the cars from *The Secret of the Ruby Dagger*.

"No freaking way!" I shout. I sprint to the nearest car, not caring how stupid I look in front of Marlowe, who is already in the back seat of the other one.

I graze my fingers along the curved fenders, hop onto the running boards, and caress the leather seats. "How did you get them to the island?" I ask Kassidy.

Her dimples pop as she dances in excited circles. "The ferry!" She bends down to examine one of the hood ornaments. "Finding the cars was the hard part. They're not very common anymore."

I gasp. "They're originals?"

Kassidy laughs. "Actual butts from the 1920s sat in these seats."

"Is this your surprise?"

"The beginning of it," says Kassidy mysteriously. She glances at her phone. "We should go. I want to get to Ashwood Manor before sunset." She piles into the car with Blaine, Fergus, and Ellison. "Looks like we're out of room here," she tells me with a wink. "You'll have to join Marlowe."

I roll my eyes and follow Chloe to the other car, where Marlowe sits reading a thick cloth-bound book. He nods at us, then buries his head back in its pages.

Chloe examines Marlowe's volume as we drive away from the ferry station. "*Anna Karenina*," she says, reading the gilded title. "Any good?"

Marlowe raises his head again, black curls blowing in the breeze as our driver accelerates up a winding road dotted with bluebells. The sun highlights the smattering of freckles under his eyes. His skin is almost as dark as mine—courtesy of his Greek mother—and it's remarkably smooth, like a pebble washed clean by the ocean.

"It's romantic but sad," he replies. He turns to me. "I believe there was a film adaptation in the 1930s."

I'm so taken aback both by his knowledge of the movie's existence and by his speaking to me that I stumble over my words. "With Greta Garbo. It's one of Kassidy's favorites."

"Do you and Kassidy watch a lot of old movies?" asks Chloe.

"Tons," I reply. "Kassidy loves the glamour of the Jazz Age. She wants to be a costume designer."

Chloe sighs. "I read her fashion column in the school newspaper every week, but I still can't put a good outfit together."

There's an uncomfortable silence while I try to think of something to say. None of us had hung out with Chloe before Nestor invited her to prom, so I know only three things about her: She's been top of our class since freshman year, she plays lacrosse, and her mom is a big-shot executive at some Chinese investment firm.

"Did you have a good time at prom?" I finally ask.

Chloe's eyes get wide, like I've just asked to read her diary. Her hand spasms, and she drops her purse on the floor of the car, spilling lipstick, a wallet, and a little red vial. The bouncing car sends the bottle rolling until it hits one of my sneakers. I pick it up and look for the brand name, but there's no label or even a spray nozzle. Just a black screw cap.

Chloe snatches it out of my hand and scoops the other dropped items back into her bag, then sits up straight, cheeks flushed with exertion. "Prom was so much fun," she says. "I'm a terrible dancer, but I loved it anyway."

My journalist's nose for gossip prickles at her reaction to my question. But before I can press her, we take a bend in the road and Ashwood Manor comes into sight.

"Oh, wow," mutters Chloe, and even Marlowe looks up from his book with interest.

The estate is perched near the top of the hill overlooking the ocean. Waves batter the cliffs below, white foam dashing itself against the rocks before being flung into the swirl of the sea. The gray stone of the house is salt-washed, like it was once underwater. Terraces full of roses and rocky trails run down the hill to the ocean, and so many wildflowers surround the property it gives the impression of a colorful blur, like a Monet painting. A dense pine forest rises in the distance beyond the house, dark and imposing.

It's like someone has lowered a Technicolor filter over my eyes. I could never have guessed from the black-and-white scenes in *The Secret of the Ruby Dagger* just how bright and alive the gardens would be or how many shades of gray the sun would illuminate in the stone. And yet there's something cold and reserved about the house itself, as if it had absorbed the notorious reclusiveness of its original owner.

"I can see why they turned this into a museum," says Chloe. "It's gorgeous."

"Wait until you see the inside," says Marlowe. "It's like walking into a time capsule."

"How have you been inside?" I ask. Theodore Ashwood permitted the film crew to shoot only the facade and grounds, so I've never even seen a picture of the interior.

Marlowe flushes, like he's revealed something he wasn't supposed to. "My mom's on the museum board with Mrs. Logan. The owner gave us a private tour a few weeks ago. Didn't Kassidy tell you?"

I shake my head. "I guess she wanted to surprise me," I say, trying not to sound jealous. Typical Kassidy. Keeping secrets to spare my feelings.

The cars pull into the gravel drive in front of Ashwood Manor. A line of staff dressed in old servants' uniforms stands outside. All of them look a lot like my parents, and I'm reminded with startling clarity that I don't belong here. My friends spend their summers visiting beautiful places around the world while I've rarely traveled more than ten miles from my apartment.

My family has gone on vacation only once. My mom drove me and Caye to a busy beach town near Boston when I was fourteen, but my sister got sick and we had to leave early. With the cost and difficulty of accommodating Caye's wheelchair, we never tried again.

I watch the drivers hand our luggage to the footmen, who struggle to lift the heavy cases up the steps. The excitement that followed me from Harker to Sparrow Island is replaced by dread. I can't let that be my life. I can't do what my mom and dad did when I was little. Soaking their hands in ice after long days at work, arguing about what bills could be delayed longest, fighting with hospitals about Caye's care.

One of the footmen tries to grab my backpack, but I shake my head and jerk the straps so tight I know I'll have marks on my shoulders. Thinking about Caye has reminded me what's at stake. No one can see the knife. I'll get only one shot. I have to make sure I don't miss.

4

Marlowe is right. Stepping into Ashwood Manor is like walking into a perfectly preserved time capsule.

Chloe's mouth drops open as she follows me and Kassidy into the foyer. "This place doesn't even seem real," she says.

Blaine laughs. "My mom would hate this décor," he says, looking at the furniture and curios with the practiced eye of someone whose mom designs houses for a living. "It's the opposite of minimalist."

Unlike its weather-beaten facade, the interior of Ashwood Manor is warm and welcoming. A magnificent staircase winds from the entry hall up to a second level. Rich oil paintings hang on the walls, while panes of stained glass filter the dying sunlight into shards of color across the oak floors. Carved sideboards overflowing with fresh lavender diffuse a sweet, delicate perfume through the hall.

My jeans and T-shirt feel shabby, like I'm an anachronism the house might purge at any second.

The stout footmen lug our bags upstairs while we roam the first floor. At the back of the house, Kassidy and I find a drawing room with a baby grand piano and stiff velvet couches surrounding a roaring fire. The room is formal but comfortable—the kind of place guests might play card games and drink fizzy whiskeys.

Tall French windows framed by fluttering indigo curtains stand wide open. Kassidy and I step through them onto the flagstone terrace.

The patio overlooks an explosion of wildflowers carpeting the hill. At the end of a long, dusty path bordered by rose gardens, a sheer cliff drops straight into the water. Except for the distant sound of waves and the buzzing of nearby bees, it's silent.

"I can't believe we're actually here," I whisper, not wanting to break the calm. "Marla Nevercross drank cocktails on this terrace." I point to the cliff. "That's where Cara Ashwood threw the ruby dagger after killing her sister's husband."

Kassidy smiles and squeezes my hand. I consider mentioning her private tour but decide against it. I know Kassidy. The tour didn't matter to her, but this moment does.

"I think it's time for the final surprise," she says.

I follow Kassidy back to the foyer, where the others are waiting. She takes a deep breath, and my heart flutters with anticipation.

"I know you want to see your rooms and unpack," says Kassidy. "But first, I need to tell you why we're here."

"Because it's a badass house on a private island?" says Ellison, like no other explanation is required.

Kassidy smiles. "It's more than that. We're standing in a piece of film history."

"Here we go," mutters Fergus.

Kassidy waves an arm around at the antiques and art. "Theodore Ashwood built this house in 1926 with the money he made selling alcohol during Prohibition," she says. "He used to host wild parties here—"

"Like mine," says Blaine with a wicked smile.

Kassidy scrunches up her nose. "His make yours look like children's birthday parties." Blaine's face grows dark, but the rest of us laugh. "Theodore's teenage daughter, Cara, who he called Sparrow, desperately wanted to be a movie star, so Theodore told Fabrizio Ricci that he could shoot his next film at Ashwood Manor if he cast Cara in one of the lead roles. So Ricci did." Kassidy's expression grows soft. "And she was perfect. So perfect the other lead fell in love with her and convinced Cara to run away from Sparrow Island and her father."

Kassidy pauses for effect, but everyone except Marlowe and me is scrolling on their phones, barely paying attention. So I chime in. "Is that when Theodore became a recluse?" I ask.

Kassidy shakes her head. "After she ran away, Cara's life became as tragic as a Ricci film. She started drinking, left the actor for the manager of a speakeasy, and died alone in a seedy Boston motel." Kassidy sighs. "When he lost his Sparrow to the same thing that made him rich, Theodore Ashwood shut himself up in Ashwood Manor and never set foot on the mainland again. Everything you'll see in the house this week—the couches you sit on, the plates you eat off, the showers you bathe in—those are his last, lonely memories."

There's a moment of silence.

"Way to kill the mood," says Blaine.

Kassidy grins. "I know how to bring it back to life. I have a surprise for all of you."

Something about Kassidy's voice makes people look up from their phones in alarm. There's a sudden tension in the hall, like electricity is zipping between our bodies.

"This isn't just a week at Ashwood Manor," she says, her voice shaking a little. "It's a theme party. A completely immersive

1920s experience. We're going to dress and act and eat like we're at one of Theodore Ashwood's house parties. Tennis, cocktail hours, fancy dinners, card games, dancing—every detail will be as close as we can get to living at Ashwood Manor like the original inhabitants."

I gasp and cover my mouth. A cascade of film images flashes in front of my eyes. Gowns and striped stockings and parasols and glasses of champagne. Stolen kisses under staircases and walks in the garden.

Kassidy smiles at me, and I remember her words on the yacht: *Everything I did, I did for the two of us.*

I look around to see how the others are taking her announcement. Marlowe, who I glance at first, doesn't react at all. Blaine groans and holds his head in his hands. Fergus plays it cool, but it's obvious he's thrilled; if it involves costumes and acting, he's always game. Chloe seems a little apprehensive but smiles all the same. And Ellison just looks amused.

"If we want it to be realistic, I'll need to bunk with the staff," he says. "Pretty sure Black dudes weren't playing a lot of tennis at fancy estates back in the day."

Kassidy flushes bright red. She always tries so hard to think of flaws in her plans. I watch her wonder if she's made a giant error.

"I'm kidding, Kass," Ellison says with a laugh. "But how are we going to dress like it's the 1920s? I don't know about the rest of you, but I mostly packed basketball shorts and T-shirts."

Kassidy recovers her composure with relief. "Each of you will find period outfits cut to your size in the armoires upstairs. Mr. Jimenez, the butler, will send all your regular clothes and cell phones back to the mainland with the drivers so nobody is tempted to cheat on the theme."

Almost everyone gasps in unison.

"Our phones?" asks Chloe.

"You can't be serious," says Ellison.

Fergus stops scrolling to stare at Kassidy in disbelief.

Even Marlowe shifts uncomfortably.

"No way I'm giving up my phone," says Blaine.

"Then no way will you be included in the week," says Kassidy with a shrug. "The yacht returns to the mainland in an hour. Anyone who doesn't want to play by the rules can go home. No hard feelings."

Angry red patches appear on Blaine's cheeks. The others don't look happy either. But no one makes any motion to leave.

"All of your parents know about the surprise," continues Kassidy. "They have the landline number in case they need to reach you. But only use the phone if absolutely necessary, because technically Theodore Ashwood didn't own one."

The butler steps out of the shadows, startling everybody. He holds out a leather satchel. Kassidy turns off her phone and drops it into the case. The others type frantically, no doubt telling friends and social media feeds why they won't be online for a week. I compose a quick note to my mom:

> Cell phones being returned to the mainland.
> Tell Caye I ♥ her and will see her soon.

When I place my phone next to Kassidy's, a weight I didn't know was there melts off my shoulders. For the first time ever, I'll be out of my mom's reach.

Kassidy smiles once everyone puts their phones in the bag. "You can give Mr. Jimenez the clothes you brought after you've changed into your evening wear." She points at Blaine. "*All* your clothes, including that watch. TAG Heuer timepieces looked completely different in the 1920s."

Blaine's eyes widen. "You think I'm going to send my seven-thousand-dollar watch back to the mainland with strangers?"

Kassidy scoffs. "No one's going to steal your stupid watch. If I make an exception for you, everybody will want to keep things, and then it won't seem real." She turns to face the rest of us. "You'll find daily schedules and copies of an etiquette book in your rooms if you want to improve your performance."

"Screw that," mutters Blaine, looking mutinous.

Kassidy ignores him. "There are two hours until we meet back downstairs for cocktails. The etiquette books have pictures of how to put on your suits and dresses and how to do your hair. If you need any help, you can ring for the maids, who have been prepared for the week."

"You even trained the staff?" whispers Chloe, with something that sounds like awe.

Kassidy nods. "About that. This is not *Downton Abbey*. Don't flirt, interrupt, or otherwise communicate with the staff about things that aren't relevant. If you need another blanket for your bed, that's relevant. If you want to bang the hot footman in the garden, that's not. Got it?"

Ellison pretends he's outraged by the rule, while everyone else half laughs.

Kassidy claps her hands together. "You can head to your bedrooms and get dressed. Izzy, you and I are sharing."

Worn Persian rugs carpet the upstairs hallway, while heavy curtains frame the picture windows. I peek into each room as we pass. They're all furnished differently, but they have the same amenities: ashtrays, stationery, candlesticks dripping with yellow wax, and ironstone bowls for washing up. My heart swells as I imagine my friends in their period clothes—brushing lint off their tuxes and shaving with straight blades in front of too-small mirrors. I realize it's not only me pretending to be something I'm not this week; for once, we're all pretending.

Our room is twice the size of the others. An enormous canopy bed supported by dark carved posts is pushed against the wall on the left. To the right is a miniature sitting room with a chartreuse chaise longue, a coffee table, and a crackling fire. A narrow closet is tucked next to a cherry armoire that looks like something out of a fairy tale.

Kassidy closes the heavy door and locks it with the brass key that's sitting in the keyhole.

"This is where Marla Nevercross stayed during the six-week film shoot," she says. "Anne Ashwood told me Theodore's room was next door. He used to sneak into Marla's bed after dark."

"Gross," I say. "Wasn't he twice her age?"

Kassidy nods. "He donated tons of money to her cheetah rescue, so maybe that's why she liked him. Anne says the affair ended when Cara ran away. Theodore blamed Marla for keeping Cara's secret romance from him." She walks over to the window, where the sun is setting behind the white pine forest. "Everyone else has their own room, but this is the biggest and it has a dreamy bathroom, so I figured you wouldn't mind sharing. Especially since I'll spend most of my nights with Blaine."

She glances at me shyly. "Are you happy with the surprise?"

I join her at the window and squeeze her hand. "It's perfect," I say. "I didn't realize how much I needed something like this."

Kassidy leans her forehead against the window, fogging up the glass with her breath. "I think Blaine does too," she says.

"He didn't make honor roll this semester, even with all the senior blow-off classes he took."

I stiffen. "Have you asked him why?"

"He says playing Hamlet was exhausting." She draws a heart in the condensation with her finger, then drags a crack down the center. "I don't know. Maybe there's another girl again."

Guilt roils my stomach. "I'm going to have a bath before cocktail hour," I say, walking away from the window before she can press me about Blaine's cheating.

"Don't take too long," she says, erasing the heart with a swipe of her hand. "We're already behind schedule."

The bathroom is glorious. I hang my towel over the brass doorknob and cross the cool hexagonal tile in bare feet. After filling the claw-foot tub with hot water and vanilla bubble bath, I sink into it with a deep sigh. The lone bathtub at my apartment is so shallow that only the lower half of my body is ever covered with water while the upper half freezes, and I can never bathe too long because someone else always needs to come in.

Who needs cocktail hour? I think. Better to soak in the tub all evening, watching bubbles pop and pretending I'm a film starlet with a secret lover next door.

Then I remember Marlowe is waiting downstairs in a tux, and I scramble out of the bath, anxious to see him.

Kassidy is already dressed in a bronze evening gown, and she looks so amazing I squeal. "You're a Roaring Twenties goddess!"

She smiles. "Grab whatever you want. I've been ordering clothes and accessories for months."

I riffle through the open trunks. Kassidy's thought of everything: jewelry, headbands, stockings, feathers, and hair-curling supplies. Even the luggage is period-appropriate.

I check out the drape of some long pearls in the mirror. "Does Chloe want to get dressed with us?" I ask. "There's enough here for ten people."

Kassidy purses her lips and pages through a hardcover on vintage hairstyles. "She can ring for a maid if she wants help," she says.

The coldness of her voice isn't lost on me. "I'm surprised you invited Chloe," I say. "None of us really know her."

Anger darkens Kassidy's face. "My dad made me," she says. "His company is doing some business deal with her mom. He wants her to think Chloe and I are friends."

"She was nice enough at prom," I say, wrapping a fur stole around my neck.

Kassidy laughs bitterly. "So nice. Super nice. The nicest ever."

"I thought you liked her."

Kassidy glances at my confused face, and her expression melts back into ease. "I don't like being told who to spend time with—that's all. This week is supposed to be special."

I point to a trunk full of alcohol in the corner. "Aren't you afraid someone will tell your parents?"

She shakes her head. "The staff will be the only real adults on the island all week, and they won't care."

"Where are the dresses?" I ask.

Kassidy skips over to the armoire. "I have one final surprise."

She throws open the doors with a flourish to reveal an entire rack full of stunning gowns. Glass beads and sequins glimmer from silks and chiffons and linens. Colorful day frocks and fancy dinner dresses hang close together, formal bumping against casual in the tight space. I brush my fingers along the delicate fabrics, marveling at their perfection. In complete Kass fashion, each dress is a restored original. They must have cost a fortune.

My hand stops on a slinky emerald-green dress. "This looks like—"

"It doesn't just look like." Kassidy is beaming, bouncing on her toes. "It's the actual dress worn by Marla Nevercross in *The Secret of the Ruby Dagger*. I bought it from a collector, who won it in one of Marla's charity auctions. She didn't want to give it up," she says, "but everyone has a price."

And Kassidy's family could always pay it.

"It's your graduation gift," she explains.

I yank my fingers away from the dress. "It's too much," I protest. "I can't accept it."

Kassidy grabs my hands. "You've been my best friend since freshman year," she says. "The only one who doesn't care who my father is or how big my house is or that I'm dating one of the most popular guys in school." She smiles at me, but her gray eyes are brimming with tears. "I insist that you have it."

5

---◆---

MARIAN ACADEMY
Three Months Ago

You want to go to the rowing regatta this weekend?" Blaine asked, looking at Fergus like he'd never seen him before. "Gus, you've said a million times that watching the crew team slap water with sticks sounds as fun as being crushed to death by stage scenery."

"Nestor told me most of the school turns out for the first race of spring," said Fergus.

Blaine snorted. "I didn't realize you believed in the wisdom of the majority."

Fergus and Blaine were waiting for Izzy and Kassidy in the courtyard, which was enclosed like a greenhouse in a peaked-glass dome. Even in the middle of winter, students could eat lunch on the lawn and bask in balmy humidity. The flower beds had been freshly turned by one of the school gardeners, and violets with sunburst centers perfumed the air with a sickly sweetness Fergus had come to associate with the coming of spring.

"Why do you *really* want to go to the race?" asked Blaine.

"This is our last semester at Marian," said Fergus. "If I don't go now, I'll never see him—I mean, them."

Blaine rolled his eyes. "*Duh.* You're making a play for someone on crew." He tapped his dimpled chin like he was thinking.

"Let me guess . . . Trey? No, he's too tall for you. Haywood? He's a bit of a blond cherub. At least that's what Kassidy says. But even you couldn't be crushing on someone so obviously uninterested in guys."

Fergus peered into the doorway, willing the girls to appear. They were always late to lunch because newspaper was fourth period and Dr. Calloway apparently thought journalists could live off words alone. It wouldn't take Blaine long to land on the right answer if he kept guessing.

"Peter's a little snake," continued Blaine. "Your success rate may be low, but you don't lack taste." Then his expression changed, and he started laughing. "Have you lost your mind, Gus?" he asked. "Ellison only dates other badass athletes, and you are—at best—a semi-badass member of the drama club's chorus."

Blaine pointed at a reclining male figure tossing a baseball into the air. "Lucas Routh. Gets his school uniforms specially tailored so his biceps don't split the seams." He jerked his thumb toward a tall blond guy who looked like he should be holding a surfboard on a California beach. "Sam Vesper. Models sweaters for L.L.Bean." Blaine turned back to Fergus. "Ellison's dated both of them this year. He clearly has a *type*. And you're not it."

Fergus hated the smug look on Blaine's face, like he knew everything about Ellison just because he'd spent the past six months hanging out with him. "Ellison dated Izzy," Fergus shot back.

Blaine shrugged. "Izzy's hot poor-girl vibe is catnip to guys at Marian," he said. "Plus, she's editor of the newspaper. I wouldn't put it past Ellison to date her for some front-page press."

"Ellison's not like that," said Fergus. He wanted so badly to tell Blaine about his winter-break fling. But Ellison had sworn him to secrecy, leaving Fergus to imagine those two weeks had taken place in a parallel universe where Ellison couldn't hold an oar and Fergus landed starring roles in school plays. A universe where they made sense.

Kassidy and Izzy arrived with their food. Izzy began munching on the sleeve of saltine crackers she brought from home every day, while Kassidy dug into her salad. Handmade earrings almost as long as her hair hung past her shoulders. They were all forced to wear school uniforms except on Freedom Fridays, but Kassidy was constantly adding unapproved accessories to her wardrobe.

"Why does Fergus look like his dog just died?" asked Kassidy.

Blaine shook his head. "He's chasing after Ellison, and I gave him an honest appraisal of his chances."

Fergus scowled. Blaine's transformation from best friend to jerk had barely been noticeable at first. Some unanswered texts. A few canceled plans. All easily explained by him having more lines to memorize and more rehearsals to attend than Fergus. Then Blaine's mom bought the lake house after the divorce, and Blaine went from popular theater kid to thrower of Marian's best parties. Maybe Fergus should have found new friends when Blaine started treating him like an unwanted stray. But he kept hoping Blaine would get tired of his classmates using him for drugs and alcohol. Now they were about to graduate, and it was too late for Fergus to leave Blaine's orbit. He had nowhere else to go.

"Since Blaine has revealed my secret shame to the world," Fergus said to the girls, "will you come to this weekend's regatta with me?"

Blaine shot Fergus a strange look. "We always go to the races."

Fergus's stomach dropped like he was on a roller coaster. "Since when?"

"Last spring," said Kassidy.

A rush of misery made the back of Fergus's neck flush. His friends—his only friends besides Nestor—had been excluding him from something fun they did together for a whole year.

"We asked you once," said Izzy softly. "You said you'd rather get your wisdom teeth pulled again."

Fergus vaguely remembered that. But it hadn't meant he *never* wanted to go. There was only one reason they wouldn't ask him a second time: They didn't want him there.

Fergus felt a familiar pressure building inside his head. Pressure that could be relieved only by throwing something and watching it shatter into a thousand pieces. He'd have to wait until the bell before he could sneak into the secret closet near the boiler room. The one with stacks of old bathroom tiles that cracked so satisfyingly against the stone wall.

A terrible image suddenly rose to the surface of his mind. For a second, Fergus couldn't speak. His stomach clenched hard, like he might be sick. Instead of tiles, it was Blaine's head he'd launched at the wall. Skull fragments littered the ground like shards of bloody glass.

Fergus forced down his nausea. "Can I go with you this weekend or not?" he asked, keeping his voice calm.

"Course, Gus," said Blaine. A smile played on his lips. "Bring some binoculars if you want a close-up of your boy. And a warm jacket. It gets colder than a nun's nips out there."

"Gross," said Izzy. "You're such a heathen."

"That's what five years of Catholic school will do to you." Blaine grinned at Fergus. "Remember Sister Mary?"

Fergus relaxed a little. The name of their fifth-grade teacher transported him back to the days when he and Blaine were so inseparable Fergus's parents joked about charging Blaine room and board. "Hairy Mary," said Fergus. "She's burned into my brain forever."

Blaine chuckled and turned to the girls. "There was this nun at Holy Cross with a super-thick mustache. She used to hit our palms with a ruler when we got math questions wrong."

"Which was often, in Blaine's case," said Fergus.

Blaine nodded. "Fergus was tired of seeing me get hit, so one morning he snuck a waxing kit into her desk drawer."

"I hoped she'd be humiliated when she found it," said Fergus.

"She opened the drawer," said Blaine. "Stared at the kit for a minute. Then opened the box and began cutting the cotton strips."

"We thought she'd lost her mind," said Fergus.

"Had she?" asked Izzy.

Blaine shook his head. "I didn't understand fractions, but of course she called on me. Usually, she slid her ruler out of her habit slowly, so we had a chance to dread the pain that was coming. But this time, she picked up a wooden stick from the kit and scooped a giant dollop of wax out of the jar. She spread the wax across my left arm and pressed a cotton strip down hard over it. Then she smiled like I was a bug she was about to crush. It was the creepiest smile I've ever seen." Blaine glanced at his arm. "She reached down and yanked the strip. Ripped the hair straight off."

"She didn't!" squealed Izzy. Kassidy laughed beside her.

"Blaine screamed like a pig being taken for slaughter," said Fergus. "I started crying. And we both got detention."

Blaine smiled. "The craziest part is that the next day Hairy Mary showed up sans mustache. She'd waxed it right off."

Everyone laughed, and for a moment, Fergus remembered what it had felt like before girls started throwing themselves at Blaine after productions and before Blaine posted himself on social media hanging out with Ellison every Saturday night. The red flash appeared back in his head, but Fergus shoved it out. In a few minutes, the bell would ring, and he could finally release the pressure. He smiled at the others while picturing shattered tiles.

6

Dressing up for movie nights with Kassidy usually feels silly, but descending the mahogany staircase in Marla Nevercross's emerald gown has the opposite effect. I hold my head high like a debutante, as if my spine wants to be worthy of Ashwood Manor's grandeur.

Kassidy's blond hair is pinned in loose waves around the side of her face, the ends nestled in a bun at the nape of her neck. She's plucked her eyebrows thin and lengthened her eyelashes so that they're spidery, giving her a haunted silent-film-star gaze.

"You're going to blow Marlowe's mind," says Kassidy, adjusting the headband hugging my chocolate-brown curls.

A delicate bracelet falls in front of my face as she tinkers with my hair.

"Is that new?" I ask.

Kassidy shakes the bracelet so it sparkles under the chandelier. "It's a graduation gift from my grandmother," she says. "She got it from her grandmother. An original diamond bracelet from the 1920s."

"It's gorgeous."

"Right? It should have gone to my mom, but my grandma said my mom's wrist is too fat to wear it, so now they're not speaking. The drama never ends with those two."

Everyone else is already sipping cocktails in the drawing room. A footman stands unobtrusively near the wall, dressed in a black waistcoat, waiting to refill drinks. I smile at him before remembering Kassidy's rule not to acknowledge the staff. It seems ridiculous that we're expected to treat them like furniture all week.

"Hey, beautiful," says Blaine, kissing Kassidy on her well-blushed cheek. Blaine looks good in everything from boxers to stage costumes, and the tailored tux Kassidy picked out for him is no exception. His hair is parted sharply on one side and brushed into a small rise on the other. He studiously avoids my eyes, which is fine with me.

Fergus leans against the baby grand piano, pulling awkwardly at his tux. He and Chloe are pretending to talk to each other while sneaking glances at the fireplace, where Ellison's tall, muscular frame is outlined against the dancing flames.

Marlowe stands near the wall with his back to the room, examining a large painting of a nymph bathing in a stream. He looks at it for so long it begins to feel like he's intentionally not turning around.

When I glance at Kassidy, she tilts her head toward Marlowe. The message is clear: *Get over there.* She's right. Italian girlfriend or not, this is no time to be a coward. He can never choose me if he doesn't know I'm an option.

I take only one step before I'm intercepted by Chloe, who rushes over with an empty champagne glass in hand.

"Your dress is stunning," she tells me, rubbing the fabric between her fingers.

Her gown is pale lavender, with a fluted fringe that skims her toned calves. She's accessorized it with layers of pearls and a headband with a white feather. The haircut that looked so unflattering with her normal clothes fits the Jazz Age perfectly, and her smoky eyes give her a hint of mystery she definitely never had when she ran through Marian's halls in her lacrosse uniform.

I can tell from the daggers Kassidy throws at her I'm not the only one surprised by how good she looks.

"The dress is my graduation present from Kass," I tell her. I glance at the twinkling heart-shaped drop nestled in the hollow of her throat. "I love your necklace."

"It was my gram's." She holds it out so I can see better. "The women in my family have been repurposing the gemstones for hundreds of years and setting them into new pieces."

Apparently, I'm the only girl at the party not wearing a family heirloom.

I lean closer to the diamond pendant and catch a whiff of something floral and earthy. I frown. "Is that Violet Ends?" I ask.

Chloe takes a step back. "Did I spray too much?"

"No, it smells good," I say. "It's Kassidy's go-to scent in the winter. That's why I know it."

And why I know it's clear and comes in a bottle shaped like oversized nail polish. Nothing like the little red vial she'd yanked out of my grasp in the car.

"Is that the perfume you had in your purse earlier?" I ask.

Chloe bites her lip. "I brought more than one." Her eyes dart to Marlowe, who's moved on to staring at a still life of fruit. "He asked about you," she says, stumbling over her words a little. "He said, 'Has Isadora come down yet?'"

Warmth spreads through my stomach. I try not to sound too eager when I answer. "He did?"

Chloe nods. "I figured your name was Isabel. I like Isadora. It's unusual."

"It's a name on my dad's side of the family."

"Was he at graduation today?"

"No, he lives in Mexico."

Chloe opens her mouth to ask another question, but I don't feel like being pitied for my sad life story. Besides, it's not her I want to talk to. I excuse myself, trying not to feel bad when her face falls.

"Should we be annoyed you find apples more interesting than us?" I ask Marlowe as I approach the wall of art.

One-half of his mouth lifts, and it's as close to a smile as I've seen from him all day. "Don't sell yourself short," he says. "There are oranges and bananas too."

"I hear all the paintings in Ashwood Manor melt at the stroke of midnight."

He tears his eyes from the still life. Now that I can see his face, the full effect of his tux hits me. He looks just as good as I'd dreamed in the bath.

"Are you suggesting I have all week to look at these paintings and should be enjoying the company of my classmates instead?" he asks.

"*Classmates?* You've known these people almost your whole life."

Marlowe glances at Blaine and Kassidy flirting near the fireplace. Chloe stands in the corner, adjusting her pearls, while Fergus plays show tunes on the piano, his highball set on top, next to the music rack.

"You're right," he says. "I'm being rude."

"On purpose?"

He frowns. "I hope not."

"You don't know?"

"Do you always know why you do things?" he asks.

I think of the knife I carefully removed from my backpack and tucked under the mattress while Kassidy was in the bathroom. "Usually," I say.

"Then you're more self-aware than I am."

He wanders over to the piano, where Blaine is now singing with Fergus. I join Kassidy near the fireplace in a huff.

"I have no idea why you like Marlowe," she says for the millionth time. "He's such a snob."

I bite my tongue before I can remind her she's in love with an attention-seeking charmer who treats his friends like butterflies he can pull the wings off of whenever their flight doesn't suit his needs.

Chloe and Ellison join in the singing. I recognize the song from the school musical Blaine starred in during spring of junior year.

We both watch Fergus lean as close to Ellison as he can while keeping his hands on the piano keys.

"Poor Gus," I say. "Still mooning after Ellison."

Kassidy shakes her head. "It's never going to happen."

"Looks like Ellison has someone else in mind," I say, tipping my chin toward Chloe. She and Ellison clink their glasses together as they harmonize.

Kassidy drains the rest of her champagne in a single gulp. "Ellison deserves better," she says.

When the song ends, Kassidy's stormy face clears. She smiles and grabs my hand. "Time to dance."

"No, no, no," I protest, but she loops her arm through mine and drags me toward the piano.

"Play 'The Charleston,' Gus!" she calls.

Usually, Fergus would bristle at being told what to do by Kassidy, but tonight he salutes her, takes another gulp of his cocktail, and begins playing the jaunty tune. Blaine sits down next to him and turns it into a duet.

Kassidy swings me into the makeshift dance area. The second she starts kicking her feet, I know what she's doing: It's the choreography from *The King on Main Street*, the movie that turned the Charleston into a national craze. Ellison and Chloe join in with a butchered version of the dance, bumping into each other as they wave their arms like those inflatable tube men outside car dealerships.

Kassidy and I bounce, sway, and tap our way around the room while the beads on our gowns swish and shimmy. We laugh, unable to keep our high spirits contained. Marlowe stands, unmoving, by the piano, and when I dare to glance at him, I find that our joy is so contagious he's grinning too.

As the last note is struck on the piano, Kassidy and I fall onto the nearest couch in a giggling heap, while everyone else claps and cheers with booze-glazed eyes. Before we have time to catch our breath, Mr. Jimenez walks through the doorway.

"Dinner is ready in the dining room," he says. With a sour expression, he gazes at Fergus's cocktail sweating on the piano. "Ms. Ashwood asked me to remind you that everything in this house is very valuable."

Blaine claps Ellison on the back with a chortle. "That's no problem," he says. "We have plenty of money."

Kassidy shoots him a dirty look. "Don't be an ass," she says. "These are priceless museum pieces. We signed those forms saying we'd be responsible if we damaged anything." She turns to Mr. Jimenez. "Sorry. We'll clean it up."

Fergus grabs his drink and does his best to wipe the pool of condensation off the wood with his tux jacket.

Kassidy and Blaine lead the way to the dining room, where a rectangular table is set with patterned china and polished silverware. Hand-painted wallpaper lines the warm wood walls. Ashwood Manor has electricity in most of the rooms, but the dining area is lit entirely by candles hanging in a bronze chandelier above the table.

Kassidy has prearranged the seating. I'm at one end of the table, next to Marlowe and across from Chloe, who is as far away from Kassidy as possible. I wonder what Kassidy isn't telling me; there's no way she's this upset about her dad forcing Chloe on our trip.

"I planned the menus by looking at old grocery lists Anne Ashwood found in the cellar," says Kassidy as a footman appears from the kitchen carrying an ornate silver bowl. "This is the meal the actors in *The Secret of the Ruby Dagger* ate on their last day of filming."

The first course is pea soup. Canned peas make me gag, but I don't want Marlowe to think I can't appreciate fancy food, so I bring a spoonful to my mouth. To my surprise, it tastes like honeysuckle and clover and springtime.

After the soup, the footman brings out a Waldorf salad, roasted chicken with pistachio cream sauce for those of us who eat meat, and a bright vegetable medley for Marlowe and Kassidy, who only eat fish. I'm so full by the time dessert arrives I'm afraid my dress will rip at the seams, but I still take a few bites of the blueberry sorbet and the light-as-air lemon chiffon cake.

"Are there any paintings you'd like to get up and examine during dinner?" I ask Marlowe, feeling more relaxed than I've been in months thanks to the champagne and the amazing food.

"I don't think that would be much use by candlelight," he says.

"What if these paintings only look good in candlelight?"

His mouth twitches. "I wasn't aware you had such a hatred of art."

"I wasn't aware you knew anything about me at all," I say airily.

A wineglass dings from the head of the table, and Kassidy stands up. I can tell from her pink face and disarrayed hair that she's drunk.

"I want to make a toast," she says, swiveling her head from person to person. "To all of you, for being willing to wear silly clothes at a country estate with no cell phones or streaming or video games so I can fulfill my dream of being a 1920s party girl before I head to college and get hit in the face with the real world. Happy graduation!"

Everyone cheers and toasts except Marlowe, who stares at me, his blue eyes black in the flickering candlelight. It feels like we're in our own quiet world, and I can't help but notice our thighs are only inches apart—so close I can almost feel his warmth radiating into my skin.

He leans over and says in a low voice: "I know you're headed to Brown in the fall, that you wish your mom didn't teach at Marian, that you love classic murder mysteries, that you only eat saltine crackers for lunch—which is terrible for you, by the way—that you let out the hems of your school skirts to make them longer, that you don't use an umbrella when it rains, and that you look absolutely incredible in that dress."

My face, which had started flushing as soon as he began to speak, now feels like it's on fire. But before I can stammer out a reply, he whispers in my ear: "I also know you're carrying a secret about Blaine that's crushing you." He looks deeply into my eyes, and my heart beats so hard I can hear it in my ears. "What I don't know is what you're going to do about it."

7

PEGASUS BOOKS
Nine Months Ago

Marlowe opened the front door of Pegasus Books on a blustery day in early September. The bell attached to the metal elbow above him jangled with a comforting familiarity. June, the store manager, acknowledged him with a nod, then went back to arranging magazines along the wall.

As Marlowe moved deeper into the store, smells that had been faint near the door grew stronger: Warm roast coffee. The tart wood pulp of new paper. Musty old walls and aged ceiling beams.

Cramped rows of books filled every inch of the flat-front building that had once been a dry goods store. Marlowe's favorite leather chair basked in a corner on the second floor, next to three casement windows, which made the most of the dim fall sun.

Every Sunday, he left the loneliness of his house and drove into town. His parents spent Saturday nights in New York City, and most of the staff took Sundays off, so for a few glorious hours each week, Marlowe was free. No driver. No housekeeper. No flying lessons or dinners at the club or black-tie social events. Just a sunny chair and a good book.

As he made his way to the creaky staircase that led upstairs, a familiar face in the mystery section stopped him in his tracks.

Izzy Morales.

Marlowe almost groaned out loud. He and Izzy had shared a few classes junior year, but he'd never spoken to her. She ran with Kassidy's set, and ever since his brother had died, he'd wanted nothing to do with Kassidy, who had attached herself to Blaine like a starving barnacle.

Anger swelled in his chest. Only two days ago, Marlowe had turned down another party invitation to Blaine's house on Pine Lake. He wouldn't confront Blaine until he didn't feel like punching his stupid face into mush. Even saying his name was disgusting; it tasted like blood and bandages.

Marlowe stared at Izzy for a few seconds before he realized what had caught his eye: She was wearing khakis and a baby-blue T-shirt under a name tag on a lanyard. The Pegasus Books uniform. She wasn't carrying around a book basket for herself; she was stocking shelves.

Great. Kassidy's best friend intruding on his Sunday space.

Izzy stopped stocking and started paging through one of the paperbacks.

"You need to pick it up, Izzy," said June, appearing from around the corner. Her hands were balled into their usual fists. "You can read on your breaks."

"Sorry," mumbled Izzy, quickly stuffing the book onto a shelf. She swung around before Marlowe could get out of her line of sight, then froze in place when she spotted him. He'd been caught staring, so he entered the row as if that's what he'd planned all along. Izzy returned to her stocking, but he could see spots of pink high on her cheekbones.

Had she recognized him? If so, she showed no interest in conversation. Most Marian students—drawn to wealth like bees to honey—would take advantage of the chance to be alone with him.

Marlowe browsed close to Izzy, reading the backs of books with fake interest. He thought it was strange he'd never noticed that she smelled like wild oranges and jasmine. The scent reminded him of a garden he'd explored in Sicily.

"Oh!" Izzy said, turning to leave and almost bumping into him with her basket. "Sorry. I didn't see you."

"It's my fault," began Marlowe, but then her swinging lanyard caught his eye. The name ISADORA MORALES was printed in bold black letters on the laminated name tag.

His mouth formed the words. A memory he hadn't thought of for years flooded his brain with such intensity he almost stumbled. He caught himself on the edge of the shelf.

"Isadora," he whispered. He hadn't meant to say it aloud. "I've never heard any of the teachers say your real name."

"You know who I am?" she asked.

"We had chemistry together," he said.

"And Modern Art. But unless you're impressed by stick figures, you probably didn't notice." Izzy's face grew distracted. "Great, the manager is glaring at me again. If I get fired on my second day, I'll probably set a record."

Then, Marlowe thought, he would have Pegasus to himself again. But as he looked into her worried eyes, his mind kept repeating her name. *Isadora, Isadora.* Without thinking about it, Marlowe grabbed a book off the shelf. He raised his voice so June could hear him. "You're right—it is in this row. Thanks for helping me find it."

Izzy's mouth dropped open.

He shot her a little smile and then walked past June. "Best

staff in Harker," he said. June's glare turned into something soft, and her fists unclenched a little.

Marlowe spent the rest of the day in his favorite chair, but he had trouble focusing on his book. He kept glancing toward the stacks and the coffee bar. Somehow, a girl who had always slid through his thoughts like water through a sieve now dwelled there.

His family's travels made it easy to avoid dating girls at school. He was casually seeing a first-year art student in Rome named Gia, who knew nothing about him except that he liked her sketches and paid for everything when he visited.

As closing time approached, Marlowe roamed the stacks. He pretended he wasn't searching for Izzy, but when June called out a final warning to bring purchases to the cash wrap, disappointment flooded his body. Until he spotted Izzy ringing up books next to June.

"Next!" called June when Marlowe reached the front of the line. He turned to the magnet carousel as if he were still shopping and told the woman behind him to go ahead. He grabbed a magnet at random and returned to his place in line.

When Marlowe approached Izzy's register, her cheeks flushed a little, but otherwise she treated him like anyone else. "Did you find everything okay?" she asked.

He stared at her for a few seconds, trying to remember how to have a normal conversation after a long day absorbed in other people's words. "I found—yes," he said. "I did." He handed her his books and the magnet.

"I could spend the rest of my sunsets with you," she said.

Marlowe froze. "What?" He tried to ignore the strange rush of adrenaline making his stomach feel warm.

Izzy held up the magnet. "That's what it says." She scanned and bagged it. "For your girlfriend?"

"It's a joke," he said quickly. "Like a white elephant gift."

"You have customers waiting, Izzy," growled June.

Izzy raised herself onto her tiptoes so she could see behind Marlowe. Then she popped back down and shoved his receipt inside the bag. "I hope your girlfriend enjoys the joke," she said. "If she thinks you're serious, you might have to propose."

"She's an Italian artist who thinks marriage is a tool of the patriarchy, so probably not," said Marlowe before he could stop himself. What was he doing? He and Gia weren't even official.

"Of course she is," said Izzy. Her voice was even, but Marlowe could feel the waves of sarcasm rolling across the counter. She handed him the bag of books with a forced smile. "Next!" she called.

As Marlowe climbed into his car, he cursed himself for not reading the magnet before he checked out. *Dumb, dumb, dumb.* Now Izzy thought he had a girlfriend.

But what did it matter? He had a firm rule: No dating girls from school. So it was strange the name Isadora continued to pulse in his head, warming him like winter sun.

As he sped up the hill to his family's compound, Marlowe's lips curved into an involuntary smile. Yes, he had a firm rule.

But rules were made to be broken.

When I wake up the next morning, Kassidy's side of the bed is empty. I think of her with Blaine, running her hands over his pale skin, along the birthmark on his upper left thigh near the curve of his—

Bile fills my mouth as I remember Marlowe's words from the night before.

What I don't know is what you're going to do about it.

At least I know Marlowe hasn't told anyone; if he had, the gossip would have spread like wildfire through the Academy.

Kassidy hasn't returned by the time I head to breakfast in a floral day dress with a Peter Pan collar. Mr. Jimenez stands at attention in the dining room, next to silver chafing dishes filled with pancakes, eggs, tomatoes, and ham. I load up my plate and sit down, idly wondering which chair Marla Nevercross chose during filming each morning.

Chloe sits across from me, cutting her ham into tiny bites. Marlowe is at the head of the table, reading the morning paper. He looks so natural, with his legs crossed and his tea in one hand, that I wonder if this is his regular morning routine and not an act to comply with Kassidy's rule to stay in character.

Ellison peers out the window through binoculars. The high

school championship ring on his middle finger glitters in the sunlight cutting through the glass.

"See anything interesting?" I ask.

"The Mermaid Regatta is this weekend," he says. "I can see some of the boats from here."

Kassidy's clicking heels announce her entrance. She's chosen bright colors for our first full day on the island: a lime-green day dress and a straw hat pinned with cloth rosettes. "Will everyone be up for tennis around noon?" she asks.

Ellison walks back to the table and picks up his cup of tea. "Sounds good to me."

"Only if we play doubles," says Fergus. "Singles is so dull."

"Count me out," says Marlowe, putting down his paper.

"Afraid you'll look stupid in 1920s tennis pants?" mocks Fergus.

"I find this era's clothes quite comfortable," says Marlowe, not rising to the bait. "But I'll play if you agree to singles. Me and you."

Fergus smirks. "Done."

At noon, we all descend the garden terraces to the tennis court. A footman follows us, carrying half a dozen rackets. Seeing the others clothed in white cotton dresses and slacks to play tennis gives me a heady feeling, like I'm watching echoes of people who walked the same rocky paths over a hundred years before.

Fergus stands on one side of the court, stretching. He's wearing the same pants and sweater as Marlowe, but he's tied a chintz silk ascot around his neck.

Blaine grins while he watches Fergus warm up. "I don't think

Marlowe knows Gus was junior state champ when we were younger."

Kassidy shrugs. "That was a long time ago."

"So?" asks Blaine, lip curling into a sneer. "I don't think Marlowe learned how to play tennis by reading about it."

The game is afoot. Fergus serves first, and it's an ace right out of the gate.

Blaine whoops with elation. "Damn, Gus! Nice shot!"

Marlowe doesn't react. He bends forward a little and bounces side to side, watching the next serve come his way. He swings at it and misses entirely.

"No wonder Marlowe didn't want to play," says Ellison, miming a forehand stroke like he wished he could take Marlowe's place.

"I wouldn't jump to conclusions," says Kassidy.

Marlowe volleys Fergus's next serve, but a few strokes later Fergus hits a line drive that slices past him. This looks like it's going to be a bloodbath, and I wonder why Marlowe insisted on playing singles.

Soon, it's Marlowe's turn to serve. His first ball flies out of bounds.

"Maybe I should play with my left hand," yells Fergus. "Give you a fighting chance."

Marlowe smiles. "I was just waiting for you to taunt me." He draws his racket behind him and serves the ball so hard it spins into a blur as it smacks inside the line.

Fergus's eyes pop wide with surprise.

Blaine doubles over, laughing. "He's a ringer!" he calls.

Marlowe's second serve is an ace too. As is his third.

"You knew?" I ask Kassidy.

She nods. "Marlowe's family compound has four tennis courts, and they keep a pro on staff. I've always told him he would kill on Marian's team, but he says he doesn't like organized sports." She grins. "He's one of the best players at our country club."

Fergus never earns another point and goes down in straight sets. His face is bright red when he comes over to the sidelines.

"Better luck next time, old boy," says Blaine, clapping Fergus on the shoulder.

"You think this is funny?" snaps Fergus.

"Maybe you should focus more on the piano and less on athletes"—Blaine winks at Ellison—"I mean, athletics."

Fergus slams his racket on the ground, forcing Chloe to jump out of the way as it bounces off the clay court. "Screw you!" he yells into Blaine's face. Then he storms off toward the gardens.

"What a baby," says Blaine, rolling his eyes.

Kassidy picks up the battered racket and runs her fingers over the strings, checking for damage. "You told me you'd make sure he behaved himself this week," she says.

Blaine shrugs. "How was I supposed to know Marlowe was some kind of tennis prodigy?"

Kassidy glares at Blaine, and he stops smiling.

"Fine," he sighs. "I'll go soothe the baby's sore feelings."

Marlowe walks casually back to the bench, wiping sweat off his brow.

"Good game, man," says Ellison, clearly impressed.

"You don't usually play people that far outside your skill level," says Kassidy.

"He pissed me off," replies Marlowe, wiping the handle of his racket before handing it to the footman.

"I'm sure that's the reason," answers Kassidy, with a side-eye glance at me.

"Do you want to play next?" Chloe asks Kassidy shyly from under a white visor.

Kassidy grabs two rackets from the footman and hands one of them to Ellison. "I don't think we're evenly matched," she says, then grabs Ellison's hand and guides him to the court.

Chloe steps back like she's been slapped.

I'd been so tipsy and tired the night before, I'd completely forgotten to ask Kassidy why she was being mean to Chloe. Usually, she only hates girls when they hit on Blaine, but I've never even seen Chloe talk to him.

I explore the nearby gardens while I wait for the others to get tired of tennis. After hiking along a narrow dirt path overrun by marsh marigolds, I find a trickling fountain hidden behind rosebushes so big they look like trees. Sparrows twitter as they hop in and out of the water, shaking their feathers dry after each baptism. As I sit on the edge of the fountain and watch them, I replay the image of Marlowe stretching for a tennis ball, his shirt coming untucked and revealing his brown stomach.

"I'm sick of you treating me like a second-class friend."

Fergus's voice interrupts my daydream from the other side of the rosebushes. Four years of writing for the school paper has made me immune to feeling guilty for eavesdropping, so I freeze and listen.

"You're acting like a child," says Blaine. "I'm treating you the same as always."

"This whole year, you've been all about Ellison. Ellison and his Olympic rowing trials. Ellison and all the girls chasing after him. Like you can share in his limelight if you stand close enough."

"I'm sorry Ellison doesn't want you," says Blaine icily. "But he's made that clear and you keep trying. It's pathetic."

"He might want me," says Fergus, his voice growing louder. "You don't know."

Blaine laughs. "Keep dreaming."

"Why are you being such a jerk when I'm only here to support you? Just get it over with so we can leave."

"I told you. Not until the end of the week. I'm not ruining Kassidy's vacation. I owe her that."

My stomach sparks with nervous electricity. Has Blaine decided to tell Kassidy the secret?

"Screw cocktail hour," yells Fergus. "I'm starting right now." Footsteps pound away, up the main path to the house.

"Gus, wait!" trails Blaine's voice.

Two seconds later, a figure steps out of the rosebushes.

"That was interesting."

I almost fall into the fountain.

"You shouldn't sneak up on people," I say, righting myself and then glaring at Marlowe.

He snorts. "Pot, meet Kettle."

"I was sitting here before they arrived. I couldn't help but hear."

"Sounds like there's trouble in paradise," he says.

If he thinks I'm going to confirm his suspicions about Blaine, he's wrong. "Kassidy's side of the bed was empty this morning," I say. "So all is good in paradise."

Marlowe shrugs. "Sex doesn't mean anything."

I wonder if Marlowe's ever slept with anyone. A romance-novel tableau of him draped across a couch while his artist girlfriend paints him pops into my mind. *Of course he has.*

"Blaine and Kassidy already booked flights between their colleges for the whole first semester," I say. "They're committed to each other." But I sound unconvincing, even to my own ears.

"What else could that have been about?" pushes Marlowe.

My cheeks start to burn. There's no way I'm having this conversation with him. "I think lunch is probably ready," I say, standing up. I need space to think. If Blaine has decided to tell Kassidy, I don't have much time left to act.

"I doubt they're serving saltines," he says dryly.

My eyes snap up to his. I'd fallen asleep the night before turning his words over in my head. "You don't even sit with us at lunch," I say. "How do you know about the saltines?"

"Maybe I'm observant."

"And the other stuff. How did you know?"

"I think you're right about lunch," he says abruptly. He walks back through the bushes, leaving me alone in front of the fountain, wondering and worried.

9

CHLOE'S HOUSE
Five Weeks Ago

Chloe sat on her bed, staring at her phone. Blaine's text dots had been blinking for almost three minutes. He was either writing one of the long messages that had been so common only a week ago or he was rewriting his text over and over.

The message was short.

> i'm just confused right now. and this thing between you and me is making it worse.

Chloe's hands tightened around her phone. This *thing* was the first time she understood what people meant when they said they were in love. For the past few weeks, all she could think about was Blaine. It was like everything else had faded to gray.

Her thumbs flew over the screen.

> you told me it was over with kassidy.

> it is.

> i'm tired of making her feel bad. and making you feel bad.

every day i wake up and tell myself
i'm going to be honest with everyone.
then i'm not.

this makes me feel guilty too.

did I ever tell you my dad used to bring
his girlfriend to our house when i was at
holy cross?

didn't even try to hide it from
my mom.

what a jerk.

i'm no different.

i've been too much of a coward to tell
kass we don't have a future.

i'll break up with her soon so she
has the summer to process.

if she's alone in another state
without her parents and izzy, she
might fall apart.

Chloe's eyes stung with tears. This was the Blaine she'd fallen
for. The guy who was sensitive. Who was capable of thinking
about other people. The Blaine of the past week—who'd been
alternately ghosting her and sending single-word responses—
was a stranger.

Chloe wanted to reassure him that she wasn't trying to issue
an ultimatum.

i'm not asking you to break up
with kassidy immediately. or
anyone else you're seeing.

Chloe paused, then tapped the BACK button to delete the last line. She didn't want to make him feel guiltier, even though she desperately wanted to know if she was the only other girl. But it wasn't worth derailing the conversation over his denials.

> i only want us to keep doing
> what we're doing.

What they were doing made her head spin. Somehow, they'd gone from nothing to everything in a single night at Ellison's after-prom party in Boston. She wasn't proud of how it had happened. But she never wanted it to end.

> for now.

Chloe breathed a sigh of relief. Being with Blaine was like looking at a rainbow and discovering hundreds of previously unimaginable colors. Everything was new. She daydreamed about him during class, watched for his red hair in the halls, felt like she might burst into flames when his car pulled into her driveway. It was intoxicating, like only the good parts of being drunk.

Of course, there was a dark side too. Chloe had been too busy with school and sports to date much, so she'd never had a reason to be jealous before. Now jealousy plagued her thoughts like an unwelcome guest. When Chloe wasn't thinking about Blaine, her mind spiraled around the suspicion that she wasn't the only other girl in his life.

She was glad senior year was nearly over. She'd clinched the valedictorian spot and lacrosse season had ended, so none of her teachers or coaches noticed her distraction. Her mom—

typically sharp-eyed—had been preoccupied with the deal she was negotiating with Kassidy's father.

Chloe felt a bit breathless as she typed.

> are we still on for the lookout
> after school tomorrow?

Blaine reacted to her text with a thumbs-up.

It wasn't the excited response Chloe wanted. But it was enough.

10

───────◇───────

There's tension in the drawing room when Kassidy and I walk in later that evening. No one's singing Broadway tunes, and instead of playing the piano, Fergus is sitting in a corner chair vaping and spinning a sparkling cigarette case in his hand. The open bottle of wine on the table next to him shows he's made good on his threat to start cocktail hour early.

Kassidy and I have chosen different looks than the night before. My dress is gauzy and black, with a scoop back, and my hair is slicked close to my head in wavelets. Kassidy's wearing a tiered eggplant drop-waist dress covered in gold beads. Her hair is wrapped in a silk scarf dripping with delicate lace.

Mr. Jimenez hands us each a sidecar, that evening's cocktail. It's cold and tart.

Ellison approaches me. "Good, isn't it?" he says. "I've never had a drink like this."

"The rowing team doesn't indulge in fancy cocktails after races?"

He laughs. "They're bigger fans of tapping kegs, you might remember."

We both blush. Ellison must be pretty tipsy already to forget our unspoken vow of silence about the very embarrassing few weeks we spent dating at the end of junior year.

In what I later decided was stress-induced insanity brought on by finals, we felt within days of meeting that we were soulmates destined for eternal love. But when Ellison's rowing buddies stole our love letters out of his backpack and started quoting cringe lines about my "fiery Spanish soul" in the locker room, he broke up with me.

I was devastated until I met Marlowe and realized that the guy who'd stereotyped me with the wrong nationality probably wasn't my soulmate, just a hot guy I had good chemistry with.

Marlowe approaches and saves us from any more awkwardness. "Someone should take that bottle away from Fergus," he says. Fergus has moved to the piano and started banging on it at random, like a five-year-old.

I sigh. "I'll talk to him."

Fergus rolls his eyes when I sit down. "Don't you get tired of always being the designated therapist?"

"I came to ask if you'd play a song for me."

"You're better than them, you know," he whispers. "They're all assholes."

"Why are you here, then?" I ask, wondering if he'll tell me what he and Blaine were arguing about earlier.

He keeps slamming the keys. "Because I'm a nostalgic idiot," he says. "I thought this would be a last hurrah with Blaine, since we're supposed to be best friends. I should have known he would spend the week sleeping with Kassidy and fawning over Ellison."

I put my hand on his to stop the jarring noise. "You're going to college in a few months. You don't have to see any of us ever again if you don't want."

He looks at me with tears in his eyes and wine on his hot breath. "Why do you all hate me?"

"No one hates you, Gus. That's the alcohol talking. Now will you play me my song?"

His lids look heavy. "Which one?"

"'Someone to Watch Over Me.'"

He smiles a little. "I played this at Blaine's Christmas party sophomore year."

"That was a fun night," I say. "This can be a fun night too."

"Do you think someone will want me in college?" he asks softly as he plays.

"Plenty of guys wanted you at Marian, but you always chased the ones who didn't," I say impatiently. "You can throw a pity party, but no one's going to attend. None of us feel sorry for someone who has everything going for him."

Fergus flushes pink with pleasure. The fire of his insecurity requires constant quenching, and although I'd never noticed it before, he's right: It's usually me throwing the water.

"Marlowe's into you," he says, slurring his words.

My heart jerks out of rhythm. "What makes you think that?"

"We had AP Calculus and British Poetry back-to-back this semester. But instead of going from class to class, he always went the long way, through Kennedy Hall. I got curious and followed him for a few days until I figured out why. He wanted to pass your locker."

"He never talked to me in the hallway," I say. "He always just nodded."

"You were the only person he nodded to. He did it every day so he could see you."

Mr. Jimenez announces dinner. Kassidy has placed Marlowe across from me. Ellison and Fergus sit facing each other, while Blaine's at the head of the table, with Kassidy on his right and Chloe on his left.

Keep your friends close and your enemies closer. The saying pops into my head out of nowhere. Maybe the sidecars are stronger than they taste.

As Kassidy predicted, none of the staff has balked at serving us alcohol, though I feel like they've been staring at us with sullen eyes. I shudder at how indulgent all this must seem to them.

Everyone looks sunburned, and there's an oppressive awkwardness in the air. Kassidy tries to mask it by asking a footman to move the gramophone into the dining room.

"Tonight's meal was Cara's favorite," says Kassidy, reaching for a tiny fork. "Bon appétit!"

The first course is chilled raw oysters, which I refuse without worrying what Marlowe thinks. I'm thankful for the music so I can't hear the others slurp down the gooey messes inside the shells. Luckily, the sweet corn chowder the footman brings out next more than makes up for the starter. It's not quite as perfect as the pea soup from the night before, but it's hearty and garnished with fresh thyme from the garden.

I glance across the table and find Marlowe staring at me again, the salmon mousse on toast in front of him neglected. Had he really spent last semester seeking me out every day? If so, why had he never stopped to talk?

Fergus holds up his glass for more wine as the footman sets out dessert—brown-sugar ice cream topped with summer peaches. Fergus's scowl has been getting deeper and deeper as he's watched Ellison chat with Chloe about Princeton's rowing team.

"Your mom was at my house the other day," Kassidy says to Chloe. Everyone stops eating their ice cream and looks at them.

Chloe seems surprised Kassidy is addressing her directly. "Her company is working on a deal with your dad," she says.

"It must be complicated," says Kassidy. "She didn't leave until almost two in the morning. And it wasn't the first time I've heard her sneak out of our house."

My heart speeds up. It's not hard to figure out what Kassidy's insinuating, although I have no idea why she's doing it in front of everyone. But Mr. Logan having an affair with Chloe's mom? I try to picture Kassidy's quiet, stern dad having a passionate fling, but every cell in my body rejects the image. Unless it's part of the same midlife crisis that made him buy the motorcycles we stole after he left them sitting in the garage for two years. But how could Kassidy not have told me?

"My mom's a hard worker," replies Chloe with a chill in her voice.

"You two have a lot in common, then," says Kassidy with one of her fake wide smiles.

Red blotches spill across Chloe's cheeks. But it's Blaine's face that startles me. He glares at Kassidy, and for a second her smile wavers.

"Only a really hard worker could be valedictorian *and* land a lacrosse scholarship to USC," says Ellison, gallant as always.

"Ellison knows all about effort," slurs Fergus, his eyes unfocused. "How else could he have passed physics?"

The whole table falls silent at the exact second the record on the gramophone runs out. It thumps dully as it spins without a needle. A footman hurries to turn it over, but Fergus holds up a hand to stop him.

"What do you mean?" asks Ellison.

"You were failing," says Fergus. "They would have withheld your diploma. But then Mr. Benson"—he sticks his tongue out and blows a raspberry—"mysteriously died. So Dean Halliwell filled in. And everyone knows he never fails athletes."

Ellison's hand tightens around his wineglass. "Mr. Benson's death wasn't mysterious," he says. "He had a heart attack."

"I'd say that's pretty mysterious for a fifty-year-old marathon runner."

"You should have some water," I tell Fergus, hoping a distraction will help him hop off this impending train crash.

Fergus ignores me and keeps talking. "Mr. Benson's death was *super* convenient for you. That's all I'm saying."

Chloe laughs at his obvious subtext. "Ellison, murder a teacher?" she says. "Who would believe that?"

Fergus turns to the head of the table. "Plenty of people. Right, Blaine?"

Blaine starts fidgeting with his silverware. I have the sudden urge to get up and run out of the dining room, but my legs feel like lead.

I know where this is headed; I was there when Blaine got high as a kite at one of his parties and started spouting off dumb theories about people at school.

"Shut up, Gus," hisses Blaine. But the damage is done.

Ellison's mouth falls open. "*You* spread that rumor?" he asks, almost dropping his wineglass. Some of it sloshes over the rim and trickles like blood across the white tablecloth.

"It was just a joke," says Blaine, shifting uncomfortably. "It's not like I believed it. I was just screwing with people's heads."

"And lives," yells Ellison, bringing his fist down so hard the silverware rattles.

Everybody jumps, and Chloe covers her mouth with her hand. Only Marlowe looks calm and unaffected, and I kind of hate him in that moment.

"Dude, calm down," says Blaine, looking alarmed. "I'm sorry. It was a joke I made when I was trashed."

"That joke got me interviewed by the cops!" says Ellison.

This is news to me. Blaine's rumor flew around school for a few weeks and then died. I didn't think anyone outside Marian would take it seriously.

"My mom was horrified," continues Ellison, his voice shaking. "We have all this money, but I'm still just the Black kid being accused of murder because I struggled with a single class in four years. She had to threaten to sue the school to keep the interview off my permanent record."

Blaine looks ill. "I had no idea," he says. "I'm really sorry." This time it sounds like he means it.

"Then how did you pass physics?" asks Fergus, who looks pleased with the effect his needling has produced.

"I got a tutor," spits Ellison. "Like plenty of other people at school."

"Must have been a pretty good tutor to raise you from an F to a B," says Fergus. My mind flashes back to Fergus bragging about how well he scored on his AP Physics exam.

Ellison narrows his dark eyes and looks straight into Fergus's beady ones. "That was *all* he was good at."

Fergus turns red and begins spluttering. He rises like he's going to launch himself across the table at Ellison.

"Who are you to talk about failing, Fergus?"

Fergus is so shocked to hear Marlowe speaking to him that he sits back down heavily in his chair. "I don't know what you mean," he replies hotly.

"You forget I was Ms. Mahadi's homeroom assistant."

Fergus's face goes, if possible, an even darker shade of scarlet. "I had one bad semester," he says. "But I didn't fail European History. I passed."

"Yeah, I saw the letter your parents sent," says Marlowe.

Blaine lets out a snorting laugh. "Did anyone else almost fail out of Marian?" he asks. His smile falls into a frown when he sees Ellison's glare.

Kassidy finally steps in. "This has gone far enough," she says. "Clearly, we all had some shit to say to each other, and now it's said. Blaine, you apologized to Ellison. Gus, it's your turn."

I can tell he's about to object, so I clear my throat loudly. When he sees my face, he shuts his mouth so hard I hear his teeth click together.

"I'm sorry, Ellison," he mumbles, looking at his hands. "I know you didn't kill Mr. Benson."

"Excellent. That's over, then," says Kassidy.

"Your turn," I say, and her head swings over to me so fast I'm afraid she'll get a cricked neck. We have a wordless exchange with our eyes. I can tell she's pissed, but Chloe has no control over whether her mom has an affair with Kassidy's dad. And Kassidy's hurt feelings are no reason to treat Chloe like a bitch for the rest of the week.

Chloe looks stricken by my suggestion. "Please don't apologize," she says in a rush.

Now that Kassidy knows Chloe doesn't want it, the apology comes easily. "I'm sorry I called your mom a home-wrecker." Kassidy rises from the table with an unfinished cocktail in her hand. "Let's put this behind us and take some of Blaine's party favors."

There's a general murmur of approval as everyone stands up, but a kind of hazy swaying seems to affect us as we walk toward the door, like we're shaking off rubble from an earthquake.

I lean against the fireplace in the drawing room, watching Blaine pull various baggies and paraphernalia from a small case stashed under the couch. The footman places the gramophone back in the corner and turns on the record. Then he hurries out of the room with a frown.

As the first joint is passed around, I can almost see everyone physically relax. Fergus holds the joint out to me, but I shake my head. When the smell of marijuana begins to burn my nose, I leave the others and go in search of Marlowe, who never returned from the dining room. I find him in a high-backed chair in the library, reading a tiny book of poetry by candlelight.

"Good evening, Isadora," he says after I collapse into the seat across from him.

I wonder why he's using my full name. Chloe said he'd called me Isadora the day before too.

"You don't inhale?" he asks.

"I don't like drugs," I reply, wiping dust off the cover of the book on the tea table next to me.

"Me neither. But I used to."

"What changed?"

He closes his book. "My older brother OD'd."

A sharp, slicing pain tightens my chest. "I remember hearing about that when we were freshmen. That must have been really horrible."

"It was. My parents had never been very involved in our lives. Raised by nannies, the usual rich-kid story. But it broke them."

"Did you grow closer afterward?"

He shakes his head and spins one of his diamond cuff links between his thumb and his index finger. "The opposite. I think they were afraid of connecting with me after that. Of getting close and losing me too."

I trace the life line on my right palm and shiver. "I'm sorry."

Marlowe shrugs and says, "'Man hands on misery to man.'" I recognize the line from Marlowe's yearbook quote. Philip Larkin must be a favorite. "You should have taken the British Poetry class," he continues. "Ms. Chenyaka is brilliant."

"It clashed with journalism."

"Is that what you want to study at Brown?"

"If I go," I reply in a small voice. I immediately regret saying it.

Marlowe knits his brows. "You're on scholarship, right?"

"It's not about the money," I say.

"Then what?"

For a moment, silence hangs in the musty air between us.

"Did you know I have a sister?" I ask.

Marlowe frowns, as if he doesn't understand what that has to do with Brown. "Is she younger or older?"

"Caye is two years younger."

"Why isn't she at Marian?"

"She goes to school in the city, where they have a program for people with disabilities."

He looks shaken. "I had no idea."

"She needs full-time care," I say. "My mom will barely be able to do it alone, but she's insisting I go to college. I'm staying on the East Coast to be close, but it will be tough on them."

"And if your mom weren't around to take care of Caye?"

"Then it would be up to me."

He closes his eyes. "Jesus."

I stand up. "Sadly, he can't help. No one can."

Marlowe rises from his chair and moves a few steps closer, as if he wants to comfort me without making me uncomfortable. "That doesn't mean you have to do anything stupid," he says.

I laugh humorlessly. "My dad was deported when I was little, but I'll always remember what he told me when la migra came for him: 'If an eye for an eye makes the whole world blind, be sure your eye is taken last.'"

11

zzy was halfway through helping Caye eat her cinnamon applesauce when a sharp knock on the front door almost made her
drop the plastic spoon. Caye's eyes opened wide, and her arms
began to shake.

"It's fine, Caye," said Izzy. "Probably someone trying to sell
us God."

Izzy squinted through the peephole and frowned when she
saw familiar blue eyes. She twisted the dead bolt, unhooked the
chain, and opened the door.

"Hey, Blaine," she said. "Everything okay?"

He cocked his head to the side. "Why wouldn't it be?"

"Usually you text before coming over."

Blaine held up a corsage. "Kassidy asked me to pick up the
flowers from Lulu's so we don't have to get them tomorrow
before the dance. Your place was on my way home."

"Thanks," said Izzy, taking the corsage. Sprigs of baby's
breath encircled sugar plum tea roses and preserved eucalyp-
tus. "It's beautiful."

"Fergus thought so too. I just dropped his off."

Blaine walked past her and sat on the couch. He always
looked surprisingly at home in her beige apartment, as if he

didn't spend most of his time in a house that had been featured in *Maine Home + Design*.

"Hey, Caye," Blaine said with a smile. "Looks like you're enjoying that applesauce."

Caye waved a balled fist in the air and grinned. "Hi," she said, drawing out the vowel.

For some reason, Caye loved Blaine. Maybe because the color of his hair made him easier to see than other people. Or maybe she was drawn to his charm, like everyone else.

Izzy sat back down to finish feeding Caye. "Is Fergus dreading going to prom with me?" she asked. "I know he would have preferred . . . well, someone else."

Blaine laughed. "Ellison isn't even going to the dance. He's setting up the condo in Boston for the after-party." Blaine played with the frayed ends of his distressed jacket. "My dad confirmed the helicopters will be waiting for us in Portland, but we'll need to leave the dance by ten to catch them."

"Blaine!" said Caye, pushing the spoon away from her mouth.

"C'mon, Caye," said Izzy. "Blaine doesn't want to feed you."

Blaine stopped messing with his coat and hopped off the couch. "Of course I do! Give me that spoon."

Caye giggled as he sat down next to her.

"Careful, Caye. Blaine flirts with all the girls," said Izzy, turning to Blaine. "He's a Darcy in the streets but a Wickham in the sheets."

Blaine rolled his eyes. "How long have you been practicing that line?"

"Long enough to nail it."

Blaine zoomed the spoon into Caye's mouth like an airplane. "All right," he said, when the container was nearly empty.

"It's been a bumpy ride, but here's the last bite." He made the spoon dive toward Caye, but at the last minute she pressed her lips together and the spoon bumped her face, smooshing applesauce all over it.

"Oh no!" said Blaine. "A crash landing!"

All three of them started laughing. Just then, the front door opened. Izzy hadn't expected her mom back from the gym so early. Her hair was in a falling bun, and her yoga mat was bunched awkwardly under her arm.

She frowned. "What's going on?"

Blaine stopped laughing and straightened up. "Oh, hi, Ms. Morales," he said.

Izzy's mom dropped her mat and her keys on the table. "Mr. Gilbert," she said. "Don't we see enough of each other at Thursday tutoring?"

Blaine grinned. "I'm only here to drop off Izzy's corsage."

Izzy's mom glanced at the flowers. "They're lovely," she said. "Kassidy has a wonderful eye." She looked around. "Is she here too?"

"She's at the country club with her parents," said Izzy. "They do dinner with the Wests on Fridays."

Rumbling thunder shook the apartment.

"You better get going, Blaine," said Izzy's mom, pointing outside. "The news said Valley View Road might flood."

The soft patter of droplets splashing the window alerted Caye to the storm. "Rain!" she screamed.

"It's one of her favorite things," Izzy explained to Blaine. "But she hates lightning. Go figure."

Izzy cleaned Caye's face, then wheeled her out to the covered sidewalk next to the courtyard. Their mom and Blaine followed.

Sheets of water drenched the rectangle of grass the apartment provided for recreation.

Caye clapped her hands together and laughed as the falling drops blew mist onto their faces.

Blaine smiled. "I bet I can make Caye like the rain even more," he said. Without any hesitation, he vaulted over the short wrought-iron fence surrounding the grass and ran into the middle of the courtyard. He pulled out his phone and tapped a button. A song from a movie he, Izzy, and Kassidy had recently watched came blasting through the speakers. Blaine started dancing like a house on fire. His arms and legs punched the air with wild abandon. When the song hit the chorus, he spun around and shook his butt like a rhythmless Shakira.

This was too much for Caye. She squealed with delight. Even Izzy's mom was smiling.

Blaine kept dancing until the song ended and he was completely soaked. "Bye, Caye!" he called, leaping over the other end of the fence and sprinting through the parking lot to his Jaguar.

"Only Blaine could have stage presence in the rain," said Izzy with a laugh, turning to her mom.

But the smile had dropped off her mom's face.

"What?" asked Izzy.

"You know how I feel about you having boys at the apartment when I'm not here."

Izzy flushed. "It's not like that," she said. "He was just dropping off my corsage."

"That's not what it looked like when I came in," said her mom. "Not to mention I'm his teacher. I've worked hard to build a professional image. I don't like walking into my own living room and looking like a sweaty mess in front of your friends."

"I'm sorry," said Izzy. "I didn't know he was coming by."

Izzy's apology seemed to only make her mom angrier. "I don't want to see Blaine alone with you again, whether I'm here or not," she snapped. "You should remember that friends like Kassidy don't come along every day."

Izzy's blush deepened, and her hand gripped the top of Caye's wheelchair so hard it hurt. "What's *that* supposed to mean?" she asked.

Her mom crossed her arms and looked Izzy dead in the eye. "You know exactly what I mean."

12

———◇———

Breakfast is a silent, strained affair the next day. I'd slept poorly, woken by raised voices that rolled like ghostly echoes down the hall, as if Ashwood Manor were replaying arguments from past occupants.

It occurs to me that fancy clothes and a beautiful estate can't erase human drama, and I wonder how many people have sat unhappily in this dining room, clothed pristinely while their emotions raged as violently as the sea.

Kassidy suggests we all go swimming, but I stay behind because I don't want to deal with everyone's bad moods. She hasn't spoken to me since I challenged her at dinner. Fergus is ignoring me too.

While the others go to the beach, I spend the afternoon on the patio terrace, flipping through a Georgette Heyer mystery I found stuffed between couch cushions. A light breeze caresses my face, and the droning static of the breaking waves lulls me into a quiet calm.

Maybe swimming in the sea will make people happy again . . . Maybe the salt water will cleanse their anger . . . Maybe . . .

"Kassidy!" yells a distant voice.

"Somebody help her!"

I leap up out of my half sleep, almost falling over the glass table in front of me. Something's wrong, but for a moment my brain can't catch up to reality. Then I hear Kassidy scream.

I sprint down the garden terraces toward the sound of her voice, holding my sun hat flat against my head while its ribbons twirl wildly in the wind.

As I run, I see Blaine race across the rocky sand and plunge headfirst into the ocean. By the time I hurl myself down the rotting driftwood steps, the others are clustered on the shore.

"A riptide caught her," Ellison says when I reach them. His face is pinched with concern.

I hike up my dress and get ready to jump in after Blaine, but Marlowe grabs my arm hard. "It won't help her if you need to be rescued too," he says.

Blaine swims farther and farther out into the choppy gray sea, searching for Kassidy. Something green flashes out of the corner of my eye about a hundred yards away. It's Kassidy's bathing suit.

"Kassidy!" I shriek, tripping over rocks as I run across the beach.

Sputtering, Kassidy drags herself out of the water and onto a strip of sand. I fall on my knees next to her.

"Are you all right?" I pound her back in case there's water in her lungs.

She coughs like a seal a few times, but no water comes up. "I swam sideways, and the riptide let me out," she gasps. She stares down the shoreline. "What are they all looking at?"

"Blaine went in after you."

Kassidy stumbles over to the rest of the group, who are all trying to get Blaine's attention over the crashing waves.

"He's coming back!" says Chloe.

Kassidy throws a barbed glare her way, then turns to watch Blaine swim to land.

Blaine hauls himself out of the water, wool suit dripping heavily, gasping for breath. "What the hell were you thinking swimming out that far?" he yells at Kassidy, pulling her into a bear hug.

"I'm sorry," she says in a small voice.

Chloe lingers close to them, like she wants to join their hug, but she settles for shivering and clutching Ellison's arm. Marlowe's watching me like he's afraid I'll break down, but now that Kassidy's safe, my mind churns with a single thought: *If only the riptide had dragged Blaine and his secrets to the bottom of the sea. Then we would all be free of him.*

The beach day has been ruined. No one will get near the water, and what little laughter rises from the rocks is forced and unpleasant. When the afternoon fog rolls in, everyone packs up their umbrellas and bags with relief and returns to their rooms to get ready for dinner.

Kassidy collapses onto the canopy bed in her wet bathing suit. Our conflict from the night before has evaporated.

"That riptide was so scary," I say, chewing my fingernails. "Blaine risked his life for you."

Kassidy rolls over and stares at the ceiling. "If only he'd risk his heart for me." She sighs. "Do you think all house parties went this terribly in the 1920s?"

"Maybe you and I should come back to the room after dinner," I suggest, trying to take her mind off what happened at the beach. "We can play cards and talk about how men's wool bathing suits do *not* leave much to the imagination."

Kassidy laughs weakly. "A girls' night sounds nice."

"You should soak in the tub after being in that freezing water." I peek into the bathroom. "We're out of clean towels. I'll ask Mr. Jimenez for more."

When I get downstairs, the butler is nowhere to be found, but there's a maid in the dining room setting the table. She's not much older than me, and I wonder if she's watching our group with jealousy or eye rolls.

"Can we have some extra towels?" I ask her.

"Yes, miss," she says, and walks over to the wall, where there's a brass candelabra sculpted into three rosebuds, each holding a stubby candle. She pulls the middle rosebud, and the wall swings open to reveal a hidden passage.

"No way," I whisper, peering into the dark.

"It's just a hallway," she says.

"Yeah, but it's a secret hallway!"

She shrugs. "Only if you don't know about it."

I can't argue with that. But just because the novelty has worn off for her doesn't mean I don't want to explore.

I stop her before she enters the passage. "I can get them," I say.

She shrugs again and leaves me alone. The hidden space is narrow and long and filled with piles of extra linens, racks of vintage wines, and stacks of old hardcover books. As I grab some clean towels, I hear familiar voices coming from the other end of the passage. I hurry down the dark corridor and press my ear against the wall of what must be the library.

Blaine is speaking softly, but I can just make out what he's saying. "I can't do this anymore."

"You said you were breaking up with her." Chloe's voice is low and bitter.

"It's not as simple as that."

"Is there someone else? Somebody besides Kassidy?"

"Of course not. But we're going to college soon, and I want to have new experiences."

"Experience new girls, you mean."

"Prom night was really special, and everything that came after was great, but—"

"You were using me. I get it."

"That's not true. I just think this has . . . run its course."

"Run its course?" Chloe's words explode with shrill anger. "Like I'm some kind of virus you needed out of your system?" Now she's flat-out yelling. *"I'm* the one who ended up on antibiotics. *I'm* the one who had to go to a secret clinic so my mom didn't find out I'd screwed someone diseased! Fuck you, Blaine!"

I run out of the passage and dining room just in time to see Chloe fly up the staircase, hair in disarray and cheeks stained with tears. She slams her bedroom door so loudly I feel it shudder.

Blaine stops dead when he comes out of the library and sees me standing in the foyer. My mind is racing. *Chloe and Blaine. Blaine and Chloe.* I'm shaking so hard it's all I can do to hold on to the towels.

"All this time you were with Chloe too?" I ask with barely controlled rage.

Blaine's face flushes bright red, but he doesn't answer.

"How many hearts are you willing to break?" I say.

Blaine runs his hands through his hair, and, to my surprise, the distress on his face looks genuine. Before he can respond, something falls out of his pocket and onto the ground.

It's a phone.

He swoops down to pick it up. "Take care of Kass," he says. "She deserves better than me."

He trudges miserably up the stairs. I'd watched Blaine put his iPhone with its blue Marian Academy case in the butler's satchel. The one he dropped was the small black burner phone he hid secret texts on—texts from people who weren't his girlfriend.

"She deserves better than both of us," I mutter.

I climb the stairs in a daze. As I pass Blaine's room, his shower pipes begin to groan. Kassidy is still lying on top of the bed in her swimsuit when I enter with the towels. I'm afraid she'll notice something is wrong, but she looks as distracted and out of sorts as I do. She hops off the bed, grabs a towel from my arms, and heads into the bathroom with a mumbled "Thanks."

I sit on the bed in shock once she's gone. Is this the real reason Kassidy is being so awful to Chloe? She knows Blaine hooked up with her at prom? I guess it also explains why Nestor dumped Chloe so soon after the dance.

I shiver. If Blaine gave Chloe an STD, he might have given it to everyone he slept with.

And now he's in the room next to us, naked and vulnerable in the shower while everyone else is tucked away in their rooms getting ready for cocktails and dinner.

I hadn't expected my opportunity to come so soon. But finding out about Chloe makes me more convinced than ever that Blaine is getting exactly what he deserves. And I might not get a better chance to give it to him.

As soon as I hear the splash of Kassidy entering the tub, I'm in motion. I take the gold knife from under the mattress and carefully slide it up the sleeve of my day coat. Then I open the bedroom door and peer into the hallway. It's empty. I slip along the wall until I reach Blaine's room, listening carefully for any stray sounds over the banging of the pipes.

As soon as I touch the doorknob, a wave of panic stops me in my tracks. My heart races so fast in my ears I can't even distinguish separate beats. The knife in my sleeve feels death-cold, like it's burning my skin.

There's still time to turn back, a little voice whispers in my head. I can pretend I never stalked down the hallway hiding a weapon in my clothes. Pretend this was part of the themed weekend—an old-school murder mystery game.

Then a flood of memories blurs my vision. Caye, her little face peering at me from bed, one eye bigger than the other and both looking at me with love. Me and Kassidy playing peekaboo behind our hands while Caye throws her head back and gurgles with laughter. The memories shift, and it's Blaine in my apartment. I see him on the couch where I sleep and in the kitchen and in the parking lot. His eyes are the opposite of Caye's. Blue where hers are brown. Cold where hers are warm. Filled with suspicion instead of trust.

I take a deep breath. As the panic subsides and the anger resurfaces, I remember why I brought the knife. And as long as Kassidy never finds out what I've done . . .

I open Blaine's door as silently as a mouse and creep inside.

When I finish, I leave Blaine's room and gently shut the door behind me. I turn and find myself feet away from Marlowe.

I slap my hands over my mouth so I don't scream.

"You scared me half to death," I hiss.

"What were you doing in Blaine's room?" he asks.

My heart beats so loud I'm sure Marlowe can hear it. I pull my coat more tightly around my body. "None of your damn business. Why are you spying on me?"

"I'm not. I came up the stairs right before you left Blaine's room."

"It's not what you think," I say, but my voice cracks over the words.

"What's done is done," he says. He walks down the hall and doesn't look back.

I hurry to my bedroom, praying that Kassidy isn't out of the bath yet. The water is still draining, so at least that part of the plan has gone right. I close the door with a soft thud, jump on the bed, open a book, and pretend I've been reading.

Why did Marlowe have to come up the stairs at that exact moment? Now he's caught me, and all I can do is hope he'll keep another secret.

But I of all people know that secrets rarely stay that way.

I'm still shaking and light-headed when Kassidy comes out of the bathroom in a silk bathrobe, steam following her like theatrical smoke.

"It's all yours," she says. "Still plenty of hot water." Kassidy flips through a few dresses in the armoire before choosing a silver-sequined black gown. She lays short opera gloves and a gorgeous double-rhinestone headband on the bed before beginning to wind her curls.

I don't trust myself to talk, so I head into the bathroom without a word. I bite my nails while the bathtub fills, trying not to think about my time in Blaine's room. When I lower myself into the bubbles, my muscles relax. Marlowe is right: What's done is done. I can sink into the depths of my regrets, or I can move forward.

As my heart rate slows, my mind wanders back to sitting next to Marlowe at dinner, his hand resting gently on my shoulder. I imagine how it would feel if he brushed his thumb along my collarbone, our bodies moving closer . . .

I hear the hollow echo of Kassidy's scream for help, see her arms wave wildly as she tries to move through the riptide. I imagine her face under the salt water, eyes bulging, lungs gasping for air while her mouth and nose burn. I feel myself drift away with her on the tide.

My eyes snap open. I see toes floating through a haze of bubbles, and for a second I think I'm still dreaming. It's only when I breathe in a bellyful of water that I realize with a terrified start that I'm awake and lying at the bottom of the bathtub. Panic floods my brain like hot metal. My hands slip on the porcelain as I struggle for the surface. I push myself up and jerk my head above the water, sputtering soap. After my heart stops racing, I climb out of the bathtub, trembling with residual adrenaline.

When I enter the bedroom, Kassidy is napping. She looks thinner and younger somehow, her dark dress flowing around her lithe frame. She stirs as I tiptoe to the armoire, then rolls over and gazes at me with dull, sleepy eyes. "Is it time to go downstairs?"

"Soon," I say, my voice shaking. "I accidentally stayed in the bath too long."

Kassidy slides out of bed and paces in silence while I get ready. She stops in front of the bedroom door and tries to open it. "Did you take the key?" she asks. "It's not in the hole."

She's right. The keyhole is empty. After a few minutes of

searching, I find the key on the bathroom floor in the pocket of my crumpled coat.

"Sorry," I say. "I must have taken it when I locked the door."

As I pin my hair, I consider telling her about the conversation I overheard between Blaine and Chloe. Then again, if she doesn't know the details of their relationship, I could make things worse.

This is all Blaine's fault. He tells women he wants to be with them, and they always believe him. I cringe as I think of the letters written in his messy scrawl, hidden in a pillowcase at my apartment.

Eventually, everyone finds out he's a liar.

13

The drawing room is quiet when we arrive. Ellison sits on the sofa in his black tux, holding what appears to be sparkling water. He jumps when he sees us, his left leg bouncing nervously.

"You look wired," I say.

He gives a short, barking laugh. "I drank too much tea at breakfast. That loose-leaf is crazy strong."

I try to recall if I'd seen him drink an unusual amount of tea, but, pathetically, the only person I can remember from breakfast is Marlowe.

Fergus wanders into the room, looking disheveled in his wrinkled suit, and sits at the piano. "A drink, my good man," he says in a loud, theatrical voice.

Mr. Jimenez hands him that evening's cocktail: a corpse reviver, made with a splash of absinthe. Fergus gulps it down and holds out his empty coupe glass. "Hit me again," he says. Apparently, he's determined to go on another bender.

Ellison keeps glancing over at him, but Fergus ignores all of us and plays a slow, sad tune that does nothing to dispel the tense atmosphere.

Chloe glides in with puffy red eyes. There's an eerie calm about her. She grabs a corpse reviver from the tray and joins

Ellison on the sofa. Her eyes flash to Kassidy, and a look of sympathy crosses her face.

Kassidy stands by the fireplace, gazing into the flames and holding an untouched glass of champagne in her pale hand.

Marlowe enters the drawing room. "Evening," he says. No one answers him. He walks past me without meeting my eyes. No doubt he thinks the worst of me sneaking out of Blaine's room.

A wave of anxiety shakes my legs when I think of Blaine upstairs. *It's for the best,* I remind myself. Blaine has hurt so many people. Spurned their friendship and love. Lied and spread rumors. Created thunderstorms of tears. So why can't I stop the regret pricking my heart?

After another fifteen minutes of awkward silence, dinner is announced.

"Where's Blaine?" asks Marlowe, looking around the room.

Kassidy is roused from her fire staring. "He must have lost track of time," she says, with a quick glance at her wristwatch.

Fergus stumbles away from the piano. "Or he's trying to avoid someone."

Deep-red splotches pool in Chloe's cheeks. Ellison's left leg bounces faster.

"I'll go get him," says Kassidy.

The rest of us drift into the dining room.

Just as the footman drapes a napkin over my lap, a heart-wrenching scream shatters the silence.

Fergus's eyes bulge. "What the——"

I'm on my feet first, shoving back from the table so hard my chair falls to the ground. My heels drive a sharp pain into my calves as I bound up the stairs, but I don't slow down. I sprint across the hallway right as Kassidy stumbles out of Blaine's room and falls to the ground, dry-heaving and wailing.

"Kass, what's wrong?" I ask, dropping to my knees. I wrap my arms around her to steady the convulsions that are rocking her body so hard I'm afraid she's going to break her teeth.

The others run by me and enter the room in a flurry. I hear shrill, terrified screams from Fergus and Chloe.

"Fuck! No, no, no, no, no," Ellison's deep voice cries. "Everyone stay back!"

"Somebody help him!" shrieks Chloe.

Kassidy is crying so hard she's hyperventilating.

"Kass, you need to calm down," I say. "Take little breaths."

Someone darts out of the room and across the rugs to the stairs, but I don't see who.

Ellison comes out and kneels beside me. "I'll take Kass to your room. She can't stay out here."

He picks her up like a rag doll. I follow him as he carries her through the open door and places her on the bed before leaving again. Kassidy's dark sequins reflect the flame of the dripping yellow candle on the side table. Her tears are coming slower now, but her face is frozen in a mask of horror.

I drape a blanket across her legs and run my hand over her hair soothingly, but my mind is racing. I need to know what everyone saw.

"I'll be right back, Kass."

She doesn't even appear to notice me, so I slip into the hallway. Fergus is on the ground, sobbing. Chloe is leaning against the wall, sucking in huge gulps of air, while Marlowe tries to calm her down. He glances at me as I pass, his face unreadable.

I take a deep breath and steel myself for the horror that lies within. Then I enter Blaine's room.

Nausea roils my stomach. Blaine is on the ground near the bathroom, facedown, one arm above his head and the other contorted awkwardly beneath his torso. A towel is wrapped around his bottom half, but he's not wearing a shirt. There are jagged bloody gashes on his back and dark-red pools of blood next to his body.

Ellison is kneeling, but he pops up when he sees me. He stuffs something into his pocket with a deft motion and stares at me with wide eyes. I realize he expects me to say something.

"What happened?" I whisper.

"Somebody stabbed him," he says, his voice quivering, though I can't tell if it's with fear or rage. "A lot."

I look at the blood with fascination and disgust. It's hard to believe it's all from one person. Blaine's body looks staged, like Marian's theater crew decided to produce *Hamlet* at Ashwood Manor, complete with the stabbing victim. Blaine's final role, at school and in life.

I hope Ellison won't see the storm of guilt and hope making my muscles twitch. "Did you find the knife?" I ask, taking care to keep my voice from trembling.

Ellison shakes his head. "I looked around—it's not here."

"We need to call the police."

"Marlowe already did," he says. "They're on their way, but it'll take time. They have to take the ferry across, and it's going to storm."

As if on cue, a crack of thunder rattles the house.

Kassidy's wails rise above the sound. I take one last look at

Blaine before I rush next door to check on her. She's half out of bed now, clinging to the blanket with both hands. "Blaine!" she gasps. "Blaine!"

I run over and wrap an arm around her, gently guiding her back toward the pillow. Her diamond bracelet catches on the lace fringe of the blanket. I try to pull them apart, but the fabric begins to tear. I finally get the clasp unhooked and place the bracelet in the drawer of the side table for Kassidy to find later. "Let's lie down," I say, treating her like I do Caye when she has one of her nightmares. "Everything's going to be fine."

Kassidy doesn't resist and collapses back into bed. I sit and watch her chest rise and fall while the sight of Blaine's lifeless body flashes into my mind every few seconds. The grandfather clock ticks quietly in the corner, the hands moving so slowly I feel like I'm trapped in one of those dreams where time is a solid fog. Rain pelts the house in a steady stream. My dark eyes look back at me in the dripping window.

What did Marlowe say to the police on the phone? Did he tell them he'd seen me creep out of Blaine's room hours before we found his body?

No. He was downstairs for only a few minutes. And it's unlikely they asked him for too many details on the 911 call. I probably don't have to worry about the police knowing my movements or motives.

Yet.

Two hours later, there's a loud pounding at the front door. I jerk out of my stupor and jump up, moaning as my neck twinges from being slumped uncomfortably in a chair. Kassidy doesn't stir.

I hurry into the hallway and meet the frightened eyes of the others.

"It's the cops," whispers Fergus. "I saw them from my window, driving up the hill."

We go downstairs as a group to find that Mr. Jimenez has already opened the front door. His unsurprised face indicates that someone told him about Blaine.

Rain falls in heavy bands outside, glittering in the headlights of the vehicles lining the drive. Two police officers in dripping uniforms step through the door. Other people, dressed in all-white disposable suits, pull cases from a van. An ambulance stands by, but the EMTs stay inside.

"We got a report of a possible death at this address," says one of the officers, a middle-aged man with a giant blond mustache and bald head. "Which of you made that call?"

Marlowe steps forward, his face serene. Only his messy curls give any sign that something upsetting has happened. "I did. One of our friends has been stabbed. He's dead."

"Where is he?" asks the officer with a disturbing lack of urgency.

"Upstairs," says Marlowe. "We can show you."

The officer frowns at us, and I realize how ridiculously out of place our period clothes must look. "I can find him," he says. "You folks stay here with Officer Merin."

He disappears up the stairs.

Officer Merin is young and plump. Her black hair is slicked back into a tight ponytail. "Are you having some kind of costume party?" she asks doubtfully, examining our dresses and tuxes.

"It's a 1920s party," I say. "We just graduated from high school."

"Is anyone under eighteen?"

We all shake our heads.

She eyes us with suspicion. "None of your parents are here?"

"Like we said, we're all eighteen," repeats Ellison defensively.

I wait for Officer Merin to ask us what happened, but she just walks around the house and takes notes. The officer with the blond mustache comes back downstairs. He motions for Officer Merin to follow him outside. Through the open front door, I see them talk to the ambulance driver and then to one of the people in white.

"That's the forensic team," says Marlowe, to no one in particular.

After a few minutes, the officers come back inside, trailed by a half dozen people in white and one tired-looking woman in a sharp suit carrying a doctor's bag.

"Officer Young and I need all of you to go to the big room with the fireplace and wait for us," says Officer Merin. "Is anyone else here besides the five of you?"

"The staff," says Mr. Jimenez, who has been lurking in the shadows near the front door. "Four of us total. We sleep in the old servants' quarters."

"Only four in a house this big?"

"There were others that helped us prepare for the week, but they returned on the ferry yesterday."

Officer Merin exchanges a glance with Officer Young. "Please ask your staff to remain at Ashwood Manor until they're interviewed," she says. "Anyone else?"

I speak up. "Kassidy. Blaine is"—I stop, realizing that Blaine's life belongs to the past—"Blaine *was* her boyfriend. She's upstairs."

Officer Young's mustache twitches. "Why isn't she down here?"

"She had a breakdown," I reply, "but she finally fell asleep, so we left her in bed."

"We'll need you to stay downstairs while the scene is processed," he says. "It may take a long time, but we cannot allow you near your friend's room. An officer will be posted at the drawing room door for your safety."

A collective chill descends on the group. *Our safety.*

Violence has seeped into the dark hallways of Ashwood Manor, and now one of us is dead.

14

---◆---

MARIAN ROWING REGATTA
Three Months Ago

March came in like a lion—if that lion wandered the Arctic desert instead of the Sahara.

"I'm freezing my balls off," grumbled Fergus, stuffing his hands into the pockets of a jacket Ellison had once complimented.

"That's what happens when you choose style over warmth," said Blaine with a smirk.

Fergus and Blaine sat in lawn chairs at the edge of Pine Lake, waiting for the first rowing regatta of spring to begin. The sky was overcast, and a stiff breeze stung Fergus's eyes. Small waves capped with angry white froth lapped the shore.

"Lots of chop," said Blaine. "Ellison won't be breaking his state record today."

"Unless the wind shifts," said a voice on their right.

Fergus swung his head around. Marlowe stood alone near a group of elderly women wrapped in so many furs they looked like a herd of chinchillas.

"Grab a seat," said Blaine, pointing at an empty chair next to Fergus.

Marlowe's voice was as cold as the morning air when he responded. "My dad's waiting for me at the boats."

Blaine's eyes followed Marlowe as he wove through the crowd toward the clubhouse. "Why does he treat me like I spend my free time murdering puppies?"

"He probably hates everybody who was at the party where his brother OD'd," whispered Fergus, glancing around to make sure none of their classmates were nearby.

Blaine shook his head. "I was in Boston that weekend," he said. "A townie threw a rager at Harker Fields that spiraled out of control. Bet they got some bad shit from a dealer downtown."

Out of the corner of his eye, Fergus saw two juniors he didn't know by name nodding significantly at Blaine.

"Speaking of . . . ," said Blaine with a grin. He grabbed the leather bag he always carried and met the juniors near the woods bordering the lake. It wasn't hard to figure out why they'd signaled him. Midterms were coming up, and Blaine did a steady trade in Ritalin and Adderall every March.

"Here they come," yelled a voice in the crowd.

A dozen athletes in blue Marian tracksuits jogged out of the clubhouse. The shoreline erupted in cheers and claps.

Fergus whipped out his binoculars. Ellison was easy to spot: He was the only Black crew member, and he towered over the other athletes.

Doubt crept down Fergus's spine. Would Ellison be angry if he knew Fergus's eyes were on him? He'd told Fergus to act like they didn't know each other at school, but he hadn't said anything about the races.

Blaine returned to his chair just as the sun peeked out from behind the gray clouds. The breeze shifted in an instant, like someone had thrown a switch.

"It's a tailwind!" called Blaine.

The spectators shifted restlessly. All at once, the state record was back in play.

Blaine stood up to get a better view. "My man has a chance!" he hooted.

A red streak of possessive rage shot across Fergus's vision. *Ellison's my man,* he thought. He hurried to his feet and adjusted the focus on his binoculars.

Ellison's slim boat was lined up in the lane closest to them. Fergus could see his strong back muscles tensed and ready for the starting signal. The bell sounded, and six sculls shot away from the dock.

Fergus's mouth dropped open as Ellison pulled ahead of the other rowers. He'd expected Ellison's athleticism to be impressive, but he hadn't known how graceful he would look as his oars cut the water with a rhythmic beauty. He pumped his legs forward and back, forward and back. Heat rose in Fergus's cheeks. Why had he never come to a regatta before? He felt the loss of all those mornings he could have watched Ellison glide across the lake, past ecstasies he could never recover. He knew one thing: He wouldn't miss another race.

Fergus dropped his binoculars to his chest when the racers rowed closer. The look on Ellison's face was one of intense concentration.

"Go, Ellison!" yelled Fergus, caught up in the moment.

Ellison's eyes darted to where the crowd stood cheering him on. When he spotted Fergus, the front of his scull swerved. Ellison straightened his boat in a single stroke. But it was too late. It took several more strokes to get back to cruising speed.

By the time he crossed the finish line, he was a dozen seconds shy of his state record.

The crowd clapped with obvious disappointment.

Blaine frowned. "I've never seen him lose control of his boat," he said. "I wonder if he hit a bad patch of water."

Fergus put his head in his hands, completely mortified. Even if no one else understood why Ellison had lost focus, Fergus knew. And worse: Ellison knew too.

He *had* to apologize.

After the other races ended, Blaine grabbed his bag and stood up. "I'm going to the clubhouse to see if Ellison's coming to my party."

"I'll ask him," said Fergus quickly.

Blaine shot him a mocking grin. "If you want to see Ellison in the locker room, just say so." He sat back down on his lawn chair. "Party starts at sunset. Don't park in front of the neighbors' houses. He knows the drill."

Assistants were placing boats back in their racks in front of the clubhouse. Fergus didn't see any Marian tracksuits outside, so he followed a few athletes from the other school into the boys' locker room, trying not to draw attention to himself. He walked along the rows of lockers, but Ellison was nowhere to be found.

A blond boy in a white towel came around the corner, almost running into him. It was Haywood, another rower on Marian's team.

"What are you doing in here, Barnes?" he asked. "Trying to sneak a peek?"

Fergus glared at him. "You've got nothing worth peeking at."

Several other crew members came out of the showers and gathered behind Haywood, who laughed as he ripped off his towel. "You sure about that?"

Fergus wanted to bolt out of the locker room. But he knew he'd take even more crap from Haywood and his buddies if he fled. Instead, he looked down.

"Haywood?" he said. "More like Not-a-lot-of-wood."

The grin fell off Haywood's face. The other guys whooped and laughed.

Suddenly, all six feet, six inches of Ellison appeared from around the corner. He stopped dead when he saw Fergus.

Haywood glanced at Ellison, then back at Fergus. He grinned like a cat that had cornered a mouse. "I get it. You want to hook a bigger fish than me." Haywood stepped back so Ellison and Fergus could face each other. The other guys waited nervously to see what Ellison would do.

Fergus shrank back when he met Ellison's eyes. He'd never seen him so angry. Fergus's voice trembled when he spoke. "Blaine wanted me to remind you about his party tonight."

"Tell him I'll be there," said Ellison curtly. "Now get lost. The locker room is for athletes, not mathletes."

The guys laughed louder than the joke deserved, but Fergus's need to make things right with Ellison was stronger than their derision. "I wondered if we could talk—"

Fergus didn't even see Ellison move. One minute, Ellison was ten feet away, and the next, he had Fergus by the throat, pressed against the lockers.

"We have nothing to talk about," spat Ellison. "I'm tired of you following me around. I'm not interested, and that's my final word. Now piss off."

He let go of Fergus's neck so abruptly Fergus fell to the floor in a heap. Ellison stalked back through the group of boys, who looked at him with a mixture of glee and fear.

Then Ellison turned around and dug the blade into Fergus's heart:

"Like I need another stalker."

15

———◇———

D o you think it was one of the staff?" asks Chloe in a soft
whisper.

It's the first word anyone has spoken in over an hour.

"Why would one of them kill Blaine?" asks Ellison. He's
back to bouncing his leg up and down.

"Drugs," says Marlowe, as if the answer is obvious.

He's on the settee in the corner, bow tie still stiff around his
neck, twirling an unlit clove cigarette around like a pen.

"Why would anyone kill Blaine for bringing some pot?" asks
Chloe. "It's not even illegal."

I glance toward the cop stationed at the door, but he's got
his back turned and is chatting animatedly to another cop, a
pretty woman with an elfin face. Our collective nightmare is
their Monday shift.

"What if someone broke into the house?" I suggest. "It's not
exactly a fortress. There's plenty of doors and windows to sneak
through."

"That's what happened. I'm sure of it." Everyone turns to
look at Fergus, who has been crying and playing "My Heart
Will Go On" over and over on the piano.

I feel a deep pang of sorrow. His best friend is dead, and the
last words he spoke to him were in anger. Without help, he'll

self-destruct. I try to think of something I can do for him. Then I shake my head. *Stop trying to fix everything for everyone.*

But something *has* been fixed. I've stuffed down my feelings, kept them locked away so tightly I barely feel them, but a humming thrill still runs through my guilt. Blaine is dead, and I'm free.

I catch Marlowe watching me and rearrange my face into something more mournful.

"It's the only explanation," I say.

"No. It's not," retorts Marlowe.

The rest of us drop into silence again. We know what he means.

"I want to go home," moans Chloe. She buries her head in a sofa pillow, crushing her feathered headband, and begins to cry.

Hours pass. I hear screaming, but I've been dozing off and on in front of the fire, and I can't tell if the sound is coming from inside my head. Then loud footsteps pound down the stairs, and I hop up, wide awake.

Fergus bangs once on the piano keys before he follows me and Marlowe into the hall. Ellison and an exhausted Chloe hurry on our heels. I'm afraid the police guard might stop us, but he's walking into the foyer too.

There's a jangling metal thrum at the top of the stairs. Two EMTs are carrying a gurney. As soon as I see the black body bag, I begin to shake. The scene drifts by in slow motion: Chloe's wail and near faint as Ellison supports her against his body. Fergus grasping the banister hard enough to crush the wood. Marlowe staring stoically at the gurney as it passes.

But the cops aren't watching the body; they're watching us. They're staring at our horrified faces, at our grief, at our secret shames, and it feels like they're waiting for the smallest hint of guilt. A twitch of a smile, the downcast eyes of a person who can't endure what they've done, the alert face of someone deriving a twisted pleasure from watching Blaine's body be removed from Ashwood Manor. Any indication that one of us turned a sparkling graduation party into a crime scene.

Now I understand that they aren't concerned for our safety at all.

They think one of us did it.

As soon as Blaine's body is rolled out of the house, time finds its normal path. Officer Young approaches us. "Your friend woke up and tried to rush into the victim's room," he says, smoothing his blond mustache. "The doctor had to sedate her. If she's not better in the morning, let the detectives know."

"Detectives?" Ellison's ears have perked up.

"We're only the attending officers. Homicide detectives have been assigned to the case. They'll be here tomorrow at nine." He checks his watch. "That's six hours from now."

"But I want to leave in the morning!" cries Chloe.

"We ask that you remain here until you're interviewed by the detectives. They'll tell you when you're free to go."

Officer Merin snaps her notepad shut. "We need the clothes you were wearing this evening," she says. "You can go upstairs and change. We'll bag whatever you remove."

"No," says Ellison.

Officer Merin's eyebrows fly upward. "We need them for testing," she protests.

"Do you have a warrant?" he asks.

We all shift uncomfortably. Ellison's mom is an attorney, but she spends more time on television than in the courtroom.

"The detectives will have one tomorrow," says Officer Merin, pursing her lips like she's bitten into a lemon.

"I guess we'll see then what the scope of the warrant is."

Officer Young narrows his eyes. "You been in trouble with the law before, son?"

My mind goes back to what Ellison told us about being interviewed by the police when Mr. Benson died. But he doesn't mention that.

"Not every Black guy has a history with the cops," snaps Ellison.

Officer Young turns so red I'm afraid the capillaries in his face might burst. "I can't wait to see which of you did it," he growls.

He and Officer Merin turn on their heels and exit Ashwood Manor without a backward glance.

"Can they really keep us here, Ellison?" asks Chloe in a small voice.

Ellison frowns. "I don't think so," he says. "But they can probably make it very unpleasant for us to leave."

IT'S PAST FOUR in the morning, and the house is silent. I've been sitting on the chaise next to the dying fire in our bedroom, waiting. The sedative the doctor gave Kassidy worked so well she didn't even open her eyes when I helped her into her pajamas. The ticking of the grandfather clock threatens to lull me to sleep, but I force myself to stay awake by pinching the skin on my wrists every few minutes.

I have a loose end to tie up, and it can't wait.

When it feels like even the worst insomniac must have fallen asleep, I creep out of our bedroom. Blaine's door is open, with yellow tape stretched across the door frame. I duck underneath the tape and head for his armoire, where his suits are hanging. I use my nightgown to pop open the doors so I won't leave fingerprints, and then slide my hand into the left pocket of Blaine's dinner pants, where I hid the gold knife.

The pocket is empty.

My gulping gasp cuts through the darkness. I shove my hand into the right pocket, in case my memory is playing tricks on me.

It's empty too.

I clutch at every pair of Blaine's pants, not caring if the sharp tip stabs me, waiting for the hard metal outline to appear beneath my fingers. When it doesn't, I run my hands over the shelves, reaching all the way into the corners. But there's nothing.

My knife is gone.

Waves of panic crash over me. I see the shadow of Blaine's body on the ground, surrounded by splashes of red. My stomach lurches, and I head for the door. Just as I'm about to duck back underneath the yellow tape, I hear soft footsteps.

Someone is walking toward me.

I rush back into the room, running as lightly as I can in my silk slippers, and climb into the armoire. Blaine's clothes smell like vintage oak and body spray. I don't dare snap the doors shut all the way, so I crouch inside, staring through the gap.

Someone pads quietly across the wood floor, then stops. There's a dull click, and the white glare of a flashlight floods the room. I hold my breath, hoping whoever it is won't hear my gentle rustling, but the intruder is busy crawling on hands and knees near the bed.

I risk peering a little farther out the cracked doors. The flashlight is bright enough for me to see the outline of the person's thick black curls.

Marlowe.

I gasp, throwing my hands over my mouth to stifle the sound, but it's too late. He jumps to his feet and sprints away, leaving the room in darkness.

I take deep breaths to stop my heart from racing. If Marlowe had caught me in Blaine's room a second time, he probably would have called the police straightaway.

But why was Marlowe in Blaine's room at all?

I wait for what feels like hours before leaving my hiding spot, in case Marlowe decides to spy. But the hallway is silent and dark, and I climb into bed without waking Kassidy. The first hints of dull sunlight are already breaking through the fog. I try to sleep, but I can't. The question won't stop churning in my head: *Where is my knife?*

KASSIDY DOESN'T STIR when the maid knocks on our door at eight o'clock, but I haul myself out of bed, eyes glazed with exhaustion. It feels completely demented to pick a fancy dress from our armoire, but I have no choice, since Kassidy sent our normal clothes back to the mainland. Her idea had seemed like a charming touch at the time, like casting our real lives aside for a week of fantasy, but now I feel like a horror sideshow, like a little girl playing games while the world burns. I can only imagine what the detectives will think about how we look. Probably like kids so out of touch with reality we could be killers.

Before I leave the room, I put a looking glass in front of Kassidy's mouth to make sure she's breathing. It seems like nothing is wrong with her besides a powerful sedative. I stroke her hair, but she doesn't respond. Last night's drama was only the beginning; she's going to be entirely inconsolable. I silently promise to be strong for her, no matter how long it takes or how much it hurts. I will not let my choices ruin her life.

No one talks at breakfast. I sneak a glance at Marlowe, who has tired lines under his eyes. He stares back at me with an inscrutable gaze. I imagine asking him why he was in Blaine's room, but then I'd have to admit I'd been in there too.

The storm, which had quieted during the night, is raging again. Dark clouds hang over the ocean, lashing the windows with rain. The fog makes Ashwood Manor feel claustrophobic, like not even light can penetrate its walls.

We jump when the knocking comes, even though we've all been watching the clock like hawks. Mr. Jimenez answers it, some words are exchanged about where to hang coats, and then two detectives enter the dining room like grim reapers ready to snatch secrets from our souls.

There's a man and a woman. The man is in his late thirties, tall and skeletal, with sharp cheekbones and piercing blue eyes. He's not attractive, but he has a sallow Victorian vibe, like he sits by fires drinking sherry and reading depressing poetry. He would look more at ease in our 1920s outfits than the faded dad jeans and button-down cream shirt he's wearing. His expression is bored and languid, like he's seen the world and found it wearisome.

The woman's appearance is startling. She's so tiny she resembles a fragile bird, but she's wearing an enormous black dress that wouldn't be out of place at a steampunk funeral. Tortoiseshell glasses perch on her snub nose, and her giant black eyes blink slowly as she looks around at all of us. She's olive-skinned and has a mountain of rich black hair piled on top of her head. Her skin is smooth, but a thick streak of silver hair tucked behind her petite ear suggests she's at least forty.

"Thank you all for agreeing to meet with us this morning," says the male detective in a rangy drawl, and I picture sweet tea and tractors. He must have made his way up the East Coast from whatever southern part of the country he calls home. "I'm Detective Cates, and this is Pilar de León. You might recognize her name from the news. She works for the police in an unofficial capacity."

We all turn to each other with uncomprehending looks.

"What do you mean, 'unofficial capacity'?" asks Ellison suspiciously.

"I am a consulting detective," she says. Her voice is melodic, and I can tell I'm not the only one surprised to hear her accent. It's like my dad's, and I wonder if they're from the same state in Mexico. "The police graciously permit me to accompany them on cases I find interesting." Her eyes sparkle mischievously at Detective Cates, whose mouth is set in a firm line, giving the distinct impression that her presence at Ashwood Manor was not his call.

"Why do you find this case interesting?" asks Marlowe.

She smiles delightedly. "An excellent question, Mr.—"

"West. Marlowe West."

"Like the detective!" Her words are soothing, like someone running their fingers down a xylophone. "I do love the Jazz Age." She glances around. "As do you, it seems."

"We're having a themed graduation party," I say, and immediately regret drawing attention to myself. She stares at me for a beat longer than the others, as if I'm a puzzle she's trying to decipher. Then she moves on.

"What a horrible thing to happen during such an important time of your life," she says sympathetically. "I see most of you haven't even touched your breakfast. That's to be expected in a tragic situation like this." She peers around with her giant eyes, like she's trying to determine which of us devoured our eggs and toast with no concern over Blaine's grisly murder. I look at the uneaten food in front of me with relief.

Detective Cates clears his throat. "We're going to interview you one by one today. You're free to roam this lower level and the grounds, but please stay off the top floor so we can search it."

"With what warrant?" asks Ellison, his dark eyes narrowing.

Detective Cates grunts. "I heard one of you was well-informed." He hands Ellison a piece of paper with an inky scrawl across the bottom.

"This says you can only examine Blaine's bedroom and bathroom."

"That's all we'll need," says Pilar de León with a sweet smile. "If you have any sense, you will have gotten rid of anything incriminating between last night and today, so we don't expect to find much."

We all freeze at the word *incriminating*. At that moment, a giant crash of thunder booms outside, rattling the dining room windows.

"Don't look so terrified, mis cariños," she says, with a twinkle in her eye. "Five of you are innocent."

16

How dare they accuse us, when someone could have broken in!" says Fergus, pacing the length of the drawing room. "If that's what they call police work, they'll never solve Blaine's murder."

"You think someone sailed across the ocean, hiked up the hill on foot, broke into the house when it was still daylight, crept up the staircase, and murdered Blaine, without anyone seeing or hearing them?" asks Ellison dryly.

Fergus stops in his tracks. The ridiculousness of this scenario isn't lost on him. "There's still the staff," replies Fergus, beginning his anxious walk again.

Detective Cates appears in the doorway. "We'd like to talk to"—he looks down at a notebook—"Kassidy Logan."

"She's asleep," I say. "The doctor gave her a strong sedative last night."

But as if she'd heard us talking about her, Kassidy glides into the drawing room still dressed in her white nightgown, looking more like a ghost than a living person. Her blond hair is disheveled, and she's barefoot.

Detective Cates surveys her placidly, as if messed-up looking girls wander into his investigations every day.

Kassidy walks past the detective without a glance, sits next to me on the couch, and puts her head on my shoulder. "Blaine's gone," she whispers. "He's not in his room anymore."

Detectives Cates clears his throat. "Kassidy Logan?"

Kassidy stares up at him with glazed eyes. "Did you take Blaine?"

"I'm sorry, but the doctor took him last night."

"I didn't get to say goodbye," she says, tears dropping onto her cheeks.

I expect Detective Cates to choose someone else to interview, now that he's seen that Kassidy isn't in a normal frame of mind, but he presses on.

"Ms. Logan, we'd like to ask you a few questions in the library."

She grabs my hand. "Only if Izzy comes."

"We'd prefer to speak to you alone."

"She doesn't have to speak to you at all," says Ellison, crossing his arms.

Detective Cates's face tightens, but he answers calmly. "Bringing Izzy is fine."

The library is dark and cool. Rain splashes softly against the arched windows. The rose gardens are visible through the fog, and for a second I can almost see Marla Nevercross strolling arm in arm with Cara Ashwood through the flowers. I shiver. Blaine's death has tainted the film forever.

Kassidy doesn't let go of my hand as we sit down on two chairs near a wall of floor-to-ceiling bookshelves. Pilar de León is perched on the edge of a periwinkle couch like a bird in a cage, the tiers of her ebony dress cascading onto a plush rug. Beside her, Detective Cates flips a page in his notebook and licks the tip of his pen.

A swell of panicky adrenaline courses through my body. I have the urge to tell them everything, just to make this day end.

Before I lose my nerve, Mr. Jimenez shuffles in. "Would you like anything to drink?" he asks the detectives.

"Some strong tea would be lovely," says Pilar de León.

After Mr. Jimenez backs out of the room, she sighs. "How pleasant it is to be waited on. I wish I could spend the whole day in this library, reading and drinking fizzy lemonade." She takes in the floral wallpaper and the chandelier hanging in the center of the room. "Whose idea was it to stay at Ashwood Manor?" she asks.

Kassidy smiles a little through her tears, which have continued to trickle down her face. "Mine," she says. "Izzy and I love the 1920s. I thought this would be a special place to celebrate our graduation."

"For my graduation, we traveled through the underground catacombs in Guanajuato, where almost two thousand souls reside," says Pilar de León dreamily. She turns to Detective Cates. "And you?"

"I spent graduation night in my bedroom, listening to records," he replies curtly.

"Always a loner," she says with a smile.

Detective Cates returns to his notes. "You arrived on Saturday afternoon?" he asks.

Kassidy nods.

"You appear to be a detail-oriented young woman. Costumes, fancy dinners, cocktails."

Kassidy looks at me helplessly.

"We're not here to police underage drinking," he says. "We only want to find out what happened to Blaine."

"Yes," she says. "I wanted it to seem real."

"Did it?" he asks.

Kassidy's brow furrows. "Sometimes. But people weren't getting along as well as I'd hoped."

"In what way?"

"Everyone was bickering. Bringing up issues from school."

"What kind of issues?" he asks.

"Stupid stuff. Rumors, old grudges—nothing important."

"You were dating the vict—Blaine?"

Kassidy nods, the tears falling faster than before.

"For how long?"

"Since freshman year," she says.

"Had you and Blaine been bickering this weekend?" he asks.

Kassidy's eyes flash. "No."

"Come now, mi cariño," says Pilar de León, the soft hiss of her accent wrapping around the word *darling* like an embrace. "In a passionate love affair like yours, there was no fighting?"

Kassidy hesitates. "We weren't fighting about anything that mattered."

I frown. Pilar de León has just charmed Kassidy into admitting to a potential motive. I glance at the consulting detective, wary of meeting her eyes. I'd been so distracted by her wild outfit and hair and glasses that I hadn't noticed her singular intensity. She watches Kassidy like a bird of prey circling a mouse.

Nerves tingle along my spine. I will have to be careful around her. I can't let her trick me into admitting what I've done.

Detective Cates clears his throat. "I know this is difficult, but please tell me what happened last night in as much detail as you can."

Kassidy squeezes my hand and closes her eyes. "We were in

the drawing room, having cocktails. Mr. Jimenez called us for dinner, but Blaine hadn't come down yet. I figured he'd lost track of time or fallen asleep, so I went upstairs to get him. When he didn't answer his door, I went in." A choking sob escapes her. "He was on the ground, covered in blood. I screamed and ran away, and then Izzy came to take care of me."

"Do you have any idea who might have wanted Blaine dead?" asks Detective Cates.

Kassidy shakes her head. "Everyone loves Blaine," she says. "Some lunatic must have broken into the house and killed him."

"When was the last time you saw Blaine alive?"

"We all went to the beach yesterday afternoon," she says. "I didn't see him after that."

"That's all for now, Ms. Logan," he says. "We may want to speak with you again, but I think you should get some rest."

We stand up to leave, but Detective Cates stops me. "We'd like to ask you a few more questions, Ms. Morales."

Kassidy stares at me with horrified eyes, but I wave her away.

"I'm fine, Kass. Go lie down in the drawing room. I'll be done soon."

She drifts out of the room like a wandering spirit. I sit back down on my chair. It feels like a giant is squeezing my chest. *It's just anxiety,* I tell myself. *If they'd found the knife, they would be making an arrest, not conducting an interview.*

Mr. Jimenez comes in, sets a tray with cups of tea and little dishes of sugar and cream by the detectives, and backs out again.

"It seems like your friend was very attached to the young man," says Pilar de León, dropping an alarming number of sugar cubes into her tea with tongs.

"They've been together for years," I say. "She loves him."

Detective Cates scribbles something in his notebook. "What was your relationship with Blaine?" he asks.

"I met him freshman year, when he started dating Kassidy."

"So you knew him pretty well."

"I guess."

"What was he like?"

It's surprisingly painful to recall Blaine's freckled face. "He loved to host parties, so we spent a lot of time at his lake house on weekends," I say. "After Winter Formal last year, he had a backyard barbecue, even though it was freezing outside. Fergus dared him to jump off the roof into the pool, and Blaine broke his foot crashing through the ice. If his parents hadn't heated the pool the week before, he could have broken a leg." I smile. "He liked to take risks, but he was a lot of fun. And he made other people more fun when they were with him."

"Did Blaine drink?"

"We all do," I admit.

"What about drugs?"

I hesitate. "Blaine did drugs at parties sometimes."

"Like what?"

I don't see the point of lying. "He smoked pot, did a little cocaine, some Molly. A few pills here and there."

Detective Cates scribbles faster.

"It sounds like a lot," I say quickly, "but he didn't do them all at once. He'd do a few lines of coke at one party. Then a few weeks later, he'd take pills with friends. He was a dabbler, not an addict."

"What kinds of pills did he take?"

"I don't know. I don't stick around when they bring out the drugs."

"Did Blaine ever sell drugs?" asks Detective Cates.

I bite my lip. If I lie and tell them Blaine dealt drugs, that might steer them in the wrong direction. But if I've learned anything from the mysteries I read, it's that lying without evidence is the fastest way to put detectives on your track. "It wasn't like that," I say. "He did drugs at parties sometimes. Lots of people do."

"Has anyone done any drugs this weekend?" asks Detective Cates.

My flushed face gives the answer away. "A little marijuana."

"Who brought it?"

"Blaine."

"Does he always bring the drugs?" pushes Detective Cates.

I stare at him. "Do you really think Blaine was killed over some party drugs?" His insistence makes me wonder if Marlowe tipped him off with this theory. My heart speeds up. If so, that means he hasn't sold me out.

Pilar de León raises an eyebrow. "Murders are usually the result of a mundane list of motives," she says. "Anger, money, illegal substances."

"What about revenge?" I ask before I can stop myself.

"It's true that there are motives you see less often. Revenge, jealousy, hate." She arches her eyebrow higher. "Do you know someone who sought revenge against your friend?"

I shake my head. I didn't sneak into his room with my knife for revenge, did I? He *had* threatened to expose the truth. And I hated him for being willing to ruin my life. But it wasn't revenge. I only wanted to protect the secret.

"Do you know if Blaine was seeing anyone besides Kassidy?" asks Detective Cates.

I definitely don't want them walking down that path. "No idea," I lie.

Detective Cates stares at me hard. "Our officers spoke with the staff this morning," he says. "One of the maids heard Blaine and Chloe arguing in the library yesterday."

Ugh. They already know. Did the maid also see me talking to Blaine afterward? I try to backtrack. "I heard they hooked up at prom," I say. "But I don't know if it's true."

Detective Cates licks his pen again and then keeps writing. Pilar de León doesn't take notes.

"Did Kassidy know about Chloe?" he asks.

Now I see how people get their tongues tied in police interviews. It's hard to know which lies to tell on the fly. "I'm not sure," I say. That's when I figure out where he's heading with his questions. "But I've seen Kassidy find incriminating texts at lunch and be making out with Blaine by dinner. Him hooking up with Chloe at prom would have been a blow, but she would have gotten over it fast."

Detective Cates leans back on the couch and whistles. "She has a more forgiving heart than me," he says. "I wouldn't have invited the girl who snuck around with my boyfriend to my graduation party."

"Kassidy's dad asked her to," I say. "He's close with Chloe's mom." The detectives don't need to know the gritty details about the affair.

Detective Cates nods. "Do you know anything about Mr. Logan's business?"

"He sells protective equipment to hospitals and militaries. Why?"

"His name's on the reservation for Ashwood Manor," says Detective Cates.

"Kassidy's parents paid for everyone," I explain. "They're rich."

"But your family isn't," says Pilar de León.

I flush. "My mom's a teacher at Marian Academy."

"The profession of givers," she says. Her voice is a pleasant brook trickling over rocks. "What's it like having your mother teach at your school?"

No one has ever asked me that before. There's something direct about Pilar de León; her questions cut to the heart of the issue. I feel tempted to be honest with her, a small break from the endless untruths I'm forced to tell.

"It's humiliating," I say. "A constant reminder that I'm a charity case. I can never act out or try on different personalities, or even have a little fling, without my mom knowing. I feel watched all day long, and I hate it."

Detective Cates's mouth hangs open, but Pilar de León nods. "What a joy the thought of college must be to you," she says. "A chance to break free from the nest."

It was supposed to be.

Detective Cates clears his throat. "When was the last time you saw Blaine alive?"

I think of Blaine in the shower, the steam blocking everything but his head and chest, and my urge to be honest comes to an abrupt end.

"The same time as Kassidy," I lie.

"What did you do between the time you came up from the beach and cocktail hour?" he asks.

I work hard to keep my face passive. "I read a little and then took a long bath while Kassidy napped."

Pilar de León's eyes light up. "I bet the bathtubs here are increíbles."

I can't help but smile. "Ours is a deep claw-foot tub, and the hot water never seems to run out, even though it's an old house."

"Do you remember hearing anything while you were in the bath?" asks Detective Cates. "Maybe a loud noise or someone yelling?"

"No. But I top off the water a lot, and the pipes are as loud as train whistles."

"Is Kassidy a heavy sleeper?" asks Pilar de León.

I laugh darkly. "It takes five alarms to wake her up in the morning. Someone could have murdered Blaine in our bedroom, and she wouldn't even have rolled over."

"Do you know if Kassidy left your room while you were in the bath?" asks Detective Cates.

"I don't think so, but I fell asleep in the tub, so I might not have heard the door," I say. Then I remember. "Wait," I say, backtracking. "She couldn't have. I had the key in the bathroom with me. I accidentally took it out of the lock."

"Could Kassidy have retrieved the key from the bathroom?"

I shake my head. "Not a chance. Kassidy may sleep like the dead, but I wake up at the faintest whisper. If Kassidy had so much as cracked open the bathroom door, I would have heard her."

He nods at me. "Thank you, Ms. Morales. Right now we're

trying to get a handle on the basics. But we'll probably want to talk to you again."

My legs shake with nerves when I stand. I hope the detectives can't tell they're trembling.

"Ms. Morales, one more thing," calls Pilar de León. "Why do you love the Jazz Age?"

I grimace. "It's when all my favorite murder mysteries were written."

"Now you find yourself in one of your own." She tilts her head like an inquisitive bird. "What are the chances?"

17

CHLOE'S HOUSE
Five Weeks Ago

E arth to Chloe," said her mom. "I know it's late, but this is important."

Chloe came out of her reverie. She'd been replaying her after-school adventure at the lookout with Blaine in her head all evening. If someone had told her two months ago she'd be having sex in the back of a car at a public hookup spot, she would have suggested they get an MRI.

"What?" she asked.

Her mom stood in the marble entryway. She was still dressed in her work clothes: a silk pussy-bow blouse tucked into a gray skirt with subtle black pinstripes. She kicked off her heels and let them fall to the side like dominoes. The shadow of a burly guard pacing outside darkened the floor and then disappeared.

Chloe's mom collapsed onto the long couch, wrinkling her suit. Not that it mattered—Lola would dry-clean it the next day—but it was unlike her mom to be sloppy with her tailored clothing.

"I'm going to be home late again tomorrow," she said, rubbing bloodshot eyes. "Which means I need you to take the twins to soccer. They've been complaining that the only person who cares about them is your father, so I promised either you or I would watch them play." She shook her head. "I bust my rear every day to keep them on that money pit of a traveling team. Meanwhile, your father spends my alimony money painting terrible art and dating every gorgeous man looking for a meal ticket along the eastern seaboard. But somehow it's *me* who doesn't care about them." She untied the bow around her neck. "Has anyone considered *I'd* like to date some gorgeous men?"

Chloe wished she could put her hands over her ears. The idea of her parents dating was so gross.

Her mom wasn't finished. "Your brothers act like I've spent the past two months reviewing red-flag documents from Warren Logan's company for pleasure, instead of working past dinner every night to keep this beautiful roof over their heads."

Chloe froze. Ever since Kassidy had invited her to Ashwood Manor, she'd been afraid her mom would change her mind and ban her from going. Not that Chloe was looking forward to watching Blaine and Kassidy suck face for a week. But the property was huge, and Blaine had promised her they'd be able to sneak away from the others.

Lola entered the cavernous living room with a glass of white wine and handed it to Chloe's mom, who took it and propped her feet on an ottoman. "What do you want to do for your birthday this weekend?" she asked Chloe. "My assistant said he can get us a reservation at Toro's. You can bring Nestor if you want."

Chloe bit her bottom lip. "Um . . ."

Her mom closed her eyes and sighed. "Let me guess. Your father's taking you."

"We could go another time," said Chloe quickly. She hated being at the center of the tug-of-war between her parents. "Blaine's mom said she'd eat there every night if she could."

Her mom frowned. "Why do you keep talking about Blaine? I thought you were dating Nestor."

"Nestor and I broke up after prom," said Chloe. Discussing guys with her mom made her want to melt into the ground. "But I'm not dating Blaine," she added, to avoid awkward follow-up questions. "He's with Kassidy. We're just friends."

Chloe's mom surprised her by snorting with laughter. "I remember saying the same thing to my mother once." She looked thoughtful. "So he's the real reason you want to go to Ashwood Manor?"

When Chloe didn't respond, her mom stared silently into space, drinking her wine.

"I know you think I'm stricter than your friends' parents," she said slowly, "but since you'll legally be an adult in a few days, I'm going to share a piece of wisdom I've gathered in my fifty years on this planet." Her voice had an edge to it, like she was choosing her words carefully. "Men never leave their wives for the other woman. They say they will. But they don't."

A hot flush spread across Chloe's face. She very much did not want to know how her mom had come by this particular piece of wisdom. "We're in high school," mumbled Chloe. "No one's married."

Chloe's mom sipped her wine. "The same principle applies. And I promise you: It will hurt."

18

I can't find Kassidy in the drawing room or anywhere else. She may have snuck past the yellow tape blocking the stairs to climb back into bed, but I'm not willing to risk a confrontation with the detectives, so I stay downstairs. Besides, Pilar de León's honeyed voice is echoing in my ears.

What are the chances?

I can't sit around twiddling my thumbs, wondering what the others are saying. I need to know.

Breakfast has been cleared in the dining room, and the table is already set for lunch. After making sure the coast is clear, I approach the wall with the brass candelabra and pull the center rosebud to open the hidden door.

I realize too late that it's going to be difficult to leave the secret passage without being discovered, but there's no going back now. I head down the dark hallway, careful to avoid toppling the stacked books. When I reach the end, I sit gently on the ground, trying not to think about how many spiders have made this nook their home.

The detectives aren't being quiet like Blaine and Chloe were, so it's easy to hear them through the wall.

"Why did you want this case, Pilar?" asks Detective Cates.

There's a tinkling laugh. "Don't flatter yourself, Ben. Captain Herrera owed me for that double homicide I solved when you two were with the Chicago PD. I asked him to hire me as a consultant for a week, and he agreed."

Detective Cates's voice is sharp. "These kids will break in a day. Or forensics will turn up something. It's a routine murder. And *you* don't do routine."

"Do you believe in fate?" asks Pilar de León.

"You know I don't."

"Mine has led me here," she says. "I found something I thought I'd lost."

"At Ashwood Manor?" Detective Cates sounds incredulous.

"In this case." She pauses. "You said Young and Merin already interviewed the staff?"

"They alibied each other out," says Detective Cates. "They were in the kitchen together all afternoon, preparing dinner. None of them left each other's sight long enough to go upstairs, murder Blaine, change their bloody clothes, and return to the kitchen. The only person the officers haven't talked to is the gardener, but he's eighty years old and has worked on the property for decades."

"Did they see anything useful besides Ms. Li arguing with Mr. Gilbert?"

"Plenty," says Detective Cates. "They watched the kids much more closely than the kids watched them. Young and Merin are going to take their formal statements this afternoon."

Shame burns my cheeks. Kassidy told us to ignore the staff, and we fell in line like good little soldiers. Now our fates might hinge on something they saw. Karma's a bitch.

"I assume there's no chance someone came in from the outside?" asks Pilar de León.

"The doors and windows stay locked during the day," says Detective Cates. "Young and Merin walked the property, but there's no sign of a break-in—no broken windows or forced doors. Young talked to the security guard at the ferry station. He said with Ashwood Manor rented for the week, the only arrivals have been the staff and the kids. He confirmed that both Rolls-Royces hired by Kassidy's father left on Saturday's ferry. He also backed up the butler's story: The others who helped prepare for the week left two days ago. The bluffs are too steep to access the house from anywhere but the dock, and the Coast Guard captain that Merin spoke to says his people haven't seen any unusual boat traffic near the island. We'll talk to the ferry driver, but—you know as well as I do—stranger killings are rare. I say we're looking at one of the kids."

"Who did you ask for next?" asks Pilar de León.

"Marlowe West. His family is rich as sin. Young and Merin say he talks like he swallowed the dictionary. When he called the police from the landline, he told them Kassidy Logan sent everyone's cell phones back to the mainland for historical accuracy. Which explains why we haven't heard from any of their parents. They must not know about the murder yet. We've asked Blaine's family to keep quiet for now. Told them it would help solve the case. But once the other parents find out, they'll send flocks of lawyers out here."

"Any of the kids could have called their parents from the landline," says Pilar de León. "That they haven't suggests they want to handle this like the adults they now are."

"Then they're dumber than their pedigrees would suggest."

"Or simply more innocent."

Detective Cates emits a harsh laugh. "Please tell me Miss Consulting Detective doesn't think they're all innocent."

Pilar de León responds calmly. "I'm certain one of them is guilty of murder," she says. "I was speaking metaphorically. I think we're looking for someone pushed to commit an extreme act outside their character. I don't believe the murderer is someone naturally ruthless."

"I don't need your help to solve this case," says Detective Cates.

Pilar de León's voice is kind when she answers. "You never did, Ben."

A loud sigh startles me; Detective Cates must be leaning against the bookshelf on the other side of the passage. "I'm sorry I'm being such a dick," he says. "I just—I was surprised to see you at the ferry station this morning."

"There wasn't time to warn you. The description of the case came through late last night, and I hopped on the first train out of New York. I'm working an art heist in SoHo."

"So a few days on this murder, and then we'll go back to being strangers?"

"That was your suggestion," says Pilar de León. "Not mine."

Another sigh, and a sad drawl: "I remember. I'll go get the kid."

For a moment, I forget everything that's happened and almost run off to tell Kassidy that the Victorian sick-boy detective and steampunk witch used to be a couple and clearly still have drama, but as soon as I picture Kassidy in her nightclothes, drifting like a long-dead ghost through rooms that have seen their fair share of them, all my excitement melts away.

Footsteps clip through the room, and I hear people lower themselves onto seats.

Detective Cates gets right to it. "Mr. West, how did you come to be invited to this Roaring Twenties graduation week extravaganza?"

"I've known Kassidy for years," says Marlowe. "Our families belong to the same country club."

"What's the vibe of the week been like so far?"

"Pretty typical. Fun scenes punctuated by moments of tension. The others have entanglements that sometimes boil over to anger."

"You don't have 'entanglements'?" asks Detective Cates.

"No."

"Tell me about Blaine."

"He was always decent to me. Insecure, like all the theater kids. Covered it up by being loud and aggressively physical. He liked diving headfirst into stupid plans that everyone cheered him for. But nothing was ever enough for him. I don't think he could stand silences."

Marlowe's tone is casual and controlled. Not at all like the scowling anger he'd let slip when he talked about Blaine last December at Pegasus.

"We've heard one *girl* wasn't enough for him either," says Detective Cates. "Do you know anything about that?"

My stomach tenses. If Marlowe tells them what he knows—

"Just rumors."

I go weak with relief. Marlowe's going to keep my secret. But why? He barely knows me.

"We've already heard how Kassidy discovered Blaine's body,"

says Detective Cates. "How long was she upstairs before she screamed?"

"Only two or three minutes," says Marlowe. "Not enough time to stab him, if that's what you're thinking."

"Was anyone else ever alone in Blaine's room?"

I think of Marlowe on his hands and knees, searching frantically for something on the floor of Blaine's bedroom.

"Ellison was alone with him for ten minutes while I was in the hall with Fergus and Chloe," says Marlowe. "Isadora was with Kassidy in their bedroom."

Again with the Isadora. I need to ask him why he never uses my nickname.

"What's Kassidy like?"

"Spoiled, but that's pretty typical at Marian," says Marlowe. "She loves expensive clothes and parties. She cares about her appearance, but I've never heard her be snide about other girls. She can get a little stressed, though. I once had to stop her from throwing herself down a stairwell during finals week."

Detective Cates's voice becomes sharp. "Do you think she really would have done that?"

"She was just venting," says Marlowe. "You have to talk people off ledges a lot at Marian, both literally and figuratively."

"Sounds like a pressure cooker."

"Depends how seriously you take it."

"Do *you* take it seriously?" asks Detective Cates.

Marlowe doesn't answer right away. "I've never been sure whether I take it too seriously or not seriously enough."

"Your school's website says you've been accepted to Yale," says Detective Cates. "You must take it somewhat seriously."

So they've already started researching us. At least they won't be calling our parents for more information; like Detective Cates said, that would unleash the flood of lawyers, and the interviews would come to an end.

"I like learning," says Marlowe. "I'm not sure if that's the same thing as taking school seriously."

"Why do you think Blaine was killed?" asks Detective Cates.

"I suppose that depends who killed him."

"You think there are multiple suspects?"

"Anyone with access to the house could have done it," says Marlowe. "But I think the likeliest scenario involves drugs. He was the biggest dealer at our school."

I gasp, forgetting that I'm hidden in the passage. Luckily, Pilar de León chokes on some tea, muffling my noise. Blaine, a drug dealer? There's no way.

Detective Cates jumps on this information. "You've seen him sell drugs?"

"No."

"Then how do you know?"

"I'd rather not say."

"Has he sold drugs to you?"

"I don't do drugs."

"So you didn't smoke pot with the others a couple nights ago?"

"No," says Marlowe. "Neither did Isadora."

"Tell me about Ms. Morales," interrupts Pilar de León.

My breath catches. Why does she want to know more about me?

"Isadora's super bright," says Marlowe. "Headed to Brown in the fall. She's also funny and thoughtful, and she recommends these really amazing books." There's a shuffling of feet. "I think it's hard for her to be on scholarship. She seems ambitious for a different life."

Heat rises in my cheeks. The only way Marlowe could know about my taste in books is from the shelf talkers June uses for staff recommendations. Has he seriously been reading my favorite books? Is that why he brought *Anna Karenina*?

"Surely, Isadora has faults," says Pilar de León with a smile in her voice.

I cringe, waiting for Marlowe's assessment.

"She doesn't ask for help, even when she should." He sniffs. "And she's private. I've known her casually for a year, and I only just found out she has a sister. She's proud too. She never goes on vacation with Kassidy's family—probably because she doesn't want to accept their charity. She doesn't realize that the money means nothing to them and that all they want is her company. That's the problem with pride—it makes you selfish."

The air in the passage immediately feels heavy and close. I'd never considered the vacations from the Logans' point of view.

Detective Cates clears his throat. "Where were you before cocktail hour?"

"In my room, reading."

"Did you hear anything unusual?"

Marlowe considers. "The only thing I heard were the pipes from Isadora and Kassidy's room. I think someone was taking a bath."

"That's all for now, Mr. West," says Detective Cates.

Footsteps strike across the wood floor, but then they stop.

Marlowe's voice echoes from a distance. "Have you found any evidence of a break-in?"

Pilar de León's voice is so soft I can barely make out her words. "I think you already know the answer to that."

Marlowe sighs. "Yeah. I do."

19

Toro's was new enough that you needed connections or patience to land a reservation.

Ellison's mom wasn't short on connections.

Which is why Ellison found himself, for the third Sunday in a row, sitting at a corner table with his mom for their weekly business meeting.

Ellison's mom had taken the seat facing the bustling restaurant. She said she hated the vulnerability of having her back turned, but Ellison knew the truth: She liked to be recognized. Even though it was the weekend, she had on a full face of makeup and a power suit. Her dark hair fell in glossy, relaxed waves to her shoulders.

It didn't take long for the first fan to drop by.

A white guy wearing a sports coat and pink loafers paused at their table as he headed for the restroom. "I love your show," he said, grinning. "About time someone held those government hacks accountable."

Ellison's mom didn't pretend to be surprised. She'd told Ellison it made a better impression to act like this sort of thing happened all the time. Which, to be fair, it did.

"Always nice to meet a viewer," she said with a satisfied smile.

"Be sure to watch this week. I'm going to blow the lid off the Talia Menendez murder case."

When the man left, Ellison's mom turned her sharp eyes back on him.

"Tell me what went wrong at the regatta yesterday," she said, taking a sip of her vodka martini. She slid an olive off its metal spear with manicured nails, then popped it in her mouth. "It's not like you to lose control of your boat."

Ellison stared into the bubbles of his sparkling water. This was the worst part about his mom being his agent. Whenever he screwed up, he disappointed her twice: once as her son and once as her client. "Broke focus," he said. He tried not to remember why he'd swerved or what had come after in the locker room.

"Mistakes like that can't happen in college," she said. "Not if you want to qualify for the Olympics next year." When Ellison didn't respond, she leaned back in her chair and tapped her fingers on the white tablecloth. "I've hired Brandon Moore to train you this summer," she said.

Ellison's head shot up. "I don't want him. I want Kahil."

His mom adjusted her already-straight silverware. "I know Coach Cho prefers Kahil, but he doesn't know you like I do. Moore is a better fit."

"I want to be a team player at Princeton," said Ellison, irritation pricking his neck. "That means training with the guy Coach Cho recommended."

His mom smiled at him, but it was the smile she used on television when she thought one of the other talking heads was making a dumb argument. "Princeton needs *you*, not the other way around," she said, waving to someone Ellison recognized from his mom's tennis club. "Team spirit is a luxury you can't afford."

Ellison's stomach clenched, but before he could say anything, the waiter arrived to take their order.

"I'll have the salmon salad, dressing on the side," said his mom, handing the waiter her menu.

"I'll do the truffle burger and fries," said Ellison. His mom cleared her throat. "Actually," he told the waiter, "sub lemon broccoli for the side."

Even though Ellison could polish off a bucket of fries every day without changing his competition weight, his mom insisted he eat clean. Vegetables with every meal, no sugary drinks, and plenty of protein. At least she didn't insist he keep a calorie-tracking app like the one she updated daily. *The camera can't add ten pounds if you don't have ten pounds to add,* she liked to say. She'd be livid if she knew about the beer he drank at parties.

After the waiter left, Ellison said, "I'm eighteen. You can't force me to train with someone. It's my career."

His mom lifted a well-groomed eyebrow. "I'd like to see the state of your career without me," she said, her voice growing tight like it always did when she was challenged. "Without the money and energy I've invested in you." She pursed her lips. "Maybe I should hire a new sports psychologist too. This one doesn't seem to be emphasizing *gratitude.*"

Ellison lowered his gaze back to his water. Rebellion churned inside him. But he tried to breathe through it. He thought of the look on Fergus's face when he'd pushed him into the lockers: Fear. Betrayal. The same emotions Ellison had seen in the mirror afterward, when guilt had turned him as cold as Pine Lake.

The breathing exercises he'd learned from his psychologist weren't enough to keep his anger away. With no warning, the words he'd been thinking since his scouting trip to Princeton fell out of his mouth.

"I want a new agent."

The restaurant fell silent. At least, that's what it seemed like to Ellison. The people at the tables around them kept talking and clinking their forks, but the only sound he heard was his mom's sudden intake of breath. Her eyes went wide with shock above the small, coral O of her mouth. For the first time Ellison could remember, she was speechless.

"I didn't mean to drop it on you like that," said Ellison, hurrying to explain. "But Coach Cho says pros need pro agents, not parents. And I know you're a lawyer, but you're a criminal defense attorney."

"You didn't object to my legal expertise when I kept your transcript clean after that dirty Mr. Benson business," said his mom, finally finding her voice.

Ellison flushed. They'd agreed never to mention that again. "I know," he said. "But Blaine's dad—"

"Kyle Gilbert?" said his mom with a dark laugh. "That man couldn't negotiate a deal for a Popsicle. He's a hack."

"He represents three athletes at Princeton already," pushed Ellison. "And he told me—"

"You already talked to him?"

Ellison's face grew warmer. "At the country club. Mr. Gilbert has a membership, so he comes by when he's in town to golf with me and Blaine." Ellison wanted to spill everything now that he'd begun. "Mr. Gilbert showed me his business plans. He says I can monetize my social media accounts. He has contacts with athletic companies all over the world."

The waiter brought their entrées, but Ellison's mom didn't even glance at her salad. Her eyes narrowed as she leaned across the table. "You listen to me," she said in a hissing whisper. "I did *not* sacrifice the trial career of my dreams to corporate media parasites in order for you to pull the rug out from under me right when we're on the cusp of sponsorships."

Ellison felt like he'd been kicked in the gut. He'd never once doubted his mom had his best interests at heart, even if he agreed with Coach Cho that he'd outgrown her help. "So that's what I am to you?" he snapped. "A walking bank account?"

To Ellison's horror, his mom's eyes filled with tears. He'd gone too far. Her public image was everything to her. If she was crying in Toro's, it meant he'd hurt something deeper than her ego.

"I'm sorry," he said. "I didn't mean that."

His mom closed her eyes and wiped away the wetness. When she opened them again, they were dry and distant. "If this is the ungrateful child I've raised, I have no one to blame but myself," she said, dumping the entire container of dressing over her salad. She picked up her fork and stabbed the salmon. "But don't come crying to me when Kyle Gilbert turns out to be a leech that sucks you dry. The only people you can trust are blood." She looked up from her plate. Her expression was so cold it raised goose bumps along Ellison's arms. "Or so I thought."

For the second time in two days, Ellison's anger was replaced by a rush of guilt so deep he thought he might drown in it. As he and his mom ate their meal in silence, he drafted an apology text to Fergus in his head. *This was the last time,* he swore to himself. *No more losing my temper.*

It was a promise he wasn't sure he could keep.

20

Good afternoon, Mr. Barnes."

I'd been too preoccupied by Marlowe's assessment of me to hear Fergus enter the library.

"We're sorry to put you through this, but it's the only way to find out what happened to dear Blaine." Pilar de León's voice is soothing, like a warm blanket, as if she senses how tightly he's wound.

"What do you need from me?" he squeaks.

I hear Detective Cates flip a page in his notebook. "Why did you come to Ashwood Manor this week?" he asks.

"Kassidy invited me."

"Are you good friends with Kassidy?"

"Not really. But she's . . . she was dating my best friend."

"So you came because of Blaine?"

"He begged me to come. He wanted moral support."

"Why?" asks Detective Cates.

"Because he was going to break up with Kassidy."

A ripple of nerves shoots up my back and into my ears. Marlowe was right; there *was* trouble in paradise. Chloe was out of the picture, which left only one explanation: Blaine was going to tell Kassidy everything.

The guilt I feel is nearly overwhelmed by relief. My gold knife ended that threat forever.

"Had he already broken up with Kassidy before he died?" asks Detective Cates.

"He wanted to wait until the end of the week."

I hear scratching. Probably Cates's pen. "Were you angry Blaine pushed you to come to this graduation party?" he asks.

"No," says Fergus. "I mean, I thought he might make more of an effort to hang out. But he spent all his time with Kassidy, even though he planned to break up with her."

"Maybe he'd changed his mind?"

"I don't think so," says Fergus. "He's been acting strange all semester. Disappearing for hours after school, not answering texts. I think he's been hooking up with someone he hasn't told me about."

"Perhaps Ms. Li?" suggests Detective Cates.

"No. I knew about Chloe. She texted him constantly. He must have been embarrassed by the other girl. Otherwise, he would have told me."

I cringe. Fergus knows Blaine well.

"What were you doing before cocktail hour yesterday?" asks Detective Cates.

"Walking around the pine forest."

"Can anyone confirm that?"

Fergus sounds hesitant. "I don't know. It's only us and the staff on the property."

"What happened when you got to the drawing room?"

"I drowned my sorrows with some cocktails. The butler mixes drinks like he's trying to poison us. You'd think Kassidy's dad would have pulled out all the stops for her graduation, but the staff here isn't up to his usual standard."

"Then what happened?" pushes Detective Cates.

"The butler called us to dinner, but Blaine wasn't there yet, so Kassidy went to get him. We all ran upstairs when we heard her yelling."

"Who reached Blaine's room first?"

"Izzy. She moved so fast it was like she knew Kassidy was going to scream. She had heels on and everything."

My stomach prickles with anger. Fergus didn't criticize my speed the time I sprinted to his aid when he drunkenly crashed into a reindeer ice sculpture at Winter Formal. And my heels had been twice as high that night.

Fergus continues, his voice growing hoarse. "Ellison actually got to Blaine's . . . body first." There's an outraged sob. "He was just lying there! We'd been downstairs the whole time, drinking and moping, and he'd been bleeding to death all alone. If I'd had any idea—"

"The coroner determined Blaine died quickly," says Detective Cates. "He wouldn't have been in pain for long."

I think of all the stab wounds on Blaine's back. It didn't look that painless to me.

"Tell us more about Blaine," says Pilar de León. She sounds like a therapist, which is definitely the right approach with Fergus, who swears by the therapist he texts with twice a week.

"We've known each other since first grade," says Fergus. "He had one of those big, fun personalities people are drawn to. When we were kids, he always pushed me to do crazy things. Jump off the highest diving board. Ride our bikes down giant hills. Steal money from my mom's purse so we could buy ciga-rettes." Fergus laughs. "We coughed so hard we threw up. But that was Blaine. Always looking for the next adventure, the next dumb thing."

"He moved on from cigarettes to something a bit more seri-ous, right?" asks Detective Cates.

I know Fergus will bristle at this suggestion. "He partied some," he says. "Nothing the rest of us haven't done."

"Did you ever see him sell drugs?"

"What? No! He wasn't a dealer. He didn't need money. His dad paid giant amounts of child support."

All those high school musicals, and Fergus still can't act his way out of a paper bag. But maybe I can tell he's lying because we're friends; maybe the detectives think he sounds truly horri-fied by the suggestion.

Then something occurs to me. If Fergus is lying, that means Marlowe is telling the truth: Blaine was a drug dealer.

"We're not here to blame Blaine for his death," says Detective Cates. He sounds bored by Fergus's dramatics. "We only want to establish a motive."

"If someone from the *outside* hurt him, we need to know why," adds Pilar de León.

She has good instincts. Too good. Fergus, desperate to pin the murder on an intruder, melts like putty in her hands.

"Blaine might have sold drugs sometimes," he backtracks. "It's not like he stood on street corners. But people knew if they needed pills to study or something to take the edge off, he would have it. It was more like a public service. Marian is so stressful. Sometimes the drugs helped."

"We're going to do everything we can to find Blaine's killer," says Pilar de León comfortingly. "It's obvious how much you cared for your friend."

I can almost hear Fergus sigh with relief. There are footsteps, and then the door closes.

"Leave it to a rich kid to frame dealing drugs as a public service," drawls Detective Cates with disgust. "My cousin has been in jail for five years for selling a few ounces of weed."

I shift uncomfortably in my cramped space. Both my feet have fallen asleep, and my knees are throbbing. Maybe I can sneak a little chair into the passage after everyone's gone to bed. It sounds like the detectives are going to be here for a while, and I intend to hear everything I can.

I briefly wonder what will happen if I get caught. It's probably illegal to listen to police interviews. But more is at stake than I can risk. I need to know what everyone tells them.

"Two left," says Detective Cates.

21

IZZY'S APARTMENT
Three Weeks Ago

Blaine and Chloe stood in the school parking lot, a few feet from her black Mercedes. It was a warm day in May, but Chloe shivered underneath her coat.

Things weren't going well with Blaine. As the weeks passed after prom, his text messages had grown shorter and shorter, as did the amount of time they spent together. Chloe tried hard to quell the suspicions building in her mind, but they haunted her like whimpering ghosts. That was the curse of being the other girl: It was impossible to trust the guy you knew was lying to someone else.

"Why do you want me to drop you off at Izzy's apartment?" she asked.

"I told you," he said. "Ms. Morales is tutoring me in calculus."

Liar. No Marian teacher tutored at home. In fact, she'd seen Blaine in Ms. Morales's classroom with two other students last Thursday after school, heads bowed over Academy-issued iPads while she taught at the front.

There was only one reason he would lie about seeing Izzy. And it was the same reason he'd been lying to Kassidy.

"You can tell me the truth, you know." But even she could hear the bitterness in her voice.

"I already have a girlfriend with too many expectations to

count," sighed Blaine. "If all you're going to do is pressure me, we should end this."

Chloe's heart jumped into her throat. "No! Sorry. I'm being ridiculous. I'm just worried about this medical thing—"

"Medical thing?"

Chloe couldn't meet his eyes. He had to know, right? But the doctor said not everyone had symptoms . . .

"It's nothing," she said. "Get in. I'll drive you."

Blaine slid into her front seat. "I can't believe my stupid Jag needs a new radiator," he said. "My mom warned me a vintage car would blow through my allowance, but my dad told me they were dope."

"Sometimes Mother knows best," muttered Chloe.

After Chloe dropped Blaine off, she pulled into a parking space. Izzy's apartment building looked depressing against the blue sky, its red bricks covered with rotten black spots, like smallpox scars. Chloe tried to breathe through the nausea of imagining Blaine and Izzy together. Blaine hadn't asked Chloe to wait, so he must have arranged a ride home. But she kept checking her texts just in case.

"Pathetic," she said aloud. "You're being completely pathetic."

Even though the sky was darkening, she was afraid her shiny Mercedes might stand out in the sea of older vehicles, so she leaned her seat back. Every few minutes, she peeked over the dashboard to look for Blaine.

She wasn't sure what she was hoping to discover. Evidence Blaine was sleeping with Izzy? She wished she could walk around the corner, knock on Izzy's door, and surprise them. That would reveal the truth. But Blaine would think she was totally unhinged.

Her mind felt fuzzy. If this was love, she wanted to give it back. In no time at all, she'd gone from stable and pragmatic to someone who was spying on her not-quite boyfriend from behind a steering wheel like a freaking stalker . . .

A car alarm jarred her out of sleep. She sat up just in time to see Izzy and Blaine standing on the sidewalk in front of the apartment building. Chloe looked at the clock on her front panel; she'd dozed off for only ten minutes.

She squinted through the evening light. Whatever had happened between Blaine and Izzy clearly hadn't ended well. Izzy held Blaine's arm in a vise grip while her lips moved fast near his face. Chloe risked lowering a window to see if she could hear them.

"I swear I'll tell Kassidy," said Izzy from across the parking lot. She was nearly yelling.

Blaine shook his arm out of Izzy's grasp and leaned close to her ear. Chloe couldn't hear his response.

Izzy pushed Blaine away so hard he stumbled over the cracked concrete. "You wouldn't dare," she said.

This time, Chloe could hear Blaine perfectly. "Try me," he said. "Just fucking try me."

Squealing tires interrupted their argument. Fergus's lime-green Audi shot through the parking lot and pulled up to the curb. Once Blaine got into the front passenger seat, Fergus revved his engine and made a fast turn back out of the lot. Izzy's eyes followed his car until it disappeared around a corner. When Izzy turned, Chloe caught a glimpse of her furious face in the orange glow of the setting sun. She looked like she wanted to chase after Blaine and rip him to pieces.

Frankly, Chloe knew the feeling.

22

———◇———

The door opens and footsteps tread briskly across the floor.

"Mr. Stephens, good morning."

I hear Ellison sit down in a chair, scraping it against the wood.

"I've seen your mother on television," says Pilar de León cheerfully. "Love her. She doesn't take shit from anyone."

"Neither do I."

"Good for you. As you know, you are here freely and may leave anytime you want."

"Should my lawyer be here?" asks Ellison.

"We find that people don't like to lawyer up too quickly," she says. "Looks bad in the media. No doubt your mother knows how difficult it is to stay on the right side of public opinion."

"What do you want to ask me?"

Detective Cates takes over, and I see how they work now. She butters suspects up, and he asks the rapid-fire questions to throw them off-balance and get unfiltered answers. "We'd like to know what you thought of Blaine," he says.

"Blaine was a cool guy," says Ellison. "Liked partying, liked girls, was involved in theater. I don't know what else to say. Just a regular guy."

"We understand he liked drugs," says Detective Cates.

"He did them at parties," says Ellison. "I never saw him high at school, but if he was, he was never in trouble over it."

"Do you do drugs?"

"Nah. I get tested all the time for rowing, so I've got to stay clean."

"You probably won't get tested again until fall semester starts," says Detective Cates shrewdly. "Did you get high with the others a couple nights ago?"

"Do you really think I'm going to answer that?" asks Ellison.

Detective Cates clicks his pen in and out a few times before saying, "I read in the paper you're set for the Olympic Trials next year."

"Yeah, which is why I'd never do something stupid like murder my friend."

He's the first person to deny killing Blaine, and now that I think about it, that's strange. All of us should have done that immediately.

"Did you have any reason to kill Blaine?"

"No."

There's silence, and then: "The staff tells us you and Blaine were involved in an argument at dinner two nights ago."

"If you already know, why ask?" says Ellison.

"So you *did* have a reason to kill him."

"No," repeats Ellison. "He did something shitty to me. But it wasn't worth killing a person over."

"What did he do?"

"None of your business."

I wish I could pop out of the passage and give Ellison a high five for pissing off Detective Cates, who pauses before continuing his interrogation. "We hear you had some difficulty with physics last year."

Ellison grunts. "Your investigation must be in the toilet if you think my ability to understand thermodynamics is relevant."

Pilar de León laughs. Or coughs. It's hard to tell from inside the passage.

Her partner plods on. "You failed the class, right?"

Detective Cates has finally landed on the right approach. Ellison loses it when people say things about him that aren't true. "I didn't fail," he shoots back. "I struggled for a few months, but I ended up with a B."

"How?"

"I got a tutor."

I can hear Detective Cates scribbling notes. "Who was the tutor?" he asks.

"Fergus."

"Fergus Barnes?"

"Yes."

"Do you know if Blaine was seeing anyone besides Kassidy?" asks Detective Cates.

"I've seen him around with other girls," says Ellison. "Chloe told me he had a thing with Izzy."

I almost jump up and yell, but I stop myself in time. An old saying of my mom's pops into my head: *Eavesdroppers never hear good of themselves.*

"What's Chloe like?" asks Detective Cates.

"She's sweet," says Ellison. "I thought we were hitting it off, but she must have been pretty into Blaine, because we'd be talking and I'd catch her staring at him. She fell apart when she saw his body."

"What did you do when you entered Blaine's room?"

"Felt for a pulse in his neck."

"You didn't find one?"

"No. He wasn't breathing either." Ellison's voice gets softer. "He was still warm, though. It felt like he was alive, but he wasn't."

"What happened next?" asks Detective Cates.

"I yelled at everyone not to touch him. They were all coming over and crowding him."

"No one else touched him?"

"Not that I saw."

"Did you touch anything else in the room?"

There's a slight hesitation. "I don't think so. It all happened so fast."

I frown. If that's true, what was he putting in his pocket when I walked in?

Detective Cates continues. "Was there anything odd about how your friends reacted when they saw Blaine's body?"

Ellison answers slowly. "Maybe one thing," he says. "Izzy came into Blaine's room after everybody else, because she'd been trying to calm Kassidy down. And she had this look. It wasn't happy, exactly. But I could have sworn she wanted to smile."

Chills tingle all over my arms and legs. My stupid face always betrays me.

"Can you think of any reason Izzy would want Blaine dead?" asks Detective Cates.

"If Blaine and Izzy had a thing and she was afraid Blaine would tell Kassidy, she might."

Screw you, Ellison.

"Do you really think Isadora would sleep with Blaine behind Kassidy's back?" asks Pilar de León.

"It doesn't seem like her," admits Ellison. "But sometimes Blaine's parties get out of control and people find themselves in bed with people they shouldn't." A chair shifts on the wood floor, like Ellison has stood up. "I do know Izzy cares about Kassidy more than anyone in the world. If she did make that particular mistake with Blaine, she'd find a way to keep it secret so their friendship wouldn't be ruined."

I dig my nails into my palms. Ellison might as well have pasted a target on my back. And he's wrong about one thing. There's a person I care about even more than Kassidy, and that's Caye.

"Thank you, Mr. Stephens. We appreciate your help."

23

---◆---

Kassidy handed her glass to a woman in a caterer's tuxedo who stood behind a makeshift bar in the tented pavilion Kassidy's parents used for winter parties. The pavilion was decorated with fresh garlands and fairy lights and a dozen Christmas trees strung with bright-gold tinsel.

"Another punch, please," said Kassidy.

The woman frowned. "Virgin?"

Kassidy smiled sweetly. "Not since I was sixteen."

The woman's eyebrows disappeared into her widow's peak. "I—I meant the punch," she stammered. "Do you want the virgin punch?"

"Yes," replied a stern voice behind Kassidy. "She's underage."

Kassidy whirled around. Had her dad heard her joke? When his face didn't flush, she breathed a sigh of relief. He might suspect what went on between her and Blaine, but he would be devastated if she confirmed it.

Her dad took a sip of his own virgin punch. "I hope this party helps everyone forget the economy's in the tank," he said, gazing at the guests as they milled around the pavilion, accepting appetizers from waiters dressed like elves.

Kassidy's dad was paler than usual, and there were circles

under his eyes, hollow and bruised, like he hadn't been sleeping. "Are you feeling okay?" she asked.

He shot her an irritated glance. "Stop worrying about me all the time," he said, puffing out his chest. "I'm healthy as a thoroughbred."

Kassidy's dad and mom were older than her friends' parents; it had taken them a long time and lots of fertility shots to have her. So it wasn't surprising that the silver at her dad's temples was more noticeable than it had been at the last holiday party. It still made Kassidy's heart hurt. He would get older and older until he wasn't there anymore.

"You know I hate horses," she said, smiling a little.

"Healthy as a Galápagos tortoise, then," he said. "They live forever, right?"

Kassidy laughed at the idea of her lean, restless dad pulling his slow bulk along the ground. "Maybe Ecuador should be our next vacation destination," she said. "You can visit your tortoise cousins."

Her dad's gray eyes—almost identical to the ones Kassidy saw in the mirror every day—lit up in his face. "Speaking of trips," he said, putting an arm around her shoulder and guiding her into a little nook behind a giant Christmas tree. "I have an early gift for my favorite daughter."

"Your only daughter."

"There was no reason to try for another baby," he said. "You can't top perfection."

Kassidy bounced on the balls of her feet in anticipation. Even though she swore off presents every Christmas, her dad always managed to get her something special that changed her mind.

"What is it?" she asked.

He dug into his pocket and pulled out a black fob attached to a key ring shaped like an anchor.

Kassidy's mouth dropped open. "A boat?"

Her dad smiled and tossed her the fob. "Not just any boat," he said. "A yacht."

Kassidy caught it and gasped. "A yacht? But how? The economy . . ."

Her dad shrugged. "Our portfolio is recession-proof," he said. "Besides, one of my contacts in Portugal sold it to me for a good price. He's upgrading."

Kassidy was torn between glee and embarrassment. She loved beautiful things, but being friends with Izzy had made her aware of money in a way she hadn't been before high school.

The excitement written on her dad's face started to fade. "Is something wrong?" he asked.

"Of course not," she replied quickly, shaking the guilt out of her head. Like her dad always said, their family spending less money didn't give Izzy's family more. Kassidy hugged her dad tight. "I'm just so surprised!"

Kassidy imagined herself lying on the deck in her favorite bathing suit. Maybe a yacht would finally change Izzy's mind about coming on vacation with them. "Is it already in the marina?" she asked.

"Felipe isn't delivering it until March," said her dad. "I'm telling you about it now because I know you like time to plan trips. I'm not sure about Ecuador, but we can certainly take it down the coast for spring break."

"Can I invite my friends?" asked Kassidy.

"Only Izzy," he said. "You know how I feel about the rest of the people you hang out with." He glanced over at Blaine, who was sitting on a couch trying to balance a deviled egg on his forehead. "I mean, honestly, Kassidy."

"You need to get used to Blaine," said Kassidy in a small voice. "He's going to be around for a very long time."

Her dad sniffed. "We'll see about that."

When Kassidy returned to the couch, she snatched the deviled egg out of Blaine's hand and leaned close to his ear. "Can you *not* act like a buffoon?" she whispered. "I want my dad to like you."

"Babe, he's never going to like anyone you date," said Blaine, looking entirely unconcerned. "That's part of the Daddy's-princess package."

Kassidy flicked him in the arm. "I am *not* a princess!"

Blaine stood up and bent into an elaborate stage bow. "You're the prettiest princess in fairyland," he said like a herald. "I pledge my eternal loyalty to your realm."

Kassidy laughed. She hopped off the couch and sank into a deep curtsy. Blaine opened his mouth to keep talking, but the ding of his phone broke through their game. He pulled it out of his pocket with a frown. After a few touches of the screen, his frown grew deeper.

"Is someone texting you?" asked Kassidy, fear rising in her throat along with memories she'd rather forget.

It always started like this. Texts at strange hours. Blaine's promises that the girl was just a friend. And then, inevitably, a confession.

"No." He turned the phone to show her. "It's an email from Dean Halliwell. He says I failed my calculus test."

Kassidy's breath hissed between her teeth. "Are you in trouble?" she asked.

"Not yet," he said. "But he's adding me to Ms. Morales's tutoring group next semester." Blaine collapsed onto the couch. "This is the worst. She's such a bitch."

Kassidy sat down next to him. "Don't let Izzy hear you," she said, looking around to make sure Izzy was still inside the house, swapping her heels for a pair of Kassidy's flats.

"As if she doesn't already know," said Blaine. "Why did I let my dad talk me into taking calculus?" He mimicked his dad's baritone: "'If you want to be a business major, you'll need a strong math background.'" He groaned. "I couldn't tell him I only applied to theater programs. He would have flipped."

"You've got to stop taking your dad's advice," said Kassidy. "He doesn't know you."

Blaine scowled. "That's not true. He usually gives me great advice."

Kassidy shook her head, but she didn't argue. Kassidy had met Mr. Gilbert a few times. Like Blaine, he was charming. But there was also something smarmy about him. He looked at her like he was sizing her up for a dress.

"I'll go to tutoring with you if you want," said Kassidy. "It's not like I couldn't use the extra help."

Blaine's eyes softened. "It's fine," he said. "I'm making a bigger deal of it than it is." He leaned over and kissed her forehead. Then he whispered in her ear: "You're the *sweetest* princess in fairyland."

24

Chloe's heavy footsteps pad across the room. For someone so light, she stomps like an elephant.

"Good afternoon, Ms. Li," says Detective Cates. "Have a seat."

There's a soft thump. "Ellison told me I don't have to talk to you," says Chloe.

"That's correct," says Detective Cates. "None of you are under arrest or being detained. You may leave anytime you wish."

A chair slides on the floor as if Chloe has gotten to her feet.

"However," says Pilar de León lightly, "people generally want to cooperate."

"Why?"

Pilar de León's accented words are like velvet. "A case like this—where a wealthy, good-looking young man is violently murdered—tends to attract a lot of media attention. Most people don't want it to come out that they're refusing to talk to the police. Even if they're innocent, it looks bad. And many of your families are high-profile. I know your mother, for instance, is in the middle of a closely watched deal with Warren Logan's company. If her daughter refused to cooperate with a murder investigation . . . Well, you see where I'm going, mi cariño."

There's a thud as Chloe sits back down.

"I do want to cooperate."

Detective Cates clears his throat, like he always does before he begins. "We've had a strange report from the gardener," he says. "About loud screams on the grounds in the hours before Blaine's death."

"Screams?" asks Chloe. After a few beats, she says, "Oh, he means when Kassidy got caught in a riptide."

Detective Cates's lazy cadence turns sharp. "Riptide?"

"Kassidy went too far out in the ocean," says Chloe. "When she couldn't get back to shore, Blaine dove in after her. We were afraid he was going to drown." Her voice cracks, like she's started crying. Someone must have handed Chloe a tissue, because I hear honking as she blows her nose. "He survived the ocean only to be killed right after."

"He sounds like a brave young man," says Pilar de León.

Chloe sniffles. "He could be really thoughtful. When my prom date left me to dance with another girl, he grabbed me for a group dance with the others. No one else even noticed, but he wanted to make sure I didn't feel left out."

"Did your romantic relationship with Blaine begin at prom?" asks Detective Cates.

Another nose blow. "Who told you I had a relationship with Blaine?"

"Did you?" presses Detective Cates.

There's a long silence.

"I don't want to talk about this," she finally says.

"That's fine," says Detective Cates. I hear pages flipping. "Did you see Blaine before you went down to cocktail hour?"

"No. I hadn't seen him since the beach."

I roll my eyes, even though no one can see me. *Except for that whole firestorm in the library.* Everyone is lying about their motives and movements. It's going to take the detectives forever to untangle all the deceptions. Which is fine with me. If they turn in enough circles, maybe they'll never solve the case.

I expect Detective Cates to call Chloe out for lying, but he moves on. "Have you been in Blaine's room this week, Ms. Li?"

"Only when we found his body," she answers in a small voice.

"Did you touch anything while you were in there?"

"Ellison told us not to. I wanted to help Blaine, but Ellison said he wasn't breathing. He was already dead."

"Thank you, Ms. Li. That's all for now."

Her chair slides noisily on the floor.

"One more thing before you go," says Pilar de León. "You haven't known Blaine's friends long, so you have a more objective eye. If you had to guess, who would you say killed him?"

"I don't know," says Chloe slowly. "Someone must have hated him, to stab him so many times. And the person with the worst temper is Fergus. He lost a tennis match the other day and flipped out at Blaine for taunting him. He's been drunk and moping around like an abused dog all weekend. I know they were best friends, but Blaine seemed to have more in common with Ellison. Maybe they were growing apart and Fergus snapped."

I hear the library door shut.

"Her silence confirms the affair," says Detective Cates.

"I don't think that one will agree to stay here much longer," says Pilar de León. "She doesn't have the same ties of friendship the others do."

"We need to get what we can from them quickly," says Detective Cates. "The threat of media attention and family exposure will give us a few days, but after that we'll have to let them go. We could ask them these same questions back on the mainland.

They're all eighteen—we wouldn't even have to inform their parents we were interrogating them." There's a hint of impatience in his voice. "I'm not sure why you insisted they all stay here."

"Once they leave Ashwood Manor," Pilar de León says silkily, "and get back into their normal clothes and normal houses and back into Mommy's arms, the spell of this week will break, and poof!—they'll turn back into the children they were before they tried on being adults. This place has atmosphere. They're all stuck in costumes, going through the motions of a more formal and mature life. The isolation of this island and the possibility that one of their friends is a murderer will make them more vulnerable each day. They'll tell us whatever we want, just to get this over with."

The hairs on my arms stand up as if a cold gust has blown through the passage. Far from being an airy-fairy new age witch with her *mis cariños* and her sugar-coated sympathy, Pilar de León is as brutally pragmatic as Detective Cates. She's just much cleverer. Which makes her that much more dangerous.

Pilar de León gives a tinkling laugh. "Six murder suspects trapped in a country house! It has a certain charm, no?"

Detective Cates sighs. "It would make it so much easier if the innocent ones stopped lying their asses off."

"There would be no need for us if everyone told the truth."

Someone opens the door. "Lunch is ready in the dining room," says Mr. Jimenez.

Crap!

I hop up and rush toward the dining room before I realize it might be full of people already. Instead of risking discovery, I return to the library end of the passage. That's when I realize I have no idea how to open the door from the inside. I run my hands along the wall in front of me until my fingers bump into something shaped like a screwdriver. After a little fumbling, I pull down on the metal, and the hidden door swings open.

The library is empty. I head for the exit, but a voice in the hallway calls, "I forgot my notebook. Be right there."

I don't have time to think. I sprint to the other side of the room and leap over the back of a couch facing the fireplace. I curl myself into the tiniest ball possible, hoping Detective Cates can't see me or my long dress from his vantage point.

I hear his footsteps approach the tea table and then leave the room again.

After a few minutes, I slip into the hallway.

"Kassidy's on the terrace waiting for you," says a voice behind me.

I whirl around. Marlowe is leaning against the wall.

"You need bells on your shoes," I snap.

The edge of his mouth quirks, but then his face falls into an expression that would be more appropriate at a wake. "I thought your interview was earlier," he says. His arms are crossed, like he's ready to defend himself against my lies.

Luckily, my excuse is draped around my shoulders. "It was," I say. "But I forgot my shawl in the library." I wave the cream wrap in his direction and beat a fast retreat before he can ask me more questions.

Kassidy is sitting in a chair overlooking the gardens and the distant dark sea. The rain has stopped, but the sky is still threatening. She's changed out of her nightgown and into a gauzy peach day dress with a cloche hat. Her curls are unpinned and flowing freely, and she isn't wearing tights.

When I sit down next to her, she gives me a tiny smile.

"Sorry about earlier," she says. "The sedative they gave me was super strong."

"Are you feeling better now?"

"Not better. But more like myself." She sighs. "Which is harder in some ways."

"I'm so sorry about Blaine, Kass."

"Me too," she says. "It feels as if any minute he's going to walk over and ask me what I'm daydreaming about. Like all of this has been a drug-induced hallucination."

I want to tell her about the secret passage, but I'm afraid she'll insist on coming with me. In her current state, she might freak out if she hears something she doesn't like.

"I had our whole lives planned," continues Kassidy hollowly. "Blaine and I would see each other every other weekend during college. When we graduated, we'd both get jobs in LA, buy a house somewhere in the Hollywood Hills, get engaged, and adopt a puppy." Tears fall onto her cheeks. "I could see it all."

It's strange how you can know someone so well and still not know the secret desires buried deep in their heart. I hope more than ever she doesn't find out what I've done. It would kill me to see the soft look in her gray eyes turn to disgust if the detectives discover my knife with Blaine's blood on it.

"That would have been a really nice future," I say.

I wonder what Kassidy's life will look like now. And even more than that, I wonder what all of this means for mine.

25

PEGASUS BOOKS
Six Months Ago

Three months after their first conversation at Pegasus, Izzy caught herself staring at Marlowe while she wiped down the coffee counter. He was sitting in his leather chair, sipping a foamy latte and reading a translation of *Crime and Punishment* that had been released the previous Tuesday.

"You should talk to him instead of banging him with your eyes," said Avery, gum snapping loudly in her mouth. She was older than Izzy and had worked at the bookstore since she was sixteen. A few weeks ago, Izzy had mindlessly added a heart to one of Marlowe's to-go coffee cups, and Avery had seen it before Izzy turned the drawing into an apple. Now she wouldn't stop bringing him up.

"I don't know what you're talking about," said Izzy, wringing out her rag.

"Probably for the best," said Avery. "He dresses too nice and orders the girliest drinks I've ever seen."

Izzy was only half paying attention. "Coffee doesn't have a gender."

"What?" said Avery blankly.

Izzy turned to face her. "There's no such thing as boy drinks or girl drinks. Liking whipped cream doesn't say something about your sexuality."

Avery shook her head. "You really are one of them, aren't you? One of those Marian kids." She spit her gum into the trash and left the coffee bar.

Izzy sighed and stole another glance at Marlowe, but his eyes remained glued to his book. Even though he came into the store nearly every Sunday, he ignored her so fervently she was beginning to wonder if she'd imagined their first conversation. His kindness in keeping her out of trouble with June had snowballed into a crush so intense she sometimes forgot the alphabet when she was shelving books if he was nearby. It was beyond embarrassing.

Marlowe looked up from his book. Izzy dropped her eyes and began vigorously scrubbing the counter. Blood rushed to her cheeks as she pictured Marlowe watching her clean in her stupid blue T-shirt and baggy khakis.

When she finished, she risked another glance to see if he was still in his chair.

"Oh!" she gasped.

Marlowe was standing right in front of her, holding an empty coffee mug. His lips twitched. "Sorry," he said. "Didn't mean to scare you."

Izzy tossed the wet rag in the sink. "I daydream as much as possible when I'm working the barista station," she said.

"That bad?"

"People order drinks with so many modifications," she said, rolling her eyes. "Last week I gave somebody twenty-nine chocolate sprinkles instead of thirty, and they complained to June."

Marlowe smiled. "Would this be a bad time to order my double-shot high-whip caramel latte with oat milk?"

"Let me guess," said Izzy. "Extra caramel swirl on top?"

"Too much?"

Izzy laughed. "That's my favorite drink too. Except I do soy milk instead of oat. More sugar."

"I'll try soy, then."

As Izzy prepared his drink, she desperately tried to think of something to say that wouldn't sound like she was hitting on a customer. Not to mention a customer with a girlfriend. As she pumped shots of vanilla syrup into the mixing glass, she remembered the upcoming party.

"Are you going to Blaine's Christmas party this year?" she asked. She tried to keep her voice casual, as if she were just making conversation.

Marlowe frowned. "Have you ever seen me at one of Blaine's parties?"

"No," said Izzy, frothing the soy milk. "I figured you were always too busy jet-setting across Europe with your fancy college girlfriend."

Marlowe's jaw clenched. "What makes you think Gia's in college?"

"Isn't she?"

"Yes," he answered.

Izzy laughed. She knew it. Kassidy had told Izzy she was creating an imaginary dream girl in her head. But Izzy was positive Marlowe's Italian girlfriend was glamorous and wild, and wouldn't be caught dead admitting she packed as much sugar as possible into her coffee drinks.

"Why does that matter?" he asked.

Izzy shrugged. "It doesn't." *Of course it matters, you idiot.*

"It's just very Marian," she said, then poured the frothed soy milk into his mug. "The rest of us have to source our love lives locally." Izzy shook the can of organic whipped cream and sprayed it into a tall swirl on top of Marlowe's drink before adding a caramel drizzle. "Want approximately thirty chocolate sprinkles for good luck?" she asked.

He shook his head. "You seem to think my luck's good enough." After a pause, he looked at her with the eyes she'd been seeing in her blue-tinged daydreams for months. "Are *you* going to Blaine's party?"

"Always do."

"Why?" he asked.

"What do you mean?"

"What do you like about Blaine?"

Izzy shrugged. "He's fun. And he's Kassidy's boyfriend."

"That's enough?"

"It's a party," said Izzy, not bothering to hide her annoyance. "Not a blood oath. You drink beer and play games and relax in the hot tub."

"Sounds terrible."

Izzy rinsed out the shaker. "Sorry we don't all spend our weekends chain-smoking clove cigarettes and crying into our French wine."

Marlowe grinned. "I prefer Italian."

"So I've heard," said Izzy, smirking.

Marlowe stopped grinning. "That's not what I—"

"Izzy, we need you at the cash register," said a sharp voice by the stairs. June was standing on the top step, hands balled into fists.

"I'll be right there," Izzy called, then turned back to Marlowe. "I get it. You're deep. We're not. I'll tell Blaine to mark you down as a no."

Marlowe leaned close to her, his eyes flashing with anger. "I have good reasons for not going to Blaine's parties," he said.

Izzy took off her apron and placed it on a hook. "Forget I asked," she said. She pointed to Marlowe's mug as she left the bar. "Enjoy the coffee. I added a pump of vanilla-cupcake syrup so it would taste like dessert."

Izzy's head tingled like a fuzzy balloon as she descended the stairs. Kassidy had been right: Marlowe was a snob. For months, Izzy had told Kassidy that a snob wouldn't have helped some random student from school in front of her boss. But the more she thought about it, the more she realized that was exactly the kind of whim he could indulge in.

She needed to stop thinking about him. There were plenty of other things to occupy her mind. College applications were due. She and Kassidy were taking a day trip to see the William Wyler film retrospective in Portland. And her mom had accepted a private math tutoring job over the holidays, which meant Izzy would be on call with Caye.

Izzy would make herself so busy she'd forget Marlowe existed. Distract herself by daydreaming about meeting a guy at Brown. Someone charming and chatty who would ask her to go to an arthouse film or play mini golf, or whatever it was people did on dates in college when they weren't gazillionaires sailing across Lake Como.

Marlowe would soon be a distant memory, as insignificant to her as she'd always been to him.

26

———◇———

Dinner feels like a hollow mockery of the nights before. We've agreed to keep up the 1920s charade for Kassidy, even though she seems more interested in drowning her trauma in champagne. I whisper encouragement to take bites of food, but her hands shake so hard she can barely get the spoon to her mouth.

The only other sound in the room is cutlery clanging against china. After my second glass of champagne, I decide to get drunk. The staff won't serve us alcohol now that the cops are involved, so I serve myself. I know I shouldn't. Losing my head when the risk is this high is stupid, but my whole body relaxes as the warming fizz of the alcohol lifts my mood.

An already-tipsy Kassidy stands up and taps her glass like she did the first night to call a toast. Except this time she hits it too hard, and the glass shatters.

"Shit!" she yells.

I watch as pieces of the champagne flute fall into her soup. She stares in shock at the stem, which is the only thing left in her hand.

Kassidy's face contorts painfully, like she's about to break into sobs. Then a giggle escapes her lips. She giggles again, and I can't help it—I giggle too. Fergus slaps his hand over his mouth, but it's too late. Laughter moves through us like a contagion. Kassidy is now laughing so hard she's hiccuping for air, and Chloe is doubled over clutching a stitch in her side.

Mr. Jimenez rushes into the room to see what's going on, and the sight of his bewildered face makes us laugh even harder.

For a few minutes, we're connected in friendship the way Kassidy wanted from the beginning. And despite the horror of Blaine's murder and my crushing guilt, I know I'll remember this moment from high school most: The six of us dressed in beautiful clothes from another time, drinking champagne in a candlelit room. Marlowe's eyes meeting mine, bright, unreadable, and intense. My best friend holding my hand and laughing uncontrollably during one of the worst days of her life. All of us bound by a shared tragedy just before our real lives were about to begin.

The laughter dies out slowly, and I can almost taste the catharsis, the release of pent-up emotions from a terrible twenty-four hours.

"To Blaine," says Marlowe, holding up his glass.

"To Blaine," the rest of us repeat.

"To Blaine," says Kassidy, "who would have laughed the loudest."

I FALL ASLEEP early in a drunken stupor, only to find myself wide awake just after midnight. Kassidy is completely out, her breathing steady. Next to her is an unmarked baggie full of pills in different shapes and colors.

I grab the bag with a sick feeling. None of the pills look familiar, and I'm positive Kassidy doesn't take any medicine beyond the occasional Advil. I slide out of bed and stuff the baggie in my backpack, trying to control the anxiety tightening my throat. I wish Kassidy's parents would come and take her home. If she's chasing champagne with random pills, she's beyond my help. The detectives may be treating us like adults, but we're used to having real adults to turn to.

My head is pounding, so I put on a silk dressing gown and slippers and make my way downstairs for some water. I pass the silent billiards room, where weak moonlight shines on a racked set of numbered balls, and glance into the pitch-black dining room, which smells faintly of lobster bisque. There are candles shining in the library, and I walk into the room to see why they haven't been put out.

Chloe is sitting in a high-back chair, staring into space. She doesn't move when I enter. For one horrifying second, I think she's dead.

"You can't sleep either?" she asks, and I exhale the breath I've been holding.

"I drank too much," I say.

"We all did," she says. "I'm blaming the alcohol for what happened at dinner."

"There's a thin emotional line between laughing and crying," I say, sitting down in the chair across from her.

She looks calm, like she did in the drawing room before Kassidy found Blaine dead.

"I hope this is the most horrible thing that ever happens to me," she says.

"I'm sorry," I say. "I know you and Blaine were close."

She sighs. "Does everyone know about prom?"

I consider lying, but I realize there's no point. "I think so."

"Kassidy too?"

"She's been pretty terrible to you all week, so probably."

"I figured, based on what she said at dinner the other night," says Chloe. "She knows our parents aren't sleeping together."

I frown. With everything going on, I haven't had the chance to ask Kassidy for details about her dad. "How can you be sure?" I ask.

"My mom's company is buying a big stake in her dad's company," says Chloe. "It's been a really antagonistic deal. She hired a bodyguard and everything. Mr. Logan is being investigated by the feds because my mom uncovered something shady."

I flash back to the unusual yelling at Kassidy's house the night she told me about Ashwood Manor. Poor Kass. All these terrible things happening to her at once.

"I don't think she knows about her dad," I say. "He doesn't talk about work much."

"My mom told me her family could lose everything," says Chloe. "I think he asked Kassidy to invite me on this trip so my mom wouldn't blow up the deal."

Chloe sounds worn out, like she's too tired to guard her secrets. It's the perfect time to do some digging of my own. "Blaine told Fergus you'd been texting him a lot," I say.

Chloe's sparse eyebrows shoot upward. "We were texting *each other*," she says. "It's not like I was pushing myself on him."

"You wouldn't be the first girl who chased Blaine. He had that effect."

"I didn't!" she protests. "I wish I had my phone so I could show you. He texted me all the time after prom. Said he wanted us to keep seeing each other long-distance during college."

"What about Kassidy?"

"He promised he was going to break up with her. But after a

few weeks, he started texting less. I kept texting him, trying to figure out if I'd done something wrong."

"You should tell the detectives that."

She stands up without meeting my eyes. "I'm going to bed," she says, grabbing a candlestick off the tea table. "I'm leaving on the next ferry, whether they're done questioning us or not."

As she walks to the door, a familiar scent triggers a red-glazed memory: Chloe's vial hitting my shoe on the way to Ashwood Manor. I know the little bottle can't have anything to do with Blaine's murder, but the journalist in me hates an unanswered question.

Usually, I'd soften an interviewee up before asking about the sensitive stuff, but Chloe's almost in the hallway; there's no time to beat around the bush. "What's in the vial you have in your purse?"

Chloe swings around. "I told you," she says. "It's perfume."

Her hand spasms on the last word. She quickly clenches her fingers into a fist, but it's too late: She's given herself away. "You've been wearing Violet Ends every day," I say. "That bottle is clear, not red."

"Blaine wasn't poisoned," Chloe shoots back. "You're just trying to distract from the fact that your motive to kill Blaine is stronger than mine."

I freeze. "My motive?"

"You think people resent you because your mom's a teacher, but it's because you and Kassidy are so obsessed with each other you ignore everyone else," says Chloe. "I can't imagine you'd want her to find out you were sleeping with her boyfriend."

My face warms. "There wasn't anything between me and Blaine."

"Right," she scoffs. "He asked me to drop him off at your apartment twice last month while Kassidy was volunteering at her church."

"He came to work on Kassidy's graduation present," I say quickly.

Angry tears fill Chloe's eyes. "You two should have gotten your stories straight." She sniffs. "My mom warned me not to come this week. She said anything hosted by a Logan would be trash. But I didn't listen." She wipes the tears falling down her face with the sleeve of her pajama gown. "Blaine wasn't a great boyfriend, but he didn't deserve this."

I glare at her, outraged by the dig at Kassidy's family. "You don't know shit about what Blaine deserved," I say.

Chloe's eyes widen, and her hand grips the candlestick more tightly. She looks like she's going to say something else, but then she spins on her heel and hurries out of the library.

I don't follow her. I sit by the fire and think. If Chloe's telling the truth about the texts, Blaine had made her believe they would be a couple. Her motive is stronger than I thought. And the more reasons other people had to murder him, the less likely suspicion is to fall on me.

But what if the detectives don't find out about Chloe's texts? The longer the investigation lasts, the greater the risk the detectives will stumble on the knife with my fingerprints all over it, or that they'll break Marlowe down until he tells them he saw me sneaking out of Blaine's room.

A flash of brilliance streaks across my mind. The investigation doesn't need to drag on. I can help the detectives. Tell them what I know so they can ask the right questions.

Chloe gave me information she'd refused to share with the

detectives for the same reason I was able to get gossip at school: Marian kids have never seen me as a threat. There are no social machinations because I'm just a teacher's daughter.

But they're wrong. I am a threat. And I'm going to burn them all down to save myself.

I strip a sheet of Ashwood Manor stationery from the writing table and make a careful list, doing my best to disguise my handwriting. Then I fold the paper, place it in an envelope, and label it with Detective Cates's name.

I stare at the note. I can still change my mind and throw it into the fire. Then I remember the love letters and the photos of Blaine hidden in a pillowcase at my apartment.

I leave the note on the table, blow out the library candles, get some water, and go back to bed.

27

The last senior party of the year was at Blaine's house on Pine Lake. Reading Week started the following Monday, giving everyone plenty of time to hide hangovers from their parents and panic about all the studying they hadn't done for finals.

"I'm glad you changed your mind about tonight," said Kassidy, squeezing Izzy's hand in the back seat of the Logans' chauffeured Bentley. "Parties are so dull without you. Last Saturday, I even agreed to play Truth or Dare with Fergus. He dared me to clean Queenie with my tongue."

Izzy gasped. "Please tell me you didn't lick Blaine's cat."

"You know I never turn down a dare."

"Gross!"

Kassidy laughed. "I was picking cat hair out of my mouth for the rest of the night." She squeezed Izzy's hand harder. "So you're never allowed to skip a party again."

"That'll be easy," said Izzy. "Since Blaine's staying with his dad all summer, this is the last one."

Kassidy's laughter died, leaving a silent void in the car. "The farewell-forever party," she said softly.

They drove along the lamplit shoreline of Pine Lake. The sun had nearly set, showing off a line of dark houses staring out over the calm water. Only a few people lived on the lake full-time, and most of the part-timers wouldn't arrive until Memorial Day weekend.

Izzy wished she hadn't reminded Kassidy it was their final high school party. Izzy might be desperate to leave Marian and Harker, but Kassidy was already nostalgic for a time that wasn't even over.

Crab apple trees bursting with pink flowers lined Blaine's long driveway. Most of the lake houses were built in the traditional New England style, but Blaine's was modern and made almost entirely of glass. Kassidy had taken forever picking out a dress, so dozens of Marian students were already inside, talking animatedly with their hands and dancing to music Izzy couldn't hear. From outside, they all looked like marionettes come to life inside a monstrous dollhouse.

Blaine met them at the door. "Finally," he said to Kassidy, raising his voice above the thumping music. "I thought you'd never get here."

Kassidy scrunched her face into a childish pout, showing Blaine what she thought of his greeting. Blaine grinned and stepped back to admire her dress. "But the wait was *so* worth it."

Kassidy laughed while Blaine held out his hand to two juniors who tried to sneak by him. "You know the rules," Blaine called after them. "No keys, no drinks."

Izzy recognized one of them from her Modern Art class. "Chill, man," the junior said, showing Blaine an open app on his phone. "We took a rideshare."

Kassidy held out her hand and pretended to drop keys into Blaine's palm. "Miguel drove us."

"Good," said Blaine. "Hey, Izzy." He turned to hug her, but she sidestepped him. The idea of touching Blaine's body in front of Kassidy made her want to gag.

Kassidy frowned at Blaine's rejected arms. Izzy knew if she hung around, the situation might get uncomfortable enough for Kassidy to say something. She didn't want to have to tell another lie.

"I'm going to grab a beer," said Izzy. She hurried through the living room and out into the backyard. After a few drinks, Kassidy would forget all about it; people ignored things they didn't want to see.

A crush of students stood around the pool, grinding to music. Way too many people were sardined in the steaming hot tub, blowing huge bubbles through plastic rings that looked like they belonged to Blaine's little cousins.

Ellison stood in front of the pony keg on the patio, filling a cup with beer. He was wearing white swim trunks and a tight black T-shirt. His long feet were bare. "Can you believe we already made it through the first keg?" he asked as Izzy approached. "Going to be a crazy night."

"Sounds like I need to catch up," said Izzy, grabbing a red Solo cup.

Ellison grinned. "That's the spirit."

Blaine's backyard was as big as a park. Beyond the pool, a grassy hill sloped down to the lake. Rope swings dangled from trees on the fringes of the pine forest separating Blaine's house from its neighbor.

"Zip line!" someone hollered. Squeals went up from the dancers, and the swimmers jumped out of the pool and raced for the lawn.

Blaine's zip line ran from the top of the hill across the water until it reached a giant blow-up pool Blaine had anchored to the lake bed. Anyone who could hold on to the zip line landed in the middle of the pool, where beer cans floated like prizes. It was a point of pride to spend Blaine's parties freezing your butt off in the middle of the lake.

Ellison removed his T-shirt in one easy motion. Izzy flashed back to an encounter they'd had in the back of his SUV after one of Blaine's parties junior year. "You coming to watch?" he asked.

Izzy never zip-lined. She wasn't scared. It just never seemed appealing to glide over a cold lake that half the swingers plunged into when they couldn't hold on to the bar. But tonight Izzy's rage toward Blaine was powering a feeling of recklessness. The farther she could get away from him, the better. And the center of the lake was as far as she could get without leaving the party.

Izzy pulled her sweater over her head to reveal a long-sleeved bathing suit underneath. She chugged her beer until only foam remained at the bottom. "I'm a watcher no more," she announced while Ellison laughed. "Tonight, I swing!"

28

After a fitful night of sleep, I skip breakfast and walk through the gardens. The sun shines weakly on grounds that are inches deep in mud. Kassidy is still asleep, no doubt knocked out by her pills. The baggie makes me wonder if Marlowe and I aren't the only ones sneaking around Blaine's room.

My sage-and-cream dress snags on wet brambles, and I slap them aside with gloved hands. For a moment, I feel like Marla Nevercross, dashing through the gardens to stop Cara Ashwood from getting rid of the ruby dagger. An irrational jealousy fills my heart. What I wouldn't give to discover someone had taken my knife and thrown it into the ocean, where my fingerprints would be washed away.

I step through familiar rosebushes and find Marlowe sitting on a stone bench next to the fountain, smoking. The expression on his face is as grim as it was when he caught me coming out of the library. No doubt all my suspicious behavior has added up to an inevitable conclusion in his mind.

"Good morning, Isadora."

I sit next to him on the bench. "Why don't you call me Izzy, like everyone else?"

Pinpoints of red appear on his cheeks. "I'll tell you another time," he says. "How was your interview yesterday?"

"Best half hour of my life."

He doesn't laugh.

Despite his cold reception, it's nice to be near him, to smell the sweet smoke from his clove cigarette, to see the amber halos in his eyes. I consider commenting on the storm or the roses, but I decide to skip the small talk and say what's on my mind.

"You think I killed Blaine."

His jaw pulsates under his ear. "I don't know what to think," he says.

"You saw me come out of his room, and you think that's the last time he was alive."

Marlowe doesn't answer.

"What if I told you I didn't kill him?" I ask.

He smiles a little. "What if I told you *I* didn't?"

Buttery sunlight reflects off his dark curls. The same curls that were bent over Blaine's floor searching his room in the middle of the night.

"I'd believe you," I say. "Unlike me, you don't have a motive."

He exhales a curl of smoke. "Sure I do."

My stomach clenches. If he admits his motive, I'll have to decide whether to tell the detectives. I don't want to make that call, so I don't ask.

For several minutes, we're quiet. I hadn't noticed, when I sat down, how little room I'd left between our bodies. Every time Marlowe moves, the crisp sleeve of his suit jacket brushes against my bare arm with a soft rasp.

Tension builds in the silence, as if we're both hoping the other one will start the conversation we're having inside our heads. All the unspoken words act like they have forever to express themselves, but for all I know, the detectives are on their way to arrest me. I decide life is too short to be a coward.

"I wish we'd talked more at Pegasus," I say.

Marlowe freezes as if I've surprised him. But he recovers quickly and says, "I could hardly focus on my reading because I always hoped you'd come say hello."

Relief floods my body. All this time, it hadn't just been me thinking about us. "June would have fired me if I'd paid too much attention to you," I say. "Besides, you have a girlfriend."

Marlowe shakes his head. "I was afraid I'd given you the wrong impression," he says. "That thing with Gia"—he pauses—"I date girls outside Harker because they don't know who I am. But it's hard to get serious when you live long-distance."

"Then why didn't you come talk to me?" I ask.

"It seemed rude when you were a captive audience at work."

"We go to the same school," I say gently. "You could have talked to me there."

He frowns. "I don't think you realize how rarely you're alone at school. If you're not with Kassidy, you're with Fergus or Blaine." He finally meets my eyes. "I would have talked to you," he says. "Even with the others around. But when I said hello in the halls, it never seemed like you wanted me to say more."

"You only ever nodded in the halls," I remind him. "I figured you were being polite."

"I wasn't," he says.

We're quiet again.

"We've lost so much time," I say.

He brushes my hand with his. "It's not too late."

I'm almost overcome with nausea when I think how much I would have loved this conversation if it weren't for the horror show I've plunged us into, how I would have run back upstairs to tell Kassidy that Marlowe and I had been keeping track of each other, that it hadn't just been me watching him as we moved from class to class or as we wandered the stacks of books at Pegasus.

Instead, we're sitting here admitting our feelings while knowing one of the six of us murdered our friend two days ago.

"The ferry should have arrived half an hour ago," says Marlowe, standing up and squashing the rest of his clove. "The detectives are probably up at the house."

"What do you think of them?" I ask, reluctantly getting off the bench.

He stares at the sparrows hopping from rose to rose. "Pilar de León looks like she's having fun, and Detective Cates looks like he'd rather be anywhere else in the world," he says. "Have you noticed they're physical opposites too? She's this bright little spark plug, and he's a stretched-out taffy hangdog."

"They used to be a thing."

Marlowe looks so shocked that I laugh.

"How could you know that?" he asks.

"Maybe I'm a mind reader."

Marlowe rolls his eyes. "Or maybe you've been eavesdropping in a secret passage."

My stomach swoops with fear. "P-passage?" I say. "I haven't been . . . I mean I have, but—"

"Relax," he says. "Anne Ashwood showed us the passages on the tour. When I saw you come out of the library after the detectives, I guessed."

My heartbeat returns to a normal rhythm. "Then why aren't you in there?"

Marlowe shrugs. "I'd rather enjoy this house and its grounds than be trapped in a musty hallway," he says. "Besides, listening to the others won't make me less guilty if I killed Blaine."

A hot flush creeps up the back of my neck toward my ears. "Are you going to tell anyone about the passage?" I ask.

He gives me a withering look. "What do you think?"

"Thanks, Marlowe."

"You're welcome, Isadora."

29

BLAINE'S LAKE HOUSE
Two Weeks Ago

W hat was that about?" asked Kassidy as she watched Izzy
walk toward the pool. "She totally dodged your hug."

Blaine shrugged, but his eyes didn't meet hers. "No idea."

Kassidy frowned. "She's been acting weird. Skipping parties.
Barely talking. Have you noticed?"

"No," said Blaine. "But I don't spend time thinking about her."

"I should ask her what's wrong," said Kassidy, biting her lip.
"She doesn't like it when people pry, but I don't want her to
think I don't care."

Blaine sighed. "Don't mess up our last party worrying about
the bizarre inner workings of Izzy Morales."

Kassidy still frowned, but she nodded. "Maybe you're right."

Blaine put an arm around her shoulders. "Why don't you
make me one of your famous mojitos and get this night started
for real." He leaned close to her ear. "It's not a party until you're
here, babe."

Kassidy and Blaine walked into the kitchen, which glowed
white against the darkness outside. When the snack table came
into view, Kassidy stopped dead.

"What is *she* doing here?" she hissed.

As if she could sense Kassidy's anger, Chloe looked up from
the tortilla chip she was dipping into guacamole. She started to

smile at Blaine, but then she saw Kassidy's face, and her own grew pale. She stuffed the chip into her mouth, grabbed her beer, and hurried out the sliding glass doors toward the pool.

"The whole senior class was invited," said Blaine. "I couldn't uninvite a single person because you don't like her."

Blaine's tone was dismissive, but he watched Kassidy with anxious eyes. For a second, she felt something dark and raw: disgust for the weakness that lurked behind his good looks and cocky smile. But then the moment passed, and she felt a surge of her usual love. Blaine's strong arms were around her, not Chloe. He wanted to party with her, not Chloe. And tonight she would be in his bed, not Chloe.

Kassidy swung her hair over her shoulder and smiled at Blaine, who looked relieved. "Two mojitos, coming up!" she said.

As Kassidy muddled mint leaves and fresh lime, her thoughts returned to Izzy, trying to pinpoint what was wrong. Even though they were closer than sisters, some things in their lives stayed secret. She knew that was normal, but it still made her sad.

Kassidy added a final sprig of mint to the tall glass in her hand and gave it to Blaine. He made a chef's-kiss motion after the first sip. "Perfect," he said. Then he cupped her ass and pulled her toward him. "Just like you," he whispered.

Kassidy studied his dimpled chin and the little brown birthmark next to his ear that looked like a star. Chloe's presence had reminded Kassidy that Blaine's sweet words could hide lies. Maybe Izzy's odd behavior had nothing to do with him, but Kassidy couldn't ignore the question that burrowed into her head like an earworm: *What had he done this time?*

30

The detectives are waiting for us in the drawing room. Pilar de León is wearing another wild dress; this one is layer after layer of dove-gray silk under a lacy black vest, cinched at the waist with a tiny silver bird clasp. She's wearing high-heeled black boots that would look more appropriate at Halloween, and her glasses are blood red. I'm not at all surprised to discover she's the type of woman with a drawer full of novelty frames.

I sit down next to Kassidy, whose eyes are glazed and distant. I grab her hand, and she looks over at me with a trembling lower lip. I can't tell whether she's still under the influence of whatever pills she took the night before.

"We want to give you an update," says Detective Cates in his slow drawl. "We'll have the preliminary forensics back from Blaine's room by the end of the day."

"That's fast," says Ellison.

"They put a rush on high-profile cases," explains Detective Cates.

"Here's the problem," says Pilar de León softly, tapping her ruby fingernails on the side of the fireplace. "We're still missing some important information. So today is going to go differently than yesterday. Today, you're going to tell us the truth."

There are cries of outrage. "But we *have* been," starts Fergus.

Pilar de León holds up her hand, and everyone stops talking. "Don't bother protesting, mis cariños. It happens in every investigation. I only ask if you want to protect your little secrets at the cost of keeping this investigation going forever. Surely, you don't want your new college classmates finding out you're involved in an unsolved murder case. That's not the kind of thing you want the sorority you're rushing to see when they're evaluating you for membership."

She leans in closer. "There is *nothing* you can say that will surprise us. We've been doing this for more than a decade, and we've heard it all and then some. We're not here to report you to your parents. We're not even here to report you to the police. We want to solve Blaine's murder and get the hell off this island."

"Hear, hear," says Detective Cates under his breath. "Fergus, you're up first today. Meet us in the library in ten minutes."

Detective Cates and Pilar de León walk out the door while the rest of us shift nervously in our seats.

"I didn't even consider that the investigation could last through the summer," says Chloe. She's refused to meet my eyes all day.

"Don't let them get to you," says Ellison. "They want to get their collar and move on. They don't care about us."

"I wonder why they want to talk to me first," says Fergus, wringing his hands.

No one responds. I mumble something about getting a cup of tea and hightail it out of the room. I slip into the empty dining room, pull the middle rosebud of the candelabra, and head to the end of the passage. I sit down on the soft blanket I placed inside the night before, hoping it will help keep my legs from falling asleep.

"Look at this, Pilar," says Detective Cates. I hear paper crunching. "It's a list of suggested questions."

The note I left them. Will they trust the information enough to use it?

"One of them wants to help us," says Pilar de León thoughtfully. "Or help themselves."

"It's written on Ashwood Manor stationery," says Detective Cates. "Anyone with sense would disguise their handwriting. And all of these kids have sense."

There's a tinkling laugh. "I have an idea. Let me see it for a minute."

A door opens, footsteps fall, and someone drops heavily into a chair.

"Good morning, Mr. Barnes," drawls Detective Cates. "Thanks for agreeing to help us out again today."

"Like Ms. de León said, I want this over with," replies Fergus in a shaky voice.

"Then let's get right to it. We know you and Blaine had a fight after the tennis match. What was that about?"

I pump a triumphant fist in the air. He's using my questions.

"Who told you we argued?"

"No lies today, Fergus," says Pilar de León soothingly. "Be strong."

"Fine." Fergus is already angry. "Like I told you, I wanted him to break up with Kassidy so we could leave. He wanted to wait until the end of the week."

"So you got mad," says Detective Cates, taking back over.

"A little."

"Tell us about your relationship with Ellison."

"No." Fergus is on the verge of losing his temper. This isn't going to end well for him.

"Mr. Barnes," says Detective Cates. "Surely, you don't want it leaked to the press that you had a heated argument the day before your friend was murdered."

"Are you threatening me?"

"Of course not," says Detective Cates. "We would never release confidential information. But we're required to make reports. And those reports are seen by eyes. We rarely know how leaks happen, but they do. I don't think Blaine would want that for you."

"He might," spits Fergus. "He was a shitty friend."

And there it is. When Fergus gets mad, he loses control of his mouth.

Detective Cates doesn't miss a beat. "How so?"

"He always tried to look good in front of Ellison by making fun of me."

"And you wanted to date Ellison?"

"We hooked up last winter while I was tutoring him in physics."

My mouth drops open. Ellison and Fergus? I try to picture Ellison with scrawny Fergus, but I can't see it. Ellison's boyfriends are usually as gorgeous and ripped as he is. I guess I know why Fergus was taunting Ellison at dinner. He wanted him to admit they'd had a thing.

"You and Ellison aren't together now?" asks Detective Cates.

Fergus hesitates. "Once we went back to school after break, he acted like it never happened."

"Was he afraid of being outed?"

"No, nothing like that," says Fergus. "Everybody knows Ellison is bi. He was ashamed of having hooked up with a theater nerd." Fergus sighs. "Ellison is Marian's poster boy. Great-looking, great grades, all-star athlete. He's protective of his reputation because he's already thinking about how he'll look on a box of Wheaties. And *I* don't fit into that perfect picture. So he pretended it never happened. And when I told Blaine that Ellison might like me, he laughed and called me pathetic."

"That must have really hurt."

"It did! Because screw him!" Fergus is yelling. "If he was my best friend, he wouldn't have laughed at me all the time!"

Detective Cates picks up on his enthusiasm and raises his voice too. "So you went to his room to confront him!"

The fire leaves Fergus immediately. "What . . . ? No. I didn't go to his room."

"And there was a struggle?" pushes Detective Cates.

"No. I was mad at him, but—"

"We found his watch. Your hair was caught in the winding knob. So let me ask you again, was there a struggle?"

"No! I wasn't in his room! He asked me to hide his watch from Kassidy for the week. She told him it wasn't period-appropriate, but he didn't want to send it back to the mainland because he was afraid someone would steal it."

"Then why did we find the watch in Blaine's armoire?"

"He asked for it when we were leaving the beach. He said it didn't matter what Kassidy thought and that he wanted to wear it."

"You said you didn't go into his room," says Detective Cates.

"I didn't. He stopped by mine, and I gave it back." Fergus sounds like he's on the verge of tears. "It was the last time I ever saw him."

"That's all we need from you today, Mr. Barnes," says Detective Cates abruptly. "Please send in Ms. Morales."

Shit! I tear down the passage and press my head against the door to the dining room. I don't hear anything, so I feel around for the lever—which thankfully is in the same place on the wall as its library twin—and step out of the hidden hallway.

A very surprised maid shrieks and leaps backward, clutching her hand to her heart.

"Perdón," I say. My voice breaks over my next words. "Por favor, no digas nada."

She looks even more surprised that I'm addressing her in Spanish, but she gives me a quick once-over and nods. "No hay problema."

"Gracias," I say as gratefully as I can. There's no way to know whether she'll sell me out. But she probably doesn't want to get involved with the cops, so maybe she'll keep my secret.

I rush into the hall, but Fergus stops me at the door. He looks over my shoulder. "I just checked for you in there," he says with a frown.

"I was behind the curtain, looking out the window," I lie. "It's so stressful being around everyone else."

"I hear that," he mumbles. He looks distracted, terrified. "The detectives want you. They're so awful. They push and push and accuse you of things, like they want to pin the murder on you. I hate them."

I squeeze his arm comfortingly and head to the library. I try to look composed when I enter. The period clothes help in that way; it's hard to feel like a mess when you're wearing such constricting tights.

Detective Cates sets down the piece of stationery he's holding. I recognize my fake handwriting and try not to grin.

"Ms. Morales, we have reason to believe that you were in an intimate relationship with Mr. Gilbert."

The thing is, I couldn't leave myself off the list, or they'd know I wrote it. Ellison told them I might have been sleeping with Blaine, so it seemed safest to use that as my motive.

"Whoever told you that is wrong," I say.

"He was seen entering your house several times over the last month," presses Detective Cates.

"We were working on a graduation present for Kassidy."

The lie, which had rolled off my tongue so easily with Chloe the night before, is perfect, because the only person who can corroborate it is dead.

"What present?" he asks.

"A song," I say, lying on the fly. "Blaine wanted to do something special for Kass. But he wasn't great with words. Since I was editor of the newspaper, he thought I could help."

"Did he give this song to her?"

"She would have mentioned it if he did," I say. "She loves sentimental stuff like that."

"How is Kassidy?" he asks.

"Not good." An idea strikes me. "Could you guys bring in a therapist or something? I think Kassidy might be self-medicating, and I don't want her to take too much."

Detective Cates exchanges an alarmed glance with Pilar de León. "I'll contact my department and see what we can do."

It seems like I've thrown him off somehow, and I wonder whether he's genuinely concerned for Kassidy's safety. Then I realize it probably wouldn't look great if the police let Blaine's devastated girlfriend OD at the house they've trapped us in.

"We understand Blaine intended to break up with Kassidy this week," says Detective Cates.

I try to look shocked. "I don't believe that."

"She hasn't said anything about it?"

"No," I say. "And she couldn't keep something like that from me. If Blaine had broken up with Kassidy, I would have spent the rest of the week holding boxes of Kleenex and consoling her."

Detective Cates looks at the ceiling like he's watching a fly. "The thing is, I'm having a hard time believing you and Blaine didn't have something going on."

"Why's that?" I ask.

His eyes come off the ceiling and burn straight into mine. "Because we found your fingerprints inside his armoire."

My mouth falls open. They dusted the *inside* of the armoire for prints?

I pull myself together quickly. "Sorry, I didn't mention that because it was nothing."

"What was nothing?"

I think fast. "I touched his armoire because Kassidy put some dresses in there. She brought like thirty, and they didn't all fit inside ours. She'd forgotten to grab her evening gown before her bath, so she asked me to get it."

"We didn't see any dresses in Blaine's armoire."

"Kassidy ended up moving them when she found a closet in our room," I say, remembering the narrow door.

I'm taking a risk. I know the warrant they showed Ellison let them look only inside Blaine's room. But for all I know, they got another one that let them search anywhere. Kassidy told me the closet was so full of cobwebs and dirt that under no circumstances would we be using it, which is why she'd stuffed all the dresses into our armoire. I wish I could borrow Ellison's legal brain for the rest of the interview.

Pilar de León stands up and walks toward the fire, twisting the little bird clasp at her waist in circles. When she speaks, her words are slow and precise. "You're saying you touched the inside of Blaine's armoire when you retrieved a dress for Kassidy." She turns back to face me. "Are you *sure* that's what happened?"

Why is she giving me a chance to change my story? Do they have other evidence against me? Did one of the maids or footmen see me that night?

I don't flinch. "Yes."

Detective Cates holds up a small silver object. "We found a cuff link in Blaine's room during our search. Do you recognize it?"

I definitely recognize it. It's one of Marlowe's cuff links. I guess I know now what he was searching for on the ground. I also know if I identify the cuff link, I'll be adding to their case against him and taking the heat off me. But, infuriatingly, I can't make myself do it.

"Sorry, no."

Detective Cates looks like he thinks I know exactly whose it is, but he shrugs. "That's all for now, Ms. Morales. Please send in Mr. West."

When I leave the library, Marlowe brushes past me in the hallway. He shoots me a half grin that makes my heart speed up. I grab his arm and lean close to his ear.

"They have your cuff link."

31

BLAINE'S LAKE HOUSE
Two Weeks Ago

Marlowe had never been to the Gilberts' lake house before, but the address Kassidy had texted him wasn't far from his family's compound.

He approached Blaine's front door with a strange feeling in his stomach. He'd waited years for this moment. Now that it was finally here, he thought he'd feel nervous. But it wasn't anxiety that threatened to overwhelm him. It was grief.

Marlowe had promised Augie he would confront Blaine before he left for college. And even though his brother hadn't been alive to hear the promise, Marlowe had spent the past three years vividly imagining how it would go. Sometimes he and Blaine fought, sometimes they cried, and sometimes he killed the bastard. But at the end of the visions, there was always the possibility of imagining it a different way. Once Marlowe finished with Blaine in real life, the part of Augie that lived in the promise would die.

The front door swung open, almost hitting Marlowe on the shoulder. Music and laughter rushed toward him, like someone had turned up the volume in his head.

A guy Marlowe recognized from British Poetry stumbled through the door, his arm around a girl wearing a minidress.

"Sorry, bro," the guy said. Then he squinted his eyes. "Marlowe West? Since when do you party?"

"I don't," said Marlowe.

The dropped jaws and shrill whispers began as soon as Marlowe stepped into the foyer. Even people making out on couches unwrapped themselves to catch a glimpse of him as he made a beeline through the living room, refusing to meet anyone's eye.

He soon caught sight of the person he was looking for.

Kassidy was in the backyard, watching Blaine and his friends jump off the flat roof of the house into the pool. Her hand was wrapped around a cocktail glass full of bubbles and mint leaves.

When she saw Marlowe, she said, "You came!"

Kassidy sounded much happier to see him than usual. Marlowe wondered how many cocktails she'd already downed.

"I figured you'd be locked in your bedroom, cramming for finals," she said.

Marlowe shrugged. "I got bored and wanted company."

Kassidy's lips twitched. "Maybe somebody's company in particular?"

Marlowe stared into her alcohol-flushed face. He'd casually asked about Izzy a few times during Friday dinners at the club. At least he'd tried to be casual. But what Kassidy lacked in academic smarts she made up for with social savvy.

"Should I talk to her?" he asked.

Kassidy pretended to shake a Magic 8 Ball. "Signs point to yes," she said.

Even in the midst of revving himself up for what came next, Marlowe couldn't help but grin a little.

"Wow, she even gets a smile," said Kassidy. "You must be way into her." She leaned back and looked him up and down. "I can kind of see why she's into you."

Marlowe rolled his eyes. "That's the mojitos talking."

Kassidy giggled. "Mojito goggles." She ran toward the pool yelling, "Blaine! I want to see you through my mojito goggles!"

Marlowe watched her with narrowed eyes. Eventually, Blaine would tire of the pool and want to change into warmer clothes. That's when Marlowe would strike.

Marlowe grabbed a drink from the outdoor bar and wandered around Blaine's backyard. There was no reason he couldn't make progress on Izzy while he waited. She had grown cold since their conversation at the barista counter. But high school was almost over. If he didn't try to talk to her one last time, he'd regret it.

Marlowe had almost given up on finding Izzy when he spotted her climbing the grass hill, wrapped in an oversized blanket. Mascara ran down her face, and her curls lay flat across her forehead and shoulders. Her nose was red.

Izzy came to an abrupt stop when she saw him. "You," she said.

Marlowe almost laughed. "Did you go for a midnight swim?"

She shook her head, teeth chattering. "Been in there for hours." She pointed to the zip line above their heads. "It takes you to the lake pool."

"The lake pool," Marlowe repeated. His brain raced to catch up. "I wouldn't have pegged you for a zip liner."

Izzy took a dizzy step sideways. Marlowe realized she was drunker than she sounded. "Why not?" she asked.

"You seem"—he tried to think of a good word—"careful."

She glared at him. "I'm no coward. Not when I've got a good reason."

"What's your good reason for swinging ten feet above a freezing lake?"

Izzy's eyes darted over his shoulder and then to the ground. Marlowe turned and saw Blaine and Kassidy wrapped in each other's arms on a chaise by the pool. Ellison, Fergus, and Nestor were playing charades next to the fire pit nearby.

"What are *you* doing here?" she asked, changing the subject. "Decide to act like a normal teenager for once?"

Marlowe shrugged. "My house was too quiet, so I thought I'd give the earsplitting noise of Blaine's friends a try," he said, waving his hand in the direction of the pool, where screaming boys leapt off the roof to the sound of rap on the outdoor speakers.

"Hey, Izzy!" called Ellison. "Come get warm."

Izzy smiled and waved at Ellison. Then she stumbled closer to Marlowe, almost stepping on his toes. Her voice dropped into something low and raspy. "Why are you really here?" she asked.

For a split second, Marlowe imagined leaning forward and kissing her. Running his hands through her wet curls. Touching her nose with his. Entirely forgetting his promise to Augie and focusing on the future, not the past.

Marlowe took a step back.

He wanted to tell Izzy the truth. But he couldn't.

Izzy shrugged in the face of his silence. "Let me know when you figure it out," she said. Then she ran toward the fire pit, her blanket trailing behind her.

32

---◇---

Marlowe's grin falls into a tight line when I tell him about the cuff link. I'm not sure I'm doing the right thing by warning him, but he's kept my secrets from the detectives; it's only fair to keep his.

The same maid I startled earlier is clearing what remains of the breakfast buffet. She glances at the hidden door she'd seen me come out of.

I speak to her in Spanish. "Did you talk to the detectives about the boy who was killed?"

She nods. "They asked me questions yesterday," she says. "But I couldn't help them."

"Does anyone else on staff know anything?"

Her eyes shift uncomfortably. "It's hard to say."

That sounds like a yes. But her vagueness tells me she won't spill the details. And why would she? The staff was hired to cook and clean for a bunch of rich kids, who'd repaid their efforts by trapping them in a murder investigation.

"I'm sorry this happened while you were working here," I say. I don't know the immigration status of the staff, but my dad was always looking over his shoulder no matter where we were.

"We don't want to get mixed up with the police," she whispers.

"No one thinks you had anything to do with it."

She looks relieved. While I'm happy to put her mind at ease, I need to get back into the passage without her seeing me.

"Can you take a cup of tea to Kassidy?" I ask. "She's in the drawing room. The tall blond one."

"Claro que sí," she says, taking one last look at the wall.

I've missed the first part of Marlowe's interview, but I've arrived in time to hear Detective Cates ask the question on my list.

"Why were you sneaking around Blaine's room the night he died?"

My shoulders tense. I had to put something down on the list for Marlowe, and I want to hear his explanation as much as they do.

To my surprise, he chuckles. "I knew I heard someone else in there, though I didn't think they'd snitch."

I cringe. Does he suspect it was me?

"We're still waiting for the why, Mr. West," says Detective Cates.

"I'll tell you, but it's going to sound bad."

"The truth often does," says Pilar de León wryly.

"I was looking for something I lost."

"For this?" Detective Cates must be holding up Marlowe's cuff link.

"Yes. I dropped it in Blaine's room."

"When?"

"The day he died. Before we went to the beach."

"Why were you in his room?" asks Detective Cates.

"We were having a conversation."

"About what?"

"My brother."

"We need more than that, Mr. West," says Detective Cates tartly.

I hear a long sigh. "When I was a freshman in high school, my brother overdosed," says Marlowe. "He was only sixteen years old."

The brittle sound of a teacup clattering onto its saucer echoes through the library. "Lo siento mucho," says Pilar de León in a small, tight voice. She sounds like she wants to wrap comforting arms around him as much as I do.

But Marlowe's family tragedy doesn't stop Detective Cates, who clears his throat and continues. "What does your brother's overdose have to do with Blaine?"

"Blaine sold Augie the drugs that killed him," says Marlowe.

I clap my hands over my mouth so I don't cry out. Marlowe's words from Pegasus come back to me: *I have good reasons for not going to Blaine's parties.*

"You must have been very angry at Blaine," says Detective Cates.

"I used to be," says Marlowe.

"What changed?"

"Blaine was out of town that weekend and thought Augie had taken something he got at the party, but Augie's friends confirmed he OD'd on the cocaine Blaine sold him." Marlowe's voice cracks. "When I told Blaine what he'd done, he went so pale I thought he might pass out. He fell onto his bed and started shaking and crying. He was a good actor, but he wasn't *that* good. He said he had no idea the coke was laced with fentanyl, and I believed him."

"When did you realize you lost the diamond cuff link?" asks Detective Cates.

"Before cocktails. I had them on at breakfast, so I figured one must have popped off when Blaine gave me a hug."

"So you decided to wait until the wee hours of the morning to retrieve it?"

"Of course not," says Marlowe. "I knocked on his door to get it back."

"When?" asks Detective Cates sharply.

"I was late to cocktails because I was reading and lost track of time," says Marlowe. "So . . . maybe just before seven thirty?"

"Blaine didn't answer?"

"No. I assumed he was already downstairs. I put on a different pair of cuff links and went down myself."

"If all of this was so innocent and aboveboard, why did you sneak around in the middle of the night to keep us from finding the cuff link?" asks Detective Cates.

"Maybe I shouldn't have," says Marlowe. "But I was afraid of how it would look. And I thought if I could find it, I could avoid this very personal explanation about my brother."

"Or maybe you'd rather we didn't find a motive for you," says Detective Cates. "After all, we only have your word for it that your conversation with Blaine happened when and how you say it did."

"I can't imagine I'm the first person who didn't want to be suspected of murder," says Marlowe.

"Look at this cuff link more carefully, Mr. West," says Detective Cates.

There's a moment of silence.

"The stone is missing," says Marlowe slowly.

"Was it missing before you went to talk to Blaine?"

"I don't—I don't know." I've never heard Marlowe sound uncertain before. "It might've been."

"Are you telling me you might have worn the cuff links to breakfast without noticing a thousand-dollar diamond was missing?" asks Detective Cates.

"I've been distracted since I arrived at Ashwood Manor," says Marlowe. "I can't be certain when the diamond went missing."

There's a short pause. "That's all, Mr. West. Please send in Ms. Li."

I hear footsteps getting fainter.

"One last thing," says Detective Cates, calling across the room. "You say you heard someone in Blaine's room when you were searching for your cuff link."

"There was a noise," says Marlowe.

"Where was the noise coming from?"

Ugh. It isn't only Pilar de León who's detail oriented.

Marlowe doesn't answer immediately, and I wonder again if he suspects it was me in the room. "Near the bathroom," he says. "It was dark, so I couldn't see anything. I heard a rustling sound, and I bailed."

The armoire where they found my prints is close to the bathroom, but hopefully that won't be enough for them to connect the two things. I hadn't considered that issue when I made the list. The more I lie, the harder it is to keep my stories straight.

After Marlowe leaves, Chloe pounds her way into the library. She'd looked pale in the drawing room, and her cream dress wasn't helping her coloring. We're all getting a little sloppier with our appearances. Tieless suits, daytime heels in the evening, two-day-old hair curls. I wonder if the detectives have noticed.

"We don't want to waste your time, Ms. Li," says Detective Cates. "So we're going to come straight to it, even though our question will sound indelicate."

My stomach swoops. Chloe's lies from yesterday are about to bite her in the ass.

"Did Blaine give you a sexually transmitted disease?" asks Detective Cates.

Chloe starts sobbing almost immediately. "Please don't tell my mom," she wails.

"We won't share personal information with your parents, Ms. Li," says Detective Cates, sounding annoyed. "Are we to understand you did have a relationship with Blaine?"

"Y-e-e-es," she says, sniffling.

Inside the passage, a wave of nausea makes my head throb. I can't think of Blaine and Chloe together without feeling sick.

"The two of you argued after your return from the beach?" asks Detective Cates.

"Blaine said he wanted to be free to date other girls," spits Chloe through her tears. "He gave me chlamydia, then tossed me aside like I meant nothing."

"What did you do after the fight?"

"I ran back to my room and sat on my bed."

"And?" presses Detective Cates.

Chloe has herself back under control. "After I calmed down, I realized I was being one of those girls who defines herself by her boyfriend."

"Like Kassidy?"

"Exactly," she says. "If Blaine didn't even like me enough to break up with her, he was never going to love me like I loved him. So I decided I was through with him."

"Ms. Li, do you think Kassidy's reaction to Blaine's death is consistent with her personality?" asks Pilar de León softly.

"Definitely," replies Chloe. "He cheated on her with all these other girls, but she only had eyes for him. She's a loyal person. She met Izzy during the first week of freshman year and bonded to her like a mother duck. She sticks by her friends and the people she loves."

"Thank you," says Pilar de León. "You're free to go."

Chloe crosses the floor with her thudding footsteps. Before she shuts the door, Pilar de León calls to her. "Oh, and Ms. Li? Millions of teenagers have contracted STDs. Be safe, but don't beat yourself up. And please ask Ellison to join us."

33

n the glow of the fire, Fergus looked like he was conducting an orchestra in hell.

"King Lear!" guessed Nestor.

Ellison frowned. Fergus didn't resemble a king at all with the beach towel draped over his narrow shoulders. Somehow Ellison always got pulled into playing drunken charades at Blaine's parties, even though it bored him to tears. One of the downsides of hanging out with the theater crowd.

Fergus shook his head, then started dancing around, kicking his feet in the air.

"Peter Piper?" guessed Ellison half-heartedly.

Fergus shook his head again and drew back an imaginary arrow.

"Robin Hood," said a voice from the trees. Marlowe stepped out of the shadows, a clove cigarette in his hand.

Fergus glared at him. "Robin Hood is right," he said. "What are you doing here?"

"Same as you." Marlowe stared unblinkingly at Fergus until Fergus lowered his eyes. A memory from freshman year surfaced in Ellison's mind: Fergus suspended for throwing a heavy prop knife at Marlowe's head and getting beat down so badly by Marlowe's brother he came back to school with his arm in a sling.

"Since when does Robin Hood dance, dude?" Nestor asked Fergus.

"In *Shrek*," replied Fergus, as if stating the obvious. "Who's next?" His eyes flashed to Ellison and then away again. They hadn't spoken to each other in person since the incident in the locker room.

"You want to take a turn, Marlowe?" asked Nestor. His voice sounded pleading, like Marlowe would be doing him a favor.

Ellison rolled his eyes. Another rich-guy fanboy. He wondered if Marlowe got as tired of people slobbering over his money as Ellison did when people slobbered over his rowing. Ellison's gaze fell on Izzy, who had left the fire pit and put on Kassidy's unicorn onesie. She and Kassidy were doing cartwheels down the grassy hill toward the lake. They screamed and laughed as they half spun, half fell onto the sandy shore. Izzy hadn't cared about his rowing. Ellison snuck a glance at Fergus; he hadn't cared either.

"I'm good," said Marlowe. He looked like he'd rather eat a pile of ants than play charades.

"Blaine's prom hookup moves in for the kill," said Fergus, as if he were narrating a nature documentary.

Chloe stood next to the pool, one hand on Blaine's arm while she talked close to his ear.

"Who is that?" asked Marlowe.

"Chloe Li," said Ellison, smirking at Nestor. "Too bad I didn't go to prom with her. Bet she wouldn't have abandoned *me* for Blaine."

"Because no one could possibly reject Mr. Olympian," muttered Fergus.

Nestor laughed. "Whatever, dude. You avoided a land mine. Girl's looser than an old rubber band."

Ellison grabbed Nestor's fist so fast it looked like he was swatting a fly. Across the fire, Fergus froze.

"What the hell?" said Nestor.

"You think it's cool to sleep with girls and then bash them?" asked Ellison.

"Jesus!" said Nestor, his eyes widening with pain. He tried to pull his hand away, but Ellison kept squeezing. "I was only joking," he yelled.

"Yeah, you're hilarious," said Marlowe as Ellison released Nestor's hand. "No wonder she bailed."

"What are you even doing here, Marlowe?" snapped Nestor, as if he hadn't just been kissing his ass. "Don't you have a private plane to buy or something?"

Marlowe stamped out his clove. "I do my plane buying on Sundays," he said. "Saturdays I reserve for conversations with idiots."

As he reached down to pick up his cigarette butt, Marlowe's entire body went rigid. Ellison turned to see what he was staring at, but there was nothing strange going on near the pool. Blaine was walking away from Chloe, who sat on the edge of the water with her arms wrapped around herself.

Marlowe straightened up and started moving away from the group.

"You headed out?" asked Ellison. He wished Marlowe would stay. He was sick to death of Nestor and found that he couldn't quite meet Fergus's eyes without feeling something he'd rather not.

Marlowe nodded. "Congrats on breaking the state record today."

"Thanks, man," said Ellison.

Once Marlowe was gone, Fergus crushed his cup into the ground. "I hate him," he said.

Ellison stood up and drained the rest of his beer. "You should learn the difference between jealousy and hate." He grabbed a blanket from one of the benches in front of the fire. "See you losers later," he said. "I have a rubber band to warm up."

34

The door opens again.

"Good afternoon, Mr. Stephens," says Detective Cates.

I hear the familiar scraping of the interview chair as Ellison sits down. "I'm thinking my mom's network would be interested to know you've pressured a bunch of teenagers into staying in a house where their friend was murdered," he says.

"We don't believe any of you are at risk, but as we've said many times, you're free to leave," says Detective Cates. "Say the word, and we'll drive you to the ferry station."

"Let's get this over with," grumbles Ellison.

Detective Cates clears his throat. "We talked to the officer in charge of Mr. Benson's death, and it seems like you forgot a few details."

"Like what?" says Ellison.

"Like the fact he was tutoring you at his private residence. Like the fact you were at his house a few hours before he died."

I feel like the exploding-head emoji. I wish I could run and tell Kassidy this gossip immediately, but I sit riveted in place.

"None of that means anything," says Ellison.

"Was Mr. Benson being inappropriate with you in some way?" asks Detective Cates.

"No!" says Ellison. I hear him get up and start pacing the

room. "That's what the police thought, but it wasn't like that. Mr. Benson was a decent guy. He wanted to tutor me at school, but I asked him to do it at his house because I didn't want anyone to know I was failing."

"You had a reputation to protect," says Detective Cates.

"Yeah, exactly."

"Most teachers wouldn't agree to give up their free time and privacy like that."

"Mr. Benson loved rowing," says Ellison. "He had a son who'd been on his college team, but they were estranged. I think I reminded him of his kid."

Detective Cates presses on. "After he died, you asked Fergus to tutor you?"

"He was Mr. Benson's homeroom assistant," says Ellison. "He found out I was failing and offered to help. Said he'd keep it a secret."

"You two had a relationship?"

"Not really," says Ellison. "I felt sorry for him, and we hooked up a couple of times. I know it sounds bad, but it didn't mean anything. It was a way of thanking him for helping me with my grade."

"But he took it more seriously," says Detective Cates.

"I guess."

"Have you seen Fergus romantically since you've been at Ashwood Manor?"

The pacing stops. "Did Fergus tell you that?" asks Ellison angrily. "The last thing I need are his lies in a police report."

"It sounds like you'd do anything to protect your reputation," says Detective Cates. There's a suggestive edge to his voice, but Ellison holds his temper.

"I know it seems cowardly, and maybe it is," says Ellison. "But I've wanted to go to the Olympics since I was a little kid. I knew I had the talent. But I also knew I'd have to look twice as good on paper as everyone else. There aren't a lot of Black rowers. So maybe I got too obsessive about my image. I don't know. I didn't want anything from high school to come back and haunt me."

"Including a teacher who'd flunked you," says Detective Cates.

Ellison sighs. "Like I told the cops back then, Mr. Benson looked sick that day. He was sweaty and pale. I left early because I didn't want to catch whatever he had. My mom got ahold of the coroner's report. He'd been a drug addict in his twenties, and it had weakened his heart. His ex-wife confirmed he hadn't gotten sober until his thirties."

"So your fight with Blaine didn't bring back bad memories?" asks Detective Cates.

"Of course it did! I was pissed. But not pissed enough to stab my friend because of a rumor he'd spread eight months ago. I wouldn't stake my entire career and future on the hope that no one would hear him cry out or see me leave his room. Have you found the knife? You won't find my prints on it."

"We're still looking for the knife," says Detective Cates. "The judge continues to be less inclined than we'd prefer to expand our warrant."

My shoulders relax. *They still haven't found it.*

"You can't violate civil liberties because you might solve one crime," says Ellison.

"Spoken like your mother's son," says Pilar de León. I can tell from her voice she's smiling.

Detective Cates sighs. "Please send in Ms. Logan."

I freeze in place. Should I be there with Kassidy? Will they even let me in again?

The decision is made for me when the door shuts and Pilar de León says, "Good afternoon, Ms. Logan. I'm glad to see a little color in your cheeks. The period clothes you brought to the island are gorgeous."

"Thank you," says Kassidy, her light footsteps clicking across the floor. "I've always wanted to be a costume designer."

Detective Cates starts in quickly. "You and Blaine weren't headed to the same college, right?"

"We'd been accepted to different programs," she says. I can hear the echo of disappointment in her voice. She'd been so upset when Northwestern rejected her.

"Did you think having a long-distance relationship would be difficult?" asks Pilar de León. She sounds motherly and sympathetic. I wonder how she decides who to be firm with and who to coddle.

"That's what everyone said," admits Kassidy. "But we decided to give it a try. We'd already booked flights to see each other in the fall."

"Whose idea was that?" asks Detective Cates.

"Mine."

"You sound like a planner," he says. His voice is chummy, like he's trying on Pilar de León's softer approach. "I wish I could be like that, but I can barely get myself to work on time." I hear him flipping pages in his notebook. "You and Blaine were overheard fighting the night before he died. What were you arguing about?"

That's one mystery solved. I'd tossed and turned that night

without knowing why. My unconscious mind must have heard them.

"We were fighting about Chloe," says Kassidy in a small voice. "He cheated on me with her on prom night."

Blaine's relationship with Chloe is the information I put on the list for Kassidy. I'd wished I had something they hadn't already been told in the interviews, but I couldn't think of any other motive for her.

"When did you find out about him and Chloe?" asks Detective Cates.

"A few weeks ago. A text from her popped up on his screen while we were hanging out. It was full of hearts and kisses."

"Why didn't you break up with him?"

I can almost see Kassidy shrugging. "I loved him," she says. "And cheating doesn't mean someone doesn't love you back. It means they don't like commitment. I know he would have committed eventually."

"What are you going to do now that he's gone?" asks Detective Cates.

I grind my teeth. Now they're just being cruel.

"I don't know." Kassidy's voice catches, and she begins to sniffle. I hear a tiny nose blow. "I'd planned this whole life for us, and now it's been snuffed out. My future is gone."

Detective Cates clears his throat. "Did you see Blaine using his cell phone this weekend?"

"No," she says. "I sent all the phones back to the mainland. They would have ruined the 1920s aesthetic."

"Blaine's parents say he texted them the morning before he died," says Detective Cates.

There's a long silence. "He must have had a second phone,"

says Kassidy. "I guess he hid it from me." She sounds exhausted, like the last brick of her castle in the sky has finally crumbled.

My hands start to shake. I've been so preoccupied with how to throw suspicion off me that I haven't considered something earth-shatteringly important.

What if Blaine didn't delete the texts?

If the detectives find his burner phone and the texts are still there, then Blaine is dead for nothing. I'll feel this guilt forever and still lose everything.

They don't have the phone yet, which means it must not have been in his room. So when could he have hidden it? And where?

I debate whether to abandon the hidden passage and look for the phone. But no—the detectives don't have an expanded warrant, and no one else is looking for it. The phone can wait.

"Tell me about your dad's company," says Detective Cates.

"His company?" asks Kassidy, her voice lifting in surprise. "They make protective equipment. Like masks and gloves."

"Has he seemed more stressed than usual lately?"

"What does this have to do with Blaine?" she asks.

"We've been asking everyone about their families," says Detective Cates.

Not true.

"I haven't noticed him act any differently than usual," says Kassidy.

I'm not surprised she doesn't tell the detectives about the fight between her parents; if Chloe's right about Mr. Logan being under investigation, Kassidy wouldn't want to risk it becoming public knowledge.

"One last question," says Detective Cates. "Did you ever think Blaine and Izzy might be romantically involved?"

My stomach drops. There's no chance she knows the truth, but—

Kassidy's laugh is one of pure astonishment. "Absolutely not," she says. "They didn't even like each other very much. Why would you ask that?"

"He was seen going into Izzy's apartment several times last month."

Kassidy sniffs. "I'm sure if you ask Izzy about it, she'll have a good explanation."

"Izzy says they were working on a graduation present for you," says Detective Cates.

"That sounds like Izzy," says Kassidy, her voice thick with tears.

I cringe. If she asks, should I really pretend Blaine and I were working on a song?

The detectives thank Kassidy and send her on her way. The library door thumps shut.

I hear Detective Cates shuffling pages. "I don't buy the graduation-present story," he says. "Why would Blaine write a sappy song for a girl he was about to ditch?"

"Maybe the dead Don Juan was more torn about his decision than his friends think," replies Pilar de León thoughtfully.

"We're missing a piece of the puzzle here," says Detective Cates. "Someone is holding back information that would make everything fall into place." His notebook flips shut. "You don't think there will be another murder, right?"

"No," says Pilar de León. "But we should watch these six carefully. Guilt is more unpredictable than anger, and we don't want the killer to take us by surprise."

35

BLAINE'S LAKE HOUSE
Two Weeks Ago

It felt like Blaine stopped to talk to every single party guest after he left Chloe sitting by the pool.

Marlowe lurked in the trees, waiting. He shook his hands in the wind, drying his sweaty palms. He didn't want anything to betray to Blaine the nerves that were building with such pressure he thought he might scream into the night air and ruin everything.

After twenty minutes of laughing and dancing and taking shots, Blaine finally detached himself from his friends and went inside. Marlowe followed him through the sliding glass doors and into the kitchen. A thrill ran up his spine. He blew on his fists and cracked his neck like a fighter. It was time.

Before Marlowe could pass into the living room, a slight movement caught his eye. Kassidy stood in a dark corner of the kitchen, next to a tall plant. She was staring out the window at Chloe and Ellison, who sat by the pool with their bare legs in the heated water. Kassidy's arms were crossed over her black dress. The look on her face was one Marlowe had never seen there before.

As if she could feel his eyes, Kassidy turned in his direction. "Leaving so soon?" she asked, quickly brushing a tear off her cheek.

Marlowe couldn't afford to be waylaid, but Kassidy might get suspicious if he tried to get away from her. It would probably take Blaine a few minutes to change clothes upstairs. Marlowe had a little time.

"Not yet," said Marlowe, taking a few steps closer to her. "Everything okay, Kassidy?"

"Of course." Her voice was light but strained. "Izzy left, and Blaine's been"—she paused—"playing host, so I thought I'd take a breather." She held up her glass. "Too many mojitos plus too many cartwheels."

A dart of disappointment stung Marlowe's chest. "Isadora left?"

Kassidy nodded. "Her mom called her home. I don't think she was in a party mood anyway."

"I didn't help much," said Marlowe.

Kassidy stared at him. "I don't pretend to understand you, Marlowe," she said. "Sometimes I'm not even sure I understand Izzy. Even though I'm not your biggest fan—"

"Because you think I'm a pretentious prat," interrupted Marlowe.

Kassidy laughed a little. "You're what Izzy wants," she said. "And I want Izzy to have what she wants. So I'm inviting you on our graduation trip. It's an exclusive guest list. Only seven of us. No adults. And Izzy doesn't know about it yet, so don't spill. If you two don't find a way to fall into each other's arms by the end of the week, it's not meant to be."

Marlowe tried not to betray the rush of adrenaline making him feel alive. "Week?"

"Anne Ashwood is letting us rent Ashwood Manor," said

Kassidy. "Your mom's on the museum board, so she probably already knows about it. We leave Saturday, after graduation."

Marlowe clenched his hands so they wouldn't shake. A week at Ashwood Manor. He and Izzy could actually get to know each other, instead of exchanging awkward words over party music or at her job. And the island was isolated and wild. Marlowe could make sure no one saw him confront Blaine. Visions of how he would do it rushed through his mind.

"I'm in," he said, then headed for the front door. There was no need to follow Blaine anymore.

"Hey, Marlowe?" said Kassidy from behind him.

Marlowe spun around. In his distraction, he'd forgotten to say goodbye. "Yes?" he asked.

"If you tell Izzy I spilled about her crush, I'll push you off a cliff at Ashwood Manor."

Marlowe grinned. Hearing Kassidy make a death threat was like watching a kitten try to roar. "Noted," he said. "For what it's worth, I think you're an amazing friend."

When she smiled back at him, he understood why everyone made such a fuss about her looks. She was so bright and beautiful it was like staring at a full moon.

Marlowe left Blaine's house and slid into the back seat behind his driver. For a moment, he felt something he didn't recognize. Images from the party flashed in front of his eyes: The tense lines of Blaine's face while he listened to Chloe whisper in his ear. Kassidy's glee as she and Izzy cartwheeled to the lake. Izzy running up the hill, dripping wet. He could read the emotions that crossed her face like a favorite book: shock, embarrassment, defiance, and, unmistakably, pleasure.

When Marlowe finally understood what he was feeling, a little drop of sadness poisoned the well. He shook his head, trying not to let grief make a home. For now, he would revel in this new feeling.

Hope.

36

I t sounds like they're done with interviews for the day, and I don't want to get caught flat-footed in the passage again, so I hurry back to the dining room.

Marlowe's sitting at the head of the table, reading the paper and drinking a cup of tea. He doesn't look surprised to see me. "Is everyone telling the whole truth and nothing but the truth today?" he asks.

I sit down next to him and touch his hand. "I'm so sorry about your brother."

Marlowe nods. "Like I said: plenty of motive. I've hated Blaine for years."

"You aren't the only one," I say. "If I'd known this much drama was going on at Marian, the school paper would have been filled with nothing but gossip."

Marlowe chews his lip. "Did the detectives mention my diamond cuff link again?"

I stare at him. "No, why?"

"It's expensive. I'd like to find the stone."

Expensive? If Marlowe's family is worth as much as school rumors say, losing the diamond is like me dropping a penny on the ground.

He folds the newspaper and places it on the table. "Will you walk with me to the beach?" he asks. "We don't have much time left at Ashwood Manor."

Terror tingles down my spine. "You think they'll solve the case soon?"

"It's not that," he says. "Ellison called his mom. Apparently, the police hadn't told any of our parents what happened to Blaine until this morning. They're freaking out and threatening to send an army of lawyers to the island. There's a big storm coming, so the ferry has stopped running from the mainland until Friday. But after that, we're going home."

I feel a catch in my throat. "Did they tell *all* the parents what happened?"

Marlowe nods.

"Oh no." I put my head in my hands. "At least Kassidy can get some help," I say. "Her grief is so deep I can't cope. I'm scared she's going to find Blaine's baggie of drugs and take something she shouldn't."

"Blaine's baggie of drugs?" asks Marlowe.

"Somehow she snuck Blaine's pills out of his room, and she's been dosing herself with who knows what."

"That explains why she seems so zonked," he says. "I told her I was sorry about Blaine in the hallway yesterday, and she looked at me like she had no idea who I was talking about."

"I don't know how to go home again," I whisper.

The part of me that wonders whether I'll be going home at all rears its hideous head. *The knife.* Will they find it before we get off the island?

I feel Marlowe's warm hand on my cheek. "Let's pretend none of this is happening," he says. "For one afternoon. Our problems will still be here when we come back."

And so we do. We hike down to the beach, take off our shoes, and walk barefoot along the rocky sand, laughing as we run away from the cold water that rushes closer with each foamy wave. Being around Marlowe takes my mind off everything.

"Ellison's mom told him it's the earliest tropical storm to hit the island," says Marlowe, pointing at the sky. "She said to stay on a low floor away from windows."

Black storm clouds hover in the distance, but there's still weak sunlight as we walk. Marlowe's shoulder bumps against mine as we talk about our love of Russian classics and Wes Anderson films.

"How have you not seen *The Secret of the Ruby Dagger*?" I ask.

Marlowe laughs. "I prefer my films in color." He brushes the back of my hand. "But I'd be happy to let you change my mind."

"It's the movie Kassidy talked about when we first arrived," I say. "The one Cara Ashwood starred in before she eloped. Someone stabs Marla Nevercross's husband, and she plays detective until she discovers his murderer." Goose bumps run up my arms. "Not that I'll ever be able to watch it again after everything that's happened here this week."

Sirens go off in my head—*Stop ruining the moment!*—and I quickly steer us away from the edge of what we're at the beach to forget. "The green dress I wore on Saturday is from the film. When Kassidy and I act out the movie in front of the screen, I always play Marla Nevercross. Kassidy found her dress and gave it to me for graduation."

"Kassidy's a generous friend," says Marlowe.

"She's different than people think," I tell him, picking up a broken sand dollar. "I heard you describe her as a party girl, but she really prefers to get comfortable in pajamas and eat popcorn in her theater. If it weren't for Blaine, I don't know that she'd ever leave the house."

"Why did she like him if they don't have much in common?" asks Marlowe.

I frown. "Kassidy is loyal without reason," I say. "It's almost like she decides ahead of time what a relationship will be and then makes it happen. Once she decided she would be with Blaine, she just was." I sigh. "She had their whole life planned."

"No wonder she's so devastated," says Marlowe. He picks up a smooth rock and turns it over in his hand. "Although Blaine gave her plenty of reasons to think they might not have a life together, even if he was still here to live it."

"I know," I say. "It's blind, stubborn loyalty. He didn't deserve it." I kick at the sand. "Of course, neither do I."

Marlowe skips the rock into the ocean. I watch it bounce until it disappears into a wave. "Do you want to know why I call you Isadora and not Izzy?" he asks.

I know he's changing the subject before we can go down a dark path, and I appreciate it.

"I feel like it's just to be contrarian," I say, smiling.

He laughs. "I'm not above that, but, no, that's not why."

"So why?"

"The answer is a little intense for our first solo walk on the beach," he warns.

"You caught me coming out of the room of my best friend's boyfriend shortly before he was found murdered two days ago," I say, shoving down a wave of anxiety. "I think the bar for what qualifies as intense is pretty high."

"True," he says. "The thing is, I have a neurological condition." He sees my worried face and quickly reassures me. "It's not a bad thing. Just an unusual thing. It's called lexical-gustatory synesthesia."

"Say that five times fast."

"If I did, I would taste it."

I stop walking. "Wait, what?"

He looks at me shyly. "I taste words that I read or speak."

"Are you screwing with me?"

"Definitely not," he says, and his face is so sincere I stop doubting him immediately.

"So if you say the word 'sand'—"

"The word 'sand' tastes like a BLT. Probably because 'sand' sounds like 'sandwich.'"

"And the word 'ocean'?"

"Smoked salmon."

"How can this be a real thing?" I ask.

"Doctors think it has to do with mental connections you make when you're young," he says. "Most of the word tastes are associated with foods I ate when I was a child."

"So when you say 'Izzy'?"

"Nothing happens," he says. "Not every word triggers it."

"But 'Isadora'?"

A smile spreads across his face like sunshine. "When I was six, my dad went on a business trip. Usually, our nannies cooked all of our meals, but that week my mom gave them a holiday and took care of us herself. The night my dad was scheduled to return, she went to the store and came back with the ingredients to make a special dish her nonna made when she was a child. A twist on pasta pomodoro. My mom is Greek, but she has an Italian grandmother on her father's side, who helped raise her and her sisters. She spent four hours making the dish. Sauce simmered, pasta cooked, and I watched her with the kind of amazement a little boy feels when he realizes his mom has hidden depths.

"My dad walked in from the airport right before the dish was done. He'd brought us these little handmade puppets that I now realize are totally creepy, but which I thought were the best gift ever." He laughs. "Augie and I started playing with them, and my dad joined in with his own puppet. It's the first time I remember him playing with us, though there had to be others. Half an hour later, we sat around the dinner table, just the four of us, with no nannies or staff." He sighs. "I'll never forget that first bite. It was tangy and savory and rich and creamy—and, to this day, the most incredible thing I've ever eaten. My parents drank red wine and laughed while my brother and I played with our puppets on top of the table." He shakes his head. "It's the only time I can remember the four of us being truly alone as a family."

He reaches out and takes my hand. The warmth of it sends a wave of pleasure all the way into my shoulder. "That pasta pomodoro is what I taste when I say your name, Isadora. You taste like my favorite memory."

There are no words to express what I want to tell him, so instead I lean forward and press my lips to his. They're soft, and they taste like salt water. He wraps his arms around my back and pulls me to him. Then, without a word, we walk back to Ashwood Manor, hand in hand.

EVERYONE IS GATHERED in the drawing room when we return.

Pilar de León gazes at our clasped hands with raised eyebrows. "We were about to send out a search party," she says.

"What's going on?" I ask.

"There's a storm headed this way," says Detective Cates. "Unfortunately, we have to hunker down here until Friday morning."

A roll of thunder breaks the silence that greets his pronouncement.

"You're staying at Ashwood Manor?" asks Chloe, her eyes widening. "With us?"

"I know this is awkward and you'd rather see the back of us, so we'll be staying in the servants' quarters as much as possible."

My hand tightens around Marlowe's. Their plan is completely unacceptable. For all we know, they could arrest one of us in the middle of the night. This could all be some kind of elaborate trap. And it will make it that much harder to sneak around and find Blaine's phone.

The detectives leave the drawing room, closing the door behind them.

"Is it even legal for them to stay here with us?" asks Chloe.

Ellison shakes his head. "No idea," he says. "All I know is that when Friday rolls around, I'm out."

37

Kassidy naps while I recline on the chartreuse chaise in our sitting room. I feel like she's spent more time asleep than awake since Blaine died. When we came back from the drawing room, she'd searched around her bedside table for the little baggie of pills I'd hidden in my backpack. She glanced in my direction with a question in her eyes, but I pretended to be reading. Instead of confronting me, she collapsed on the bed with tears streaming down her face.

Only one more day with the detectives. My stomach rumbles unpleasantly when I imagine the scene at Bar Harbor station. My mom, standing apart from the other parents with Caye in tow, silent on the drive home, pretending nothing happened, all the time wondering in a tiny pocket of her mind whether I'd done it. I would sit in the apartment, waiting for the detectives to find the knife and put it all together. Then they'd come for me.

My mind returns to Blaine's burner phone. Everyone is getting ready for dinner, so it's the perfect time to look for it.

Storm clouds cast shadows on the rugs in the quiet hallway. Rain splashes the windows while low, moaning rolls of thunder move in from the ocean.

Blaine had gone upstairs after his fight with Chloe. Had he hidden the phone somewhere before he returned to his room?

I start with the hallway furniture, since that's what he would have had easiest access to. Side tables and credenzas covered with decorative vases and bouquets of fresh flowers run the length of the walls. I open all of the drawers one by one and poke my fingers into their dark recesses. Mostly, I find extra linens and dust bunnies. I shove my hands into the vases, but except for a few dead insects, they're all empty.

I check behind the heavy curtains at the end of the hallway, but there's nothing wrapped in the velvet fabric. As I turn, I catch movement outside the window. It's difficult to see through the rain, but I can just make out Ellison under a black umbrella hurrying toward the pine forest. He glances back a couple of times, as if he's making sure no one's following him, and then disappears into the woods.

What is Ellison doing out in the middle of a storm?

I hear the click of a lock from a nearby room and hop behind the curtains, wrapping myself in their bulk. Footsteps head toward the stairs. I peek out in time to catch Fergus going down to the first floor. So much for everyone being holed up in their rooms. He's probably off to sneak a drink or two before dinner.

The servants' staircase is to my left. Could Blaine have hidden the phone in the storage closet? I hadn't followed him up the stairs immediately, so there may have been time.

The closet is about halfway between the first and second floors. It's full of towels and toiletries. I dig through them to be thorough, but it seems unlikely Blaine would have hidden the phone somewhere with such high traffic.

I shut the door, spin around, and let out an embarrassingly shrill scream.

Pilar de León is standing on the step below me with an inscrutable look on her face. "Can I help you with something, mi cariño?"

"How did you get there?" I ask, putting a hand over my racing heart. "I didn't hear you come up."

"Perhaps I have a light step." She stares at me, waiting.

"I was, um, looking for towels," I say.

Pilar de León steps around me and opens the storage closet again. "It looks like you found them," she says, pointing to cream towels that are still very much on the shelf and not in my hands.

Damn it.

"How is Kassidy?" she continues, ignoring my stammering explanation. "I'm sorry we can't bring anyone from the mainland to help her until Friday."

"She's not good," I admit. "She sleeps all the time. When she's awake, she mostly cries or walks around in a daze."

"Losing someone you love is too painful for words," says Pilar de León, her face tight. "Treat her like you would a china doll caught in this storm. I know how important she is to you."

Her voice has a warning in it I don't understand.

"Will you keep working on the case once we're back in Harker?" I ask.

She shakes her head. "I will return to New York, where I have other obligations."

Hope rises in my heart. "Have you ever failed to solve a case?"

"Once," she says stiffly. "It haunts you, not to bring resolution to someone. But cold cases don't always stay cold. They can be brought back into the sunlight."

The grandfather clock in the foyer clangs seven times.

"I need to change for dinner," I say. But for some reason, I don't want to leave. I hesitate awkwardly on the staircase.

"Ms. Morales, I sense there's something you'd like to tell me. Perhaps some detail you forgot to mention in the interviews?"

Despite her intense gaze, the curves of her face are comforting, and for a moment I want to tell her. I want to tell someone, anyone, what I did, to relieve the guilty pressure inside of me. So that maybe the lies can finally end.

But that's impossible. She doesn't care about me or the others; she's a crime whisperer with a heart of steel.

"Sorry, no," I hear myself saying. "I told you everything I remember in the library."

I hurry back up the stairs and into the hallway. I hope she doesn't poke around and stumble on Blaine's phone. Maybe the police somehow missed it when they processed his room. I'll have to do another search the next time I can be sure I'm alone.

I shiver. The presence of the detectives in Ashwood Manor overnight complicates things. The last thing I want to do is get caught in Blaine's room again, but I may have no choice. After all this, I can't risk his phone falling into the hands of the police without knowing whether he deleted the texts.

DINNER IS SURREAL. The detectives, who have all but accused one of us of being a killer, are now sitting at the dining room table with us, slurping chilled cucumber soup by candlelight.

I thought they'd be sober, given the seriousness of the crime and the proximity of all their main suspects, but they're making their way through a bottle of white wine like they're guests.

Marlowe sits next to me, and every once in a while he presses his thigh against mine in a comforting way. Kassidy, the jeweled feather on her headband drooping to the side, pushes her food around in circles, while Fergus takes sips out of a flask he's stowed in his pocket. Ellison and Chloe exchange a few comments about the storm raging outside but are otherwise silent.

"Have you always lived in Harker?" Pilar de León asks the group, breaking the tense quiet.

The others nod, but I shake my head a little and hope she doesn't notice. Of course she does.

"Where did you live before this, Izzy?" she asks.

"Chicago."

"The Windy City," she says dreamily. "I worked on a kidnapping there a long time ago. The food is wonderful, but it gets so cold the inside of your nose freezes."

I don't say anything, but she continues. "I know your mom is a teacher, but what does your dad do?"

My stomach tightens. Only Kassidy and Marlowe know about my dad being deported. "He works in a restaurant," I say. The last job he'd had in Chicago was at a Mexican dive on the South Side. For all I know, he's doing the same thing now.

"I have family in the restaurant business as well," she says with delight, as if it's a big coincidence. "I've been all over the world, but I've never had fresher salsa than in the town where I was born."

"My dad makes a killer salsa," I say before I can stop myself.

Whenever I bring up my dad at home, my mom turns to stone, so I rarely get to talk about him. "When I was little, he'd sit me in a high chair and let me eat the spiciest salsa the restaurant made. My mom told him he'd give me an ulcer."

Marlowe touches my knee under the table. He's looking at me like people do at the beginning of relationships, when every personal story is a treasure to cherish. But how long will I get to keep sharing my memories with him? A rush of queasiness makes it impossible to finish my smoked quail.

After the final course is cleared, the detectives ask the butler for some sherry. The rest of us seize our chance to escape from the dining room. Marlowe grabs my hand and leads me toward the library.

"Are you coming?" I ask Kassidy.

She looks at my hand in Marlowe's with a sad smile. "I'm tired," she says. "Think I'll go to bed."

I drop Marlowe's hand. "I'll come with you."

Kassidy shakes her head. "Stay down here. I'll be fine."

She heads up the stairs and disappears around the bend. Fergus, Ellison, and Chloe follow her. None of them speak, as if they're tired of each other's company.

Marlowe and I wander into the library and sit on the couch in front of the fireplace. After a few minutes, I turn to face him. "I have to know what the detectives are saying."

"Or you could sit here with me," he replies, his eyes burning into mine.

I groan. "Please don't hold it against me."

He nods, but his mouth is set in a line of concern. I know what he must be thinking, but I can't help it; hearing their conversation is more important than Marlowe wondering if I murdered Blaine.

When I reach the wall, I realize I have no idea how to open the hidden door from the library side. "You said Anne Ashwood showed you the secret passage on the tour," I say. "Where's the lever?"

Marlowe walks up to a bookshelf and pulls on a book engraved with gold roses. The hidden door swings open.

"Come back soon," he says, kissing me on the cheek.

I've been in the passage so often I can move through it easily in the dark. I reach the end and listen.

"How's the art heist investigation in SoHo going?" asks Detective Cates. The wine has softened his voice into an even thicker drawl. "I hear the NYPD is paying you a handsome consultant's fee to assist their detectives."

"I know who did it," says Pilar de León. "I just need a few more weeks to prove it." She sighs. "It's always easy to figure out the who."

Someone jangles silverware onto a dish. "What did you mean when you said fate had brought you to Ashwood Manor?" asks Detective Cates.

Pilar de León's answer is so quiet I can hardly hear her. "Did you know I came to this country illegally when I was a teenager?"

Detective Cates sounds surprised. "You never told me that."

"I wouldn't have," she replies. "It's not the sort of thing you tell a police detective, even if you're dating him."

"When did you become a citizen?"

"I didn't," she says. "I'm permitted to stay here on a work visa for people with special skills. So long as I consult with American police departments, my visa remains valid. Nowadays, my fame in PI circles means I can cross the border without much trouble, but it was different when I was young. When I was nobody." A bottle hits the table with a heavy thud. "My family wasn't so lucky."

"That must be hard," says Detective Cates.

"It is. I have a house back in my hometown that I return to when I can, but I miss them." She pauses. "Do you remember the case I was working on when you were with the Chicago PD?" He must nod, because she continues. "It wasn't exactly a kidnapping. It was more like a missing persons search."

Before she can explain further, one of the maids interrupts. "Sorry to bother you, but we need to clear your wineglasses."

"How inconsiderate of us," replies Pilar de León in Spanish. "We'll get out of your way."

"Nightcap in my room?" asks Detective Cates, his voice getting farther away as they leave the dining room.

"I'd like that," she murmurs.

When I return to the library, Marlowe is still sitting on the periwinkle couch, reading a book by firelight. I flop down next to him.

"No luck?" he asks, putting aside the book.

I shake my head. "Not unless you count listening to Detective Cates and Pilar de León rekindle their love."

Marlowe laughs. "The mysteries of human attraction."

We sit quietly for a few minutes, listening to the rain lash the windows.

"What are you thinking about?" he asks.

"I'm wondering how many families are harmed because this country deports people who have been living here for a long time," I say. "Pilar de León was telling Detective Cates that some of her family have been deported. It's a common enough story if your family is from Mexico."

"When was the last time you talked to your dad?" asks Marlowe.

"Eight years ago," I say. "When he first left, he called all the time. But then we moved to Harker, and he stopped. My mom said he'd met another woman. I thought he might at least call for our birthdays, but he never did." I shake my head. "I never understood how someone could abandon Caye like that."

He grabs my hand. "I'm sorry. He sounds like a bastard."

I nestle into his shoulder and watch the flames.

"How did you not notice that you lost a thousand-dollar diamond?" I ask.

Marlowe tenses under my head. "It took a lot of nerve to go into Blaine's room, so I wasn't paying very close attention to my clothes." I glance up at his face. His mouth is set in an angry line. "I wish they would tell me if they found it in Blaine's room."

"Does it matter?" I ask. "You have a reason for being in there that day."

His jaw clenches. "I don't like not knowing what's going on."

"Me neither," I say. "I've listened to all the interviews, and I still have no idea where their heads are at."

"Do you even want the case solved?" asks Marlowe.

I decide not to lie. "I wish they'd forget the whole thing."

"Is that what you'll do with your secret? Forget about it?"

I sit up, startled. "I'll never forget it," I say. "But like you said, what's done is done."

"There will be other Blaines."

"You don't know that."

"Have you considered telling the police?"

I leap off the couch as if he's burned me with a hot poker. Why would he even suggest something like that? How could he have misunderstood me so badly?

"That's what I've been trying to prevent from happening!" I say, pacing in front of the couch. "That's why I was in Blaine's room. That's why I did what I . . . I couldn't let them find out," I splutter. "Can't you see how it would destroy everything I've worked for?"

Marlowe stands up and touches my cheek with his hand. "I have absolute sympathy for you, Isadora. But what you're doing is trading your future for someone else's. You should consider whether that's the moral code you want to live by."

He walks abruptly out the library door.

Rage shoots through my body so fast my vision goes blurry. How *dare* he lecture me from his golden palace. He has no idea what it's like to be me, to look at Caye every day and weigh the consequences of my actions. To help my mom and work at Pegasus and edit the school newspaper, all while trying to maintain my GPA. How easy it must be to adhere to a moral code when you're never faced with a single risk to your perfectly scripted future.

But then, just as quickly, my conscience washes the anger away, and I collapse onto the couch, so drained I feel like I might never move again.

I sit and listen to the fire and the rain—elements of the world destroying and rebuilding in a never-ending circle—and try to avoid my own conclusions. But eventually, they come.

I think I always knew what I had to do. I think I built up

a story to tell myself so I didn't have to face the only possible outcome of the secret I held so closely.

My dad had been wrong: If an eye for an eye makes the whole world blind, the only choice is to put out your own eye and stop the cycle.

Maybe if I had acknowledged that sooner, I wouldn't have brought the knife.

Maybe Blaine would still be alive.

38

Kassidy isn't in the bedroom when I wake up the next day. I hope that means all the drugs are out of her system, because I need to talk to her. If the situation with her dad's company is as bad as Chloe says, maybe she and I can escape somewhere to recover from the strain of the week. Somewhere far away from Ashwood Manor and Harker and the investigation.

Then I remember the phone call I made on the landline. It hadn't taken long; I'd been asked only a few routine questions, as if the woman on the other end regularly received anonymous reports of criminal activity after midnight. But those few minutes changed the course of my life.

You'll never be able to run from this again.

When I enter the dining room, Marlowe is at the head of the table, looking pale and drinking tea. When our eyes meet, I spin on my heel and leave the way I came in. He may have been right, but I'm still pissed at what an ass he'd been about it.

Kassidy's in the drawing room, standing in front of the open French windows, staring at the storm. When I join her, I close my eyes so I can feel the fresh mist against my eyelids.

"It's washing away our sins," she says.

"You don't have any sins, Kass."

"Have you tried to imagine going home after this?" she asks. "Scrolling through social media, swimming in my pool, eating dinner with my parents. It seems"—she reflects for a moment—"like a life that doesn't belong to me anymore."

"I wish we could run half a world away," I say, opening my eyes. "Where we don't know anyone and no one knows us."

She smiles. "By the ocean somewhere, in a little bungalow—"

"Cracking coconuts and drinking piña coladas—"

"And watching old movies after lazy days at the beach," finishes Kassidy.

We're quiet for a minute, dreaming of a future we both know we'll never have.

"I told you Marlowe was into you," she whispers.

"You're always right about guys."

Kassidy shakes her head. "If that were true, my heart wouldn't be shattered into so many pieces." She glances over her shoulder at the detectives walking into the drawing room with the rest of the group. "I wish they would just leave us alone."

"You and me both."

We leave the window and sit down on a couch. Marlowe stares at me, but I avoid his eyes. I never thought I'd say it, but I can't wait to get out of these period clothes and back into my jeans and T-shirts. And I'm clearly not alone. Marlowe's suit is missing its vest and pocket watch, Kassidy's makeup is smudged while Chloe's is nonexistent, Fergus's greaser swirl lays straight across his forehead, and Ellison hasn't shaved. I wonder if this week will spoil the era for everyone. Maybe we'll always shiver when we see a flapper dress or a *Great Gatsby* adaptation.

"We've got several pieces of good news," says Detective

Cates. "The first is that the storm is still expected to clear by tomorrow morning. All of you can leave then."

"Thank God," mutters Fergus under his breath.

"The second is that we have the forensic report back on Blaine's death."

There's an uncomfortable shifting in the room.

"We need to ask you a few more brief questions. Then you'll have the afternoon free."

"My mom has advised me not to answer anything else," says Ellison, crossing his arms.

"Future Olympian lawyers up during friend's murder investigation," says Fergus, like he's a news anchor.

"You'd do the same if you knew what was good for you," retorts Ellison hotly.

They glare at each other, but then Fergus's lip curls upward and Ellison rolls his eyes.

"Can I go first?" asks Chloe, shooting Ellison a withering glance. "I want this over."

"Come with us, Ms. Li," says Detective Cates, ushering her through the doorway.

A minute later, I hop off the couch and head for the dining room.

"Where are you going?" asks Kassidy.

"To get more tea," I lie. "I'll be back."

As I creep down the secret passage, I realize with a sinking sadness that I've spent more waking hours in this dark corridor than anywhere else in Ashwood Manor. For a moment, I picture what the week would have been like without Blaine's death: acting out my favorite movie scenes with Kassidy, kissing Marlowe in the rosebushes, laughing and eating delicious food as we all indulged in our first taste of freedom after four long, hard years at Marian. The thought of that lost past almost makes me tear up.

Detective Cates is already asking Chloe questions when I reach the end of the passage. "Ms. Li, what were you wearing the evening Blaine died?"

"Why does that matter?" asks Chloe, sounding alarmed.

"You said you wanted to get this over with," says Detective Cates. "The fastest way to make that happen is to answer our questions."

"Fine," says Chloe. "I had on a pink silk dress, black heels with silver seed detailing, and a headband."

"Did you wear any jewelry? Perhaps something with diamonds?"

Diamonds? All at once, I'm on high alert. Does this have something to do with Marlowe's missing diamond cuff link?

"My necklace has diamonds," says Chloe.

"Did you wear it that evening?"

"I never take it off."

"May we see it?"

"I guess."

There's a pause.

"Thank you, Ms. Li," says Detective Cates. "Do you remember anyone else wearing diamonds that day?"

"It's hard to remember which day was which." Chloe sounds apologetic.

"Tell us about any diamonds you remember from this week," says Pilar de León.

"I think Marlowe had on diamond cuff links at breakfast one day," says Chloe slowly. "Ellison has a diamond ring from some championship thing he won. Kassidy had on a pretty diamond bracelet the first night. And Blaine"—Chloe's voice catches—"Blaine had on his diamond watch the day we arrived." She stops. "That's all I remember."

"Did you ever see Fergus with Blaine's watch?" asks Detective Cates.

"Definitely not," says Chloe. "Blaine's dad gave him that watch for his eighteenth birthday. He wouldn't let Fergus touch it, much less wear it."

Detective Cates coughs and then says, "Did Blaine ever mention working on a graduation present for Ms. Logan?"

Chloe scoffs. "Blaine wasn't the sappy gift-giving type," she says. "Kassidy complained at prom that every time he bought her flowers, they were from the leftover bin at the grocery store."

"You've been very helpful," says Detective Cates. "We recommend you stay inside Ashwood Manor—it's getting bad out there."

I can hear the rain and wind pounding the library windows, even from the passage.

"That's it, then?" asks Chloe. "You won't need me again?"

"There's one final meeting in the library after dinner," says Detective Cates. "We'd like everyone to know where we are with the case so you can rest easy as you return to your homes tomorrow."

"Send in whoever wants to come next," says Pilar de León.

I'm surprised to hear Fergus's voice over the scraping of the chair.

"Mr. Barnes, it's bold of you to volunteer," says Detective Cates.

"Though I be but little, I am fierce."

This doesn't sound like the Fergus of the past few days. *Has he been drinking?* I wonder.

Detective Cates appears to be thinking along the same lines. "Have you had any alcohol today, Fergus?"

"No." He laughs. "I've just been feeling . . . hopeful. I know that's strange when my best friend has been murdered. But I guess that's life, right—both the best and worst things can happen at the same time."

"Love must always be surrendered to," says Pilar de León pointedly.

"What were you wearing the night Blaine died?" asks Detective Cates.

Fergus's enthusiasm is immediately quenched. "Same as all the other guys. Black coat. White shirt and vest. Black shoes. White pocket square. We had it easy compared to the girls."

"What about diamonds?" asks Detective Cates.

The detectives are obviously laser-focused on diamonds. But there's no way their target is Marlowe. He told them how he lost his. Then I remember Detective Cates's tone of disbelief when Marlowe said he hadn't noticed the diamond go missing.

My heart begins to race. If there's evidence Marlowe killed Blaine, the heat will be off me. But that's not how I want it to go. I think of the way Marlowe's lips felt on the beach, soft and hungry. *That's not how I want it to go at all.*

"My cigarette case has diamonds on it," says Fergus. "At least I think they're diamonds."

"We thought only Mr. West smoked."

"I vape. Kassidy gave me the case so it would look more period-appropriate."

"You think Kassidy lent you a case with real diamonds?"

"She likes to go all out on things," says Fergus. "But you can see for yourself." There's a shuffling sound, and footsteps get closer to the passage before they trail away again.

"We don't need anything else from you," says Detective Cates. "Send in Ms. Logan."

Kassidy's light footfalls pad across the wood floor a minute later. Even Detective Cates sounds gentle when he talks to her.

"Ms. Logan, did you lend Fergus a diamond cigarette case?"

Kassidy utters a noise of disbelief. "Of course not. They're cubic zirconia. I wanted the week to be authentic, but Fergus could have thrown a tantrum and hurled the case into the ocean."

I hear pages flipping in Detective Cates's notebook. "We've been told you were wearing a diamond bracelet the first night at Ashwood Manor."

"My grandmother gave it to me as a graduation gift," she says.

"Can we see it?"

"It's gone," she says. "It came unclasped in the water when I got caught in the riptide." Her voice cracks. "My grandma is going to be so mad at me."

"Has Ms. Morales worn any diamonds this week?" asks Detective Cates.

"Izzy doesn't really own anything like that," says Kassidy. "And nothing else I brought to the island has real diamonds in it." She finally asks the question I've been trying to work out: "What does Blaine's death have to do with diamonds?"

"We found one embedded in Blaine's body," says Detective Cates.

I'm positive Kassidy's face is as horror-stricken as mine. "What?" she gasps. "How did it get there?"

He ignores her question. "Right now we're just cataloging all the diamonds that were present at the party this week."

"Of course," she says, choking up.

"You should go lie down and get some rest, Ms. Logan," says Pilar de León. "Let us know if we can send Mr. Jimenez up with anything."

I hear slow footsteps cross the floor and then the click of a latch.

"That one is holding on by a thread," says Pilar de León.

"Did you see the latest from Captain Herrera about her family?" asks Detective Cates.

"It's a sad business," she sighs. "Her mother"—she makes a tsking sound—"I'm not sure how one person will be able to bear so much."

It sounds like Chloe was right that something terrible is going on with Kassidy's family. But what's happened to Kassidy's mom? And why can't Pilar de León ever speak plainly?

"Maybe we shouldn't talk to them after dinner," says Detective Cates.

"They deserve the truth."

"They could get the truth in Harker."

"They deserve the truth at Ashwood Manor so that five of them may leave the tragedy behind these walls," says Pilar de León. "There's no reason for it to leak into Harker or their futures."

"And the sixth?"

Pilar de León's voice becomes sharp. "A life was taken, and one cannot make excuses."

39

Ms. Morales next, do you think?" asks Detective Cates.

I don't wait to hear how Pilar de León responds. I dart into the thankfully empty dining room right as Detective Cates pokes his head around the door.

"Just the person we're looking for," he says.

A giant bolt of lightning illuminates the rose garden as I sit down on the library chair. Crashing thunder follows.

"Do you think we should be this close to the windows?" I ask.

"We're perfectly safe inside," says Detective Cates. "This isn't even the worst of it. The forecast says it'll peak this evening."

"Lightning scares my sister," I say. "She loves this stupid little song, and I have to sing it for hours to keep her calm. The funny thing is, it's a sad song about the moon losing her sister before time began and how she comes out every night looking for her. You wouldn't think it would be comforting, but it's all Caye ever wants to hear."

To my surprise, Pilar de León tears up. "There's no greater gift than siblings," she says, wiping her eyes with the edge of her silk dress.

Detective Cates stares at her like she's sprouted a third head. He clears his throat. I can guess what his next words will be. But I'm wrong. He doesn't ask me anything about diamonds.

"Ms. Morales, when did the newspaper staff meet this semester?"

"Fourth period," I tell him. "Right before lunch."

Detective Cates frowns and checks his notes. "You didn't have after-school meetings?"

"Oh," I say, understanding what he means. "The editors met on Monday evenings."

"Did you go home after school and then return for these meetings?"

I shake my head. "I was the editor in chief, so I had to lead the meetings. It was easier to stay after the final bell and prepare. But what does this have to do with Blaine?"

"We have to run down everyone's stories," says Detective Cates vaguely. "Have you ever made a police report?"

A flash of heat rises from my chest into my shoulders. "No, never."

Detective Cates scribbles something in his notebook. "Well, Ms. Morales, that's all we need from you," he says. "Please send in Mr. West."

Marlowe is standing at the end of the hall, hands behind his back.

"I'm the only one left," he says. "Since Ellison has stopped cooperating."

My voice is cold when I answer him. "They're waiting for you."

I walk toward the dining room, but he touches my hand.

"Isadora, please," he says.

I turn to face him, pulling my hand away and crossing my arms over my chest.

"I'm sorry," he says. "I shouldn't have acted like a Roman judge on high last night, decreeing what's right or wrong. I do that sometimes. It's a flaw." He shakes his head. "One of many, I might add. I don't know the context of your life or your decisions. I'm just afraid of how this investigation is going to end, afraid that I might lose you before we've really begun, and hearing that you were going to let your secret die with Blaine made me even more worried that you had . . . Well, you know."

"You *do* think I might have murdered Blaine," I whisper.

"I know the romantic thing to say is no, that the girl I'm falling for could never do something like that," he says. "The honest truth is that I find you perfectly capable of murder. You're driven and ambitious and brilliant, and protective of the people you love."

My heart leaps with a painful twang against my ribs. I feel a twisted kind of pride in his words.

"But I don't think you did it," he continues. "And I'm not only saying that because I'm attached to the idea of a future with you. It's also because"—he stops—"I don't think you would risk leaving your sister. It's not my place to talk about her. But I need you to know something. If your secret gets discovered, I'm going to help you. No—" He cuts me off when I open my mouth to protest. "The money means nothing. I won't even notice it. Don't you see how insane that is? How unfair?" He runs his hands through his curls until they look wild. "I could change Caye's life—your life—and it wouldn't even . . . I'm not saying this right. I know it's too soon to be talking about this, but I don't care if our future lasts one more day or one more year or forever. I want you to know that no matter what happens, you're going to Brown. You're not going to have to give up your future."

"It's done, Marlowe," I whisper, my voice tight with suppressed emotion. "I called the police hotline last night. I'm not sure what they'll do with it, but"—I look into his sapphire eyes—"you were right. I can't trade my future for anyone else's."

He kisses me then, grabbing the back of my head with both hands, drawing me close. He pushes me against the wall, and for the first time I'm aware of the passion behind his stoicism, the reserves of emotion he never shows to anyone.

I lose track of time. Nothing exists but Marlowe. We press against each other like the ebb and flow of the ocean tide.

"Let's go to your room," I say breathlessly, biting the edge of his lip.

"Actually, I need him to come to the library," drawls a sardonic voice.

We both spin around. Detective Cates is standing in the hallway, leaning against the banister. "In case you forgot, this is a murder investigation."

We mumble apologies, and Marlowe follows Cates obediently. But before he enters the library, Marlowe runs back to me, pulls me into an embrace, and whispers in my ear, "To be continued."

After a few minutes of standing in the hallway in a daze, I head to the dining room, feeling happy, but also feeling guilty about being happy. For a single intoxicating moment, I'd forgotten every bad thing in my life. As I enter the hidden passage, I almost knock over an entire rack of wine in my distraction. I shake my head. I need to focus.

"I told you, I have no idea where I lost the diamond," says Marlowe through the library wall. "I searched my room after our last conversation, but I didn't find it."

"What if we told you we found the diamond in Blaine's room?" asks Detective Cates.

My blood runs cold, all my happy feelings replaced by dread. Is Detective Cates saying it was Marlowe's diamond they found embedded in Blaine's dead body?

"I would say that makes sense," explains Marlowe patiently. "I knew it was possible I lost it there. Is that important somehow?"

Detective Cates ignores the question. "When you talked to Blaine about your brother, do you remember touching anything in the room? Washing your hands in the bowl? Opening the armoire? Anything?"

"I touched the doorknob," says Marlowe. "And maybe the bed frame. I looked out the window at one point, so I might have touched the sill."

"Thank you, Mr. West," says Detective Cates. "You may go resume your puppy-love routine with Ms. Morales."

Marlowe's footsteps don't move toward the door.

"If you found my diamond in Blaine's room, I'd like it back," he says.

"Unfortunately, it's been cataloged as evidence," says Detective Cates.

"When will you be done with it?"

"That's for the prosecutor to decide."

My legs begin to tremble. That sounds bad. Maybe I can ask Ellison what it means.

Marlowe doesn't respond, and I hear him move quickly across the floor.

The library door opens, and Mr. Jimenez announces, "Lunch is being served in the dining room."

"I'm going to miss the food here," says Detective Cates. "It's a lot better than grabbing a gas station burrito midday."

"What a horrifying life you lead," replies Pilar de León with a laugh.

"Do you want to meet back here after lunch to discuss what's going to happen this evening?"

"Sí," says Pilar de León.

After a few beats of silence, footsteps head toward the door, getting farther and farther away. The door clicks shut. The dining room is obviously occupied, so I press my head against the library wall, waiting to make sure no one reenters. When I don't hear anything, I pull the lever and step out of the passage.

Pilar de León is sitting in a chair, smiling at me.

Shit.

40

"Hello again, Izzy," she says. "Enjoying the interviews?"

"I, um ...," I start, but there's nothing I can say. I've been caught, and I'm at her mercy.

"It must have been very uncomfortable, sitting on that hard ground in the dark for all these days."

A hot flush spreads up my neck. "You knew I was there the whole time?"

"Indeed, mi cariño." She points toward the passage. "Everyone here knows about the hidden doors. And you're not as quiet as you think."

"Does Detective Cates know?"

Pilar de León raises an eyebrow. "Men don't listen with the same ears."

I assume that means no.

"Why didn't you stop me?"

She shrugs. "I wanted to give you the chance to play detective, especially after you provided us with clues."

I hang my head. "You knew that was me too?"

"I sent pictures of everyone's handwriting to a friend at the NYPD," she says. "Anne Ashwood provided us with copies of the liability forms you signed. My friend confirmed you were the likeliest author."

"I thought I was being so clever," I say, feeling like a complete fool.

"You are clever. But, of course, you come from a clever family."

My head snaps up. "You talked to my mom?"

Pilar de León purses her lips. "Sit down, mi cariño."

I settle on a chair at the other side of the tea table. The wind is blowing the rain at a steep angle, and I wonder if the roses will survive the attack.

"I'd like to know what you've learned from these interviews," she says. "You're a journalist. Surely you have some thoughts on Blaine's murder."

I can't tell if this is a trick or not.

"I've learned you can know people for years and not have any idea what they're doing behind closed doors," I say.

"I'm not making myself clear," says Pilar de León, gazing out the window at the storm. "I find it helpful to walk through the sequence of events. People think solving murders is about the drama—who was sleeping with the victim, who had a secret motive. But no! It's all about the timeline. Time may be an illusion, but the language of time is necessary if we're to craft our story. You've listened to everyone's interviews. Walk me through the day Blaine was murdered."

This definitely feels like a trick. Is she going to try to catch me in a lie and accuse me of murdering Blaine? She waits for me to speak, with a pleasant smile on her face. If she reports me for listening to the interviews, I might get in serious trouble. And I can't afford any more trouble.

"Well, um, breakfast was around nine," I start. "Fergus showed up closer to ten because he was so hungover. Kassidy wanted to go swimming that afternoon, but I was tired of everyone, so I read a book on the terrace instead. Before that—well, at least according to the interview I overheard—Marlowe went to Blaine's room to confront him about his brother's overdose." I stop to think. "Marlowe must not have changed into his bathing suit yet, because he was still wearing his diamond cuff links, so that tells me he went soon after breakfast, before he got ready for the beach."

"An admirable deduction," she says. "Continue."

"Marlowe may or may not have lost a diamond in Blaine's room then." I hold my trembling hands under the tea table. "How did a diamond get embedded in Blaine's body?" I ask.

"It probably fell off the murderer," Pilar de León says, "and that person inadvertently pressed it into Blaine's wound."

"Are you sure it came from the killer?" I ask.

"There are other possibilities," she says, tapping her ruby fingernails on the tea table. "The diamond may already have been on the floor. Or on Blaine."

"Could someone have left it on Blaine afterward? Like if they'd bent down to take his pulse?"

Pilar de León shakes her head. "The diamond was pressed in too deep. The coroner almost missed it."

I don't want to ask the question, but I have to know. "Was it from Marlowe's cuff link?"

She tilts her head to the side. "What do you think?"

"It couldn't have been," I say.

"Do you have such confidence in your new love that you're willing to clear him of guilt?" she asks. "Or do you have secret knowledge about who killed Blaine?"

There's no way I'm heading down that dangerous path, so I

ignore her questions and continue with the timeline, growing nervous as I approach the afternoon scenes.

"The others went to the beach while I read," I say. "I fell asleep, but I woke up when Kassidy screamed. Then I ran down to the ocean to help her."

"When did everyone return from the beach?" she asks.

I try to remember. It's not easy keeping track of time without a cell phone. "I think the grandfather clock chimed three right after we all got back to our rooms."

"But everyone didn't stay in their rooms, did they?" asks Pilar de León.

I shake my head. "I guess you know from my note that I overheard Chloe and Blaine arguing. That was around half past three. Chloe ran back to her room crying about fifteen minutes later, give or take."

I don't want to tell her about my encounter with Blaine, so I skip that part. "Then Blaine went upstairs, and I followed him soon after. I heard his shower turn on as I passed his door. That was probably just before four."

Now lie, you little liar.

"I went back to my room," I say. "Kassidy took a bath while I read. I think she was in there for about thirty minutes. Then I took a bath while Kassidy got ready for the evening. That was another hour."

"What book did you read?"

My heart misses a beat. How could I not have prepared for this question? I'd picked up a book when I returned from Blaine's room, but I was so on edge I could have been reading it upside down for all I'd paid attention to it. "It was a 1920s etiquette book," I say, well aware that the pause before my answer is suspiciously long.

"You're sure you didn't hear anything while you were in the bath?"

I shake my head. "The pipes were too loud. When I came out of the bath around half past five, Kassidy was asleep."

"Do you know if she'd been napping the whole time?"

"Probably," I say. "She was tired after getting caught in the riptide. When we went downstairs around a quarter past seven, Ellison was already there. Fergus and Chloe came in soon after. Marlowe arrived last, maybe fifteen minutes later."

"When do you think Blaine was killed?"

I frown, considering the timeline carefully before I speak. I want to make sure she doesn't think I was alone long enough to kill him. "Marlowe said he knocked on Blaine's door to ask about his cuff link around half past seven, but Blaine didn't answer. That tells me he was already dead."

"Unless Marlowe waited until everyone was downstairs before murdering Blaine," says Pilar de León.

"Too risky," I say, relieved that her theory doesn't track. "Blaine could have gone down to cocktails on time or even early, and then Marlowe would have missed his chance. Blaine also couldn't have been murdered at four, because he still would have been in the shower. The water was off when we found him, and he was wrapped in a towel and looked clean. But he hadn't changed into his dinner clothes yet. It doesn't take the guys as long to get ready, but he would have still given himself half an hour to forty-five minutes to dress. I think you could safely say he was murdered sometime between four fifteen and six thirty."

"That's still a large window." Pilar de León looks at me thoughtfully. "If you were going to murder Blaine, when would you have done it?"

I take a strangled breath. *She's not accusing you of anything.*

"I would have done it on the earlier side of that window."

"Why?"

"Because people would be more likely to be in their rooms and less likely to see or hear me. Cocktails are at seven, but there's plenty to do downstairs for someone who gets ready early. Right after the beach, people would have been showering and doing their hair and picking out clothes."

"I agree," she says, staring out into space, as if she's imagining the scene. "But why *that* afternoon? Why not the next day or the end of the week?"

"S-someone must have been angry," I stammer. "He was stabbed so many times. It had to be a crime of passion, right?"

"No, no, mi cariño! Whoever murdered Blaine chose the most opportune time. They brought a knife with them to the island. They knew what they were going to do before they did it."

I interrupt. "What if the knife was already there?"

"An intriguing possibility," says Pilar de León. "But his wounds don't match any of the knives from Ashwood Manor. And none of them are missing." She smiles. "This has been most illuminating. I typically work alone, thinking and rearranging scenes on a timeline until I can see the crime in my head, like a dramatic film, but perhaps I should consider working with a partner more often."

"Maybe Detective Cates," I say.

Her eyes twinkle. "You learned much during your spying."

That reminds me of what she said before. "You told me I was clever, like my family. Did you interview my mom?"

She stiffens. "I've met your mother, but I was referring to your father."

This pronouncement strikes me with as much force as the lightning flashing over the ocean outside.

"How do you know my dad?"

Pilar de León meets my eyes, as if weighing whether to answer my question. When she speaks, her voice is soft. "If I tell you how I know your father, you must promise to listen with an open mind."

My heart speeds up, but I nod.

"Eight years ago, I worked on a missing persons case in Chicago," she says, her face growing graver with every word. "Your father was the client who hired me."

Fear burns under my breastbone. "Who was he looking for?" I whisper.

"You and your sister."

Heat spreads through my body so quickly it feels like my face might catch fire. Whatever I was afraid she was going to say, this is worse.

Pilar de León continues. "Two years after your father was deported, your mother moved without telling him where she'd gone. She cut off all communication with him."

I shake my head. "My dad stopped communicating with *us*," I say. "My mom always wanted him to call or send money. She stared at her phone for hours every night. She was lonely without him."

"He asked me to find you," says Pilar de León, ignoring me.

"Your mother hid her tracks well. One day she was in Chicago; the next day she was in the wind. I searched and searched, but it's a big country and she could have gone anywhere. The name María Morales is so common as to be useless.

"A few years ago, I thought I might have found you. A Cayetana Morales popped up in a national health database as someone with a respiratory infection from the red algae that had been terrorizing the eastern seaboard. It's the kind of thing the government tracks in case it becomes a widespread health crisis. I took a flight to Boston and then a train to the beach community where the infection was reported. But it was a dead end. I interviewed healthcare workers at every clinic, but none of them would give me access to their patient records. I may have many connections in this country, but I can't simply waltz in and ask for medical files."

I'd been on the verge of telling her to stop lying. To stop messing with my head. But her last words ring a bell.

"My family went to Brighley," I say slowly. "Four years ago. It was a disaster. The city wasn't designed for wheelchairs, and we couldn't enjoy the beach, because toxic fumes were making people sick. Caye is more sensitive than us, and my mom had to take her to a doctor when her oxygen levels dropped. We never went on another vacation."

"I'm sure your mother was afraid after that," says Pilar de León. "Leaving the safe confines of Harker would always have been a risk." Her gaze is stony. "Eventually, I had to admit defeat. The one failure of my career. There were no leads and no hope. The only chance your father had was for your mother to change her mind about contacting him. But she never did."

"Why would she run away, though?" I protest. "Why give up child support to prevent a man who had already been deported from finding us?"

"Your mother is a jealous woman," says Pilar de León darkly. "No doubt she told you your father met someone else in Mexico. That part's true. But she lied when she said that meant he didn't want anything to do with your family. She couldn't handle being rejected, and she punished him the only way she could: She broke off his connection with you and Caye."

I'm silent, wondering if any of this is possible. I could never understand how someone who had been so involved in our childhoods could stop caring about us, and especially about Caye. When my dad came home from work, she would light up with happiness. He would spin her around in her wheelchair while she screamed with laughter. He always called her his "little star" and told her if he ever got lost, he'd find his way back by looking for her in the night sky.

Hope and horror begin to fight a battle in my heart. If what Pilar de León is saying is true, my mom has been lying to me most of my life. I wish I could say she'd never do something like that, but I find myself believing she did. "Did my dad ever get back into the country?" I ask.

Pilar de León sighs. "It wasn't worth the risk to cross the border unless he could find you. But he didn't even know where to start. Your mother moved you to a town she'd never been to, never even spoken of. And so he stayed in Mexico."

"Is he still there?"

Tears spring to Pilar de León's eyes. "I'm sorry, but your father passed away two years ago. Pancreatic cancer. It took him fast."

The sky opens, and hail pounds like rocks against the windows. Whistling gales bend the white pines in an arc toward the sea. The room sways, and I feel sick, like I'm on a fishing boat being tossed around in the storm.

It can't be true. My dad can't be dead. Not when there's so much I want to say to him, so many questions I need answered. I'd always planned to search for him once I was old enough and ask why he'd abandoned us, why he'd left Caye broken and devastated.

My mind pushes back against the sudden destruction of the future I'd imagined. Maybe Pilar de León is lying—trying to upset me so I'll let something slip about Blaine's murder.

I stand up and pace the library. "You think I'm going to believe you were investigating a murder a thousand miles away from Chicago and stumbled on someone you'd been hired to find almost a decade ago?" I ask, with a vicious edge to my voice. "Those kinds of coincidences don't happen."

"I'm here because you're here, Izzy," she says, and I hate the patient sympathy in her voice. "I have a standing request with police departments all over the country to flag your name and Caye's name. I knew you'd eventually need the police for something—a stolen laptop or a break-in or a stalker. Some crime that required you to put your information in their system. Isadora, unlike María, *is* unusual. So imagine my shock when an Isadora Morales, age eighteen, popped up on a suspect list for a murder off the coast of Maine. I hopped on a train that night to see if you were the person I was looking for. Your father had given me your picture. As soon as I saw you, I knew."

"How did you know?" I snap. "I've changed a lot since I was ten."

"You look just like your father's side of the family. The same eyes, the same ears." She smiles. "Ears are an undervalued way to identify people. I asked you some questions to confirm, but they were a formality."

I think back to the past few days and realize she'd engaged me in conversation more than anyone else. She'd asked about my parents and where I'd grown up. And she'd become emotional when I talked about Caye.

"I thought you were some big-shot detective," I say. "How did you know someone like my dad? And why would you keep searching for us after he died? I know you have a rep to protect, but not solving one case wouldn't have been the end of the world."

Pilar de León's eyes flash with anger. "Many people can detect crime," she says, tilting her chin into the air. "Clients hire me because when I accept a case, I make an oath to the only deity I recognize: truth. I vow to chase every solution to its end." She pauses. "However, there is a more personal reason for my attention to this case." Her lower lip betrays the hint of a tremor. "I knew your father. We grew up in the same town in Mexico. His sister was my childhood best friend. I swore to Noemí I would never stop searching for you and Caye.

"As you can see, I always keep my promises."

41

"Pilar de León is best friends with your aunt?" asks Kassidy, cupping her face in disbelief.

We're sitting in our bedroom, listening to the storm. Kassidy has cracked the window, and I can hear the waves crashing like accusations against the shore.

"I didn't even know I had an aunt," I say, still rocked by Pilar de León's revelations. "Her name is Noemí." I shake my head. "My mom always pretended my dad's side of the family didn't exist."

Kassidy is quiet for a minute. "Why do you think your mom lied all these years?"

"She clearly has serious emotional problems."

"She's been through a lot," says Kassidy. "She raised Caye alone while getting a college degree. And she has to be better than everyone else at the Academy to prove she wasn't hired for her last name."

"She didn't have to do it by herself," I say. "My dad could have helped."

"Financially, maybe. But do you really think your dad could have snuck back into the country? If he got deported again, your mom might have been forced to move too. I know what Pilar de

León said, but maybe your mom didn't want to risk you losing your opportunity to live here."

I hadn't considered that. Kassidy has always been defensive about my mom. I think she wishes her own mother did something more useful than redecorate their house and drink vodka tonics at the country club.

"Pilar de León says she called Noemí after she figured out I was the Isadora Morales she's been hunting all these years," I say. "When I get back to Harker, Noemí's going to invite me and Caye to stay with her in Mexico this summer. She has a house with a pool, and she's going to make it wheelchair-friendly." My voice cracks a little. "Apparently, she wants to tell us about our dad."

"What do you think your mom will say?" asks Kassidy.

"I'm not sure I care."

I'm answering Kassidy evenly, because I'm afraid if I let her see how angry I am, I might start screaming and never stop. How *dare* my mom take away our time with my dad. How *dare* she destroy Caye's happiness. I remember Caye's little face peering at the front door of our Chicago apartment every day, waiting for my dad to come home. She couldn't understand what it meant to be deported. And when he didn't arrive, she cried uncontrollable tears until we distracted her enough to forget.

And what about me? I'd always hoped my dad would be proud his daughter was not only going to college but was headed to the Ivy League. I used to dream he would sneak across the border and show up at graduation with flowers, and listen to all my high school stories and apologize for missing them. I had no idea that for two years, I'd been dreaming the impossible.

I was right to do what I did. My mother is selfish, indifferent to how she impacts others. She didn't give us the chance to know our father. And now he's dead.

"I'm so sorry about your dad," whispers Kassidy, pulling me into a hug.

I cry then. For the years my dad missed. For the times I thought he'd abandoned us. For Caye, who will never be my dad's little star again. For myself and my lost future. And I cry for my mom. No matter what she's done, I can't hate her.

When I calm down, I wipe the tears off my cheeks.

"I've never seen you cry before," says Kassidy.

I laugh weakly. "You cry enough for both of us."

"TV commercials are sad!" she retorts, and we fall back on the bed, laughing and crying at the same time.

Eventually, we stop and stare at the swirly patterns on the white ceiling.

"Ashwood Manor is purgatory," says Kassidy. "I feel like we've been here for years, trapped in endless interviews."

"Six of us dancing around five chairs, ready to jump when Detective Cates calls time," I say.

"And the sixth one out is the murderer."

There's no more laughter. What would Kassidy do if she knew my shame, knew that I'm responsible, knew that I'm as twisted and selfish as my mom?

"I'm going to take a bath," she announces, and her tone is suddenly jaunty and sparkling. "A long, glorious, soul-uplifting bath, full of oodles of bubbles. And then you and I are going to get so exquisitely dolled up no one will pay attention to Detective Cates and his case update after dinner. *You*"—she pokes me gently in the arm, her angelic face looking down at me—"are going to wear the Marla Nevercross dress. And *I* am going to wear the slinky silver confection."

"Like Cara Ashwood in *The Secret of the Ruby Dagger.*"

"Precisely," she says. "We're going to role-play the hell out of this last night, Izzy. Like Cara always said: If you have to go out, go out like a bombshell."

MOUTHS DROP OPEN when we walk into the drawing room.

Ellison whistles. "If I'd known the view would be this hot," he says, "I'd have worn sunglasses."

Kassidy giggles at the silly line. "We wanted to pretend like everything is all right for one last evening."

"It is now," Marlowe whispers in my ear, the soft fabric of his tux brushing my shoulder.

I wonder when I'll get the chance to tell him about my dad. Even though we're leaving tomorrow, I still have so many questions. Will the detectives find my knife? Did Blaine delete his texts? It's felt so good for the past few hours to know my mom isn't the only family member that cares about me and Caye. But fear has crept back in. If Pilar de León finds out what I did, Noemí won't want me as her niece.

Kassidy touches my shaking hand and smiles. "Don't get lost in being Izzy," she says.

She's right. For one night, I can be Marla and she can be Cara. Sisters. True friends. I owe her that much.

Mr. Jimenez tells us the detectives have decided to eat dinner in the servants' quarters and will meet us in the library at ten. I have a feeling Pilar de León asked Detective Cates to give us one final night unsupervised.

And so the six of us sit down to dinner at Ashwood Manor for the last time. It's strange to know we'll never be together again. The innocent will disappear into college life—relegating the tragedy to that horrible thing that happened when they were eighteen, telling the story to a few significant others as the years pass, wondering, during sentimental moments, what Blaine would be doing if he hadn't died. The murderer will be erased from their minds as an anomaly. A person they thought they knew but didn't. As if any one of us couldn't be a killer in the wrong circumstances.

The others have taken up Kassidy's cheerful mood. There's no seating arrangement, and people talk loudly over the gramophone we've moved back into the dining room so we can't hear the storm. Even though they're not as dressed to perfection as me and Kassidy, everyone else has made an effort: Tuxes are pressed. Makeup is precise. Shoes are shined. Marlowe has somehow snuck fancy bottles of champagne out of the kitchen, and the wine is helping me feel warm and free, like the past few days didn't happen.

"I'm sorry about our conversation in the library," says Chloe from across the table. The others are involved in their own conversations and not listening to us.

"No, it's me who should apologize," I say. "I shouldn't have pressed you for answers. That wasn't my place."

"I was ashamed I'd fallen for Blaine," she says. "And I wanted there to be someone else who made the same mistake."

Ellison's and Fergus's animated words at the end of the table intrude on our quieter ones.

Chloe watches them laugh together. "I thought those two hated each other," she says.

I think about what I heard in the interviews. "There's a fine line between love and hate," I say with a knowing smile.

Chloe's mouth falls open. "Fergus and Ellison?" she hisses in a whisper. "No way!" She looks stunned, like she can't believe both Blaine and Ellison rejected her in the same week.

Kassidy sits serenely next to me, staring dreamily into the candles. She's drinking the champagne in small sips, and my heart swells with happiness to see she's not abusing substances to quell her sadness.

"You really do look stunning," whispers Marlowe, drawing my attention away from the others. "Maybe after the meeting, we can pick up where we left off in the hallway."

"I think this dress might be too tight for that kind of kissing," I joke.

He leans even closer to me. "I know how to solve that problem."

I'm two seconds from suggesting we skip dessert when a sparkling flash catches my eye. I look over and see that it's just the candlelight dancing off the bubbles in Kassidy's glass as she brings it to her lips. But it triggers a memory—hazy at first, then crystallizing.

The emotional impact hits me before the image clarifies. I almost sway out of my seat with dizziness. Marlowe notices the change in my demeanor and asks what's wrong, but I hold up a silencing hand. I need to remember.

Something sparkling and dainty and delicate.

Mr. Jimenez walks in with dessert, but the chocolate mousse I mindlessly spoon into my mouth tastes like soft sawdust.

Think!

The memory moves upstairs. I see Blaine's body. There's a bed at nighttime, and it's raining.

It's like grasping at smoke; each time I try to make sense of the feeling, it slips away. I know it's important. Maybe the most important memory I have. But I also dread it and know I'd be better off not remembering it at all. Yet now that I've started, I can't stop. It's only a matter of time before it buries itself in the folds of my brain.

The drawer.

And just like that, it rushes back to me.

Before I can say or do anything, Mr. Jimenez returns and tells us the detectives have requested our presence in the library.

I follow the others, trembling with fear. I have to know if what I'm remembering is true.

"I'll be right behind you," I call out, failing to keep my voice from shaking.

Kassidy and Marlowe stare after me with puzzled expressions as I dash up the stairs. I bang open my bedroom door and head for the side table. I open the drawer, pick up what's inside, and spin it around carefully under the lamplight.

And that's when I understand.

42

stumble into the library like a zombie. The detectives have arranged the couches and chairs in a semicircle around the fireplace. I take a seat next to Marlowe but refuse to meet his eyes. I don't want him reading anything in my face.

He tries to take my hand, but I pull it away. I don't want to be touched. I don't want to be comforted. I want to sink into the floor and not exist anymore.

Even though this is supposed to be Detective Cates's meeting, he's sitting silently in a chair he's dragged in front of the door. It's Pilar de León who stands with her back to the fire, staring at all of us with a rapt expression.

"I'd like to thank you for indulging me this evening," she says. "It's the privilege of a consulting detective to do what the police cannot."

"What's that?" asks Ellison suspiciously. The colorful camaraderie of dinner is fading back to gray.

"Showboat," grumbles Detective Cates.

Pilar de León sighs theatrically. "It's true, I'm afraid. My ego can only be sated by public spectacle."

I'm having trouble focusing on what she's saying as I run through the ways I could be wrong. There must be something I'm missing.

"To begin, I would like to thank you for your patience this week," she says. "I know it's difficult to feel suspected of a crime. It weighs even on the innocent to wonder whether a miscarriage of justice will pull you into the mud." She stares around at all of us, her dark eyes lit by the orange flames of the fire. "I want to put your minds at ease. We know which one of you killed Blaine."

The room explodes with an outraged tangle of voices.

"You let us sleep with a killer in the house?" yells Ellison. He looks around like he's searching for an exit, but Detective Cates is blocking the door.

"You said you were only giving us a summary of the case!" says Chloe.

Marlowe glares at Pilar de León. "I don't want to hear this," he says. "Let us leave."

Detective Cates puts his fingers in his mouth and whistles so loudly everyone stops talking.

Pilar de León smooths out her dress like a bird whose feathers have been ruffled. "This *is* a summary of the case, mis cariños," she says. "My summary of how we discovered the murderer."

I should be terrified. But I know there's no escape. No matter what happens now, I will get what I deserve. The thought makes me feel oddly at peace. But then I remember the drawer, and that peace shatters into misery.

"In any crime, the key to the solution is always the timeline," says Pilar de León. "But it's difficult to establish a timeline when all your suspects lie." She holds up her hand before anyone can interrupt. "Lying is such an interesting phenomenon," she continues with a thoughtful expression. "Even when people are placed in a situation where to lie is to implicate oneself in the worst human act, they still can't tell the truth. Shame is some-how stronger than being accused of murder."

Detective Cates grunts from his chair.

Pilar de León nods. "I'm going to tell you the story of the day Blaine died. The real story. With the lies replaced by truths."

A flash of lightning makes the chandelier flicker. When an earsplitting boom of thunder follows on its heels, everyone gasps. It's clear we've all been holding our breath, waiting for Pilar de León to seal our fates.

"The day started at breakfast," she says. "There were foul moods and green faces from the arguing and drinking the night before. Kassidy, as hostess, felt responsible for making the week as fun as possible. So many of you were caught up in your drama that you hadn't considered how important the 1920s charade was to her, how her people-pleasing personality was desperate for your final high school memory to be a success." She turns apologetic eyes on Kassidy. "Sorry, cariño, but I must say what's true."

Kassidy blushes. Pilar de León has her pegged perfectly.

"She suggested some swimming at the beach," continues Pilar de León. "All of you except Izzy headed down in your wool bathing suits, looking the part of fashionable Jazz Age social-ites, around noon. The irritation continued by the sea. Fergus huffed off to his own corner of the beach, Marlowe walked the sand in solitude, and the other four ignored the objects of their affection.

"Then something happened that helped everyone regain their equanimity. Crises are strange like that—at the very moment you think people will pull apart, they come together. Kassidy got caught in a riptide, and Blaine, forgetting all about their fighting, dove into the ocean to save her. At the same time, Izzy sprinted from her reading spot on the terrace to the beach to help her friend."

Kassidy lets out a small sob.

"Kassidy washed up on shore, and Blaine managed to swim back to land. Understandably, people were shaken by the near drowning of their two friends, and all of you headed back to Ashwood Manor. And here," she says, "is where the lying begins."

She points at Fergus. "Mr. Barnes told us that soon after returning from the beach, Blaine knocked on his door and asked for the seven-thousand-dollar diamond-faced TAG Heuer watch he'd wanted Fergus to hide from Kassidy."

"He did," interrupts Fergus.

Pilar de León silences him with a look. "I put to you that Blaine did no such thing. So the question is: How did your hair get trapped inside the winding knob?"

"It probably got caught when I was giving it back to him," says Fergus, crossing his arms over his chest.

"No, no, Mr. Barnes. The hair wasn't just caught in the knob on the side—it was also caught under the front panel, as if someone had opened the watch. Can you explain how that happened?"

Fergus shakes his head stubbornly.

"You told us Blaine knocked on your door, you handed him his watch, and that was the last time you ever saw him."

"So?"

"Your fingerprints are the last prints on it. None of Blaine's overlay yours. How did that happen if you handed the watch to him?"

Fergus looks mutinous. "Maybe your techs messed up."

She ignores him. "Let me tell you what I think. You offered to hide Blaine's watch from Kassidy, but Blaine didn't trust you or anyone else to keep such a special gift from his father safe. He told you he was going to hide the watch himself—in his armoire, away from the prying eyes of his girlfriend."

"That's not true," mumbles Fergus.

She continues. "You were mad at Blaine the night before his murder because of the fight you'd had earlier in the day, so you went to his room while he was downstairs partying and *stole* his watch."

"What the hell, Gus!" I say, momentarily dragged out of my mental torture.

Fergus turns bright red, and I can see fury building behind his eyes. He's close to popping off, which I'm sure Pilar de León knows. "I have plenty of money," he says. "I don't need to steal a watch."

"That's not why you did it," she says. "We opened the watch. And do you know what we found?" She doesn't wait for him to answer. "Melted gears."

I think it's Ellison's horrified face that does Fergus in.

"Fine!" screams Fergus, hopping to his feet. "You want the truth? The truth is that Blaine was a bastard who threw me aside like a used candy wrapper. So I stole his stupid watch, melted the gears in my fireplace, and then snuck the watch back into his room the next day while he was downstairs fighting with his latest conquest. And then someone murdered him, and I felt so bad about the watch that I wanted to throw myself in the ocean." He glares at Pilar de León. "Is that what you want to hear?"

The edges of her mouth turn up. "It's exactly what I want to hear, though of course I already knew. Your temper is a problem for you, Mr. Barnes. You should get a new therapist."

Fergus sits down and starts ugly-crying while the rest of us stare at Pilar de León, dreading whatever she's about to say next. She looks completely unperturbed by his breakdown. My blood runs cold when I imagine her getting to me. Something tells me her friendship with my aunt isn't going to spare me from her conclusions.

"So now we know Mr. Barnes was in Blaine's room before Chloe and Blaine came upstairs after their fight. Once I realized that, I began to wonder whether Mr. Barnes ever left Blaine's room."

There's a gasp from Chloe.

"Of course I did," says Fergus thickly. He seems deflated, as if all his anger has been burned away by Pilar de León's humiliation.

"He did," says Ellison, his eyes tracing the grains of wood on the library floor.

Pilar de León turns to him. "How do you know that, Mr. Stephens?"

Ellison heaves a huge sigh. "Because he met me in the forest at four, and it would have taken him fifteen minutes to walk from the house to that part of the woods. We were out there for an hour. I can't prove it, but I also can't let Fergus take the heat for something he couldn't have done. There's no way he hid in Blaine's room after returning the watch, because he and I were . . . together at the time."

Kassidy lets out a little gasp next to me. For once, she's the last person to know juicy school gossip.

Fergus looks at Ellison with undisguised gratitude. "Thank

you," he says. "I know you would rather not have admitted that in front of everyone."

"Eh, fuck that noise," says Ellison. "I'm done being ashamed of the things I do. If someone thinks less of me because I'm tapping a thieving theater nerd, I'll wave my future gold medal in their face."

Even Fergus smiles at this takedown. My eyes meet Kassidy's. We both suppress a laugh, and for a moment everything feels normal.

As I look at her, pink-cheeked from the warmth of the fire, I realize that I would do anything, give anything, to go back to the day she told me about her graduation surprise. I would tell her our visit to Ashwood Manor could wait until the museum opened. Convince her we should celebrate with just the two of us. Maybe take a road trip to Prince Edward Island or make a last-minute dash to the Caribbean on her yacht, where I'd finally take her family up on their vacation offer. I would have left my knife at home and worried about how my thighs looked in my bathing suit, like any other teenager.

"Lovely," says Pilar de León. "Just to put your minds at ease, we do have proof of what you say. You were spotted by the rather ruffled elderly gardener, who told me in no uncertain terms that he would be reporting your group's behavior to the owner. But as none of you will ever set foot in Ashwood Manor again, I can't imagine that's too much of a consequence."

The confidence with which she states this startles me. But she's right. I'll never return to Sparrow Island. Even the thought of staying at Ashwood Manor one more night makes me want to lie on the floor and refuse to move.

Pilar de León continues. "So from four to five, Mr. Barnes

and Mr. Stephens were in the pine forest, not murdering Blaine. Don't misunderstand me," she says, wagging a finger at us. "This doesn't clear them. Blaine could have been murdered anytime between four fifteen and six thirty." She points to Ellison's left hand. "Mr. Stephens, where is your championship ring?"

Ellison frowns. "I don't see what my ring has to do with anything."

"I'll be the judge of what's relevant," says Pilar de León. "Are you refusing to answer?"

Ellison rolls his eyes and digs into his pants pocket. He pulls out the ring. A circle of dull diamonds surrounds crossed oars made of fire opals.

Pilar de León raises an eyebrow. "Why is your ring in your pocket and not on your finger?"

A small shiver runs through Ellison's arm. "It got blood on it when I felt for Blaine's pulse," he says. "I didn't want to wear it again until my jeweler cleaned it."

That must have been what I'd seen Ellison put in his pocket after we discovered Blaine's body.

"Understandable," says Pilar de León. "I can see from here that none of the diamonds are missing." She turns to Chloe. "I think it's time we check in on Ms. Li."

Chloe clutches the heart pendant on her necklace like a life preserver.

"We know Ms. Li was fighting with Blaine in the library about half past three. She returned upstairs, crying, fifteen minutes later. However, we are yet to find anyone who can say she entered *her* room. Is it possible someone heard her open and close the door to Blaine's room instead?"

Chloe shakes her head, but she doesn't say anything.

"Perhaps. You see, there is one outstanding question Ms. Li has not explained to my satisfaction."

We all straighten up, alert.

"She says she didn't go into Blaine's room before he died, and touched nothing afterward, but her fingerprints were all over his ironstone washbowl."

Seven pairs of eyes shift to Chloe's face. Her already-red cheeks are flushing an even deeper scarlet, and she sinks into her seat.

"Tell me how that could have happened, Ms. Li."

"I did go in there before he died," says Chloe in a small voice. "But not after the beach. It was the day before, after lunch."

"Why were you in Blaine's room?"

Chloe hangs her head. "I don't want to say."

"You'd rather be suspected of murder?" asks Pilar de León.

"I didn't do anything wrong," mumbles Chloe.

"We tested the soap," says Pilar de León archly.

Chloe's head snaps up. "Why?"

"Because I am outrageously thorough, Ms. Li. And do you know what we found?"

"Yes," says Chloe almost inaudibly.

"The rest of us don't," says Fergus, his nose for gossip over-riding the horror of his recent humiliation.

A giant crack of thunder shakes Ashwood Manor, rattling the library windows like an animal trying to break free of its cage. The wind is stripping the trees and bushes of all their greenery. Gusting piles of leaves and petals blow toward the edge of the cliff.

"Are you sure we should be in this room?" asks Ellison, his

leg bouncing up and down nervously. "My mom said to stay in interior rooms only."

Pilar de León turns to Detective Cates.

"We're fine," he drawls. "These old houses are indestructible."

"Ms. Li?" says Pilar de León, returning to the conversation. "I imagine you found itching powder."

Detective Cates grunts with laughter, then makes his face blank again.

Fergus looks at Chloe like he can't believe it. "Itching powder?" he says. "That's your dark secret? What are you, nine years old?"

"We can't all be watch-melting masterminds, Fergus," Chloe shoots back witheringly.

"It appears that Ms. Li wanted Blaine to be in some discomfort during his stay at Ashwood Manor," says Pilar de León. "So she brought itching powder in saline to add to his soap."

"The vial," I say. "You really did use it on Blaine."

"Not to poison him," whines Chloe. "I wanted him to feel the same itching I—" She stops, looking mortified. "I wanted to hurt him a little."

"Unfortunately, you overestimated the use of soap by teenage boys," says Pilar de León. "I don't think he ever touched it."

"Then why were her prints on the bowl?" asks Marlowe.

Pilar de León gestures toward Chloe.

"I got a little solution on my hands and needed to wash it off quickly," she says. "I accidentally shifted the washbowl, and then I moved it back so Blaine wouldn't notice anyone had been there."

"Is there *anything* you didn't dust for prints?" grumbles Fergus.

"We had a very particular reason for dusting the washbowl," says Pilar de León, and something in her tone makes my stomach tense. A buzz of suspense fills the room like static.

"Which was what?" asks Marlowe.

Pilar de León stares at us with eyes full of reflected fire. "The washbowl was the murder weapon," she announces. "Someone bashed in Blaine's head with the bowl before they stabbed him. The knife wounds would have killed him, but he was already dead."

"What?!" I scream, jumping to my feet. The others look at me like I've lost my mind. I see spots and grab on to the nearest chair so I don't faint. It's as if the blackness of the storm has narrowed my vision to a single tunnel of light.

It can't be true. Pilar de León must be wrong. She's trying to trick me. That must be it.

Suddenly, the room explodes around us. I hear windows shatter. Then it feels like a bucket of cold water is poured on my head. Wind roars through my ears, as deafening as a jet engine. The fireplace is doused by a torrential flood from above, and the electricity goes out, plunging us into total darkness.

43

get lost in the chaos of screaming and panic, but I can barely find the will to care.

The washbowl was the murder weapon. Not the knife.

Detective Cates bellows for everyone to stay calm, but no one listens to him. The room is pandemonium as people yell in the darkness and trample over glass. The rain and wind come through the broken windows, knocking us off-balance.

I turn to Kassidy to make sure she's not hurt, but the couch is empty.

There's a flash of light at the back of the room that disappears almost as quickly as it came. I look around for Kassidy, but all I can make out is the hazy outline of Detective Cates, standing by the door and directing people to get away from the windows.

Then I realize what the flash of light was.

I run to the back of the library and pull on the false book. I knock over a rack of wine in my rush down the passage, but I know no one will be able to hear it over the roar of the storm pounding Ashwood Manor.

The door at the other end is wide open. I step across the threshold to find myself in an eerily silent dining room lit by flickering candles. The storm is muted on this side of the house, even though a short passage away a cyclone is battering the library.

The unmistakable creaking of the drawing room windows breaks the silence. In my hurry to follow the sound, I almost trip over a rug in the dark hall.

The storm is still raging outside, but I throw myself through the open French windows, tearing the hem of Marla's dress as it gets caught on the sharp lip of the sill. There's a figure in the distance, running through the pouring rain. It's headed for the bluffs. I sprint down the path, soaked to the bone within minutes, my heels getting stuck in the mud and wet grass every few feet until I rip them off and run barefoot.

Kassidy stands near the edge of the cliff, looking out over the turbulent ocean, her silver dress clinging to her body. I arrive after her, huffing, my hands on my hips.

"Kass, what the hell are you doing out here?"

She turns around slowly and smiles. "Only the best of friends would have followed me in this weather."

Lightning strikes out at sea, brightening the sky like the flashbulb of an old camera. Kassidy's eye makeup drips down her face in black streaks.

"Let's go back in, Kass," I say. "You don't have to talk to the detectives anymore. We can take hot baths and go home tomorrow afternoon. Your parents can find you a lawyer."

Her voice barely reaches me over the howling wind. "So you know."

I wrap my arms around my body, trying to hold myself together. Kassidy was wrong: Ashwood Manor isn't purgatory; it's hell. "Let's not talk about it," I say.

"How did you figure out it was me?" she asks.

A soft groan escapes my throat. I know it's hopeless to fight her. Maybe if she confesses, she'll agree to go back upstairs. "The bracelet," I say. "You didn't lose it in the ocean like you told the detectives. Everything was such a blur when we found Blaine's body that I forgot I'd put it in the side table. But then at dinner, your champagne sparkled in the candlelight like it was full of tiny diamonds, and the memory came back to me. When I checked the drawer, I saw that the bracelet was missing a stone."

She nods. "The washbowl must have knocked the diamond loose when I hit Blaine." She says this simply, as if bashing boyfriends over the head is something people do every day.

"Why, Kass?" I cry, my heart aching so painfully I'm afraid it might tear in half. "Why did you do it? I thought you loved Blaine."

"I did," she says. "But he didn't love me back." Her voice is pouty, like a little girl talking to her stuffed animals. "I devoted myself to him for four years. I never so much as looked at another guy. I gave up all sorts of experiences for him during the best years of my life. And I knew he wasn't doing the same. But I could deal with that, so long as he understood it was me and him forever."

"You killed him because he broke up with you?" I gasp.

She doesn't answer. "Remember how I got caught in the riptide?" she asks. "When I washed up on shore and saw him swimming so far out, waving his arms for help, I thought he might drown. But I wasn't terrified—I was relieved. I imagined how nice it would be to know he wasn't out there living his life without me." She shakes her head. "I couldn't believe I'd thought it, and the feeling went away as soon as it came. But later that afternoon, I went into his room while you were in the bath—"

"How?" I interrupt. "I had the key to the door in the bathroom."

"There's a hidden passage in the closet that goes to the room next door," she says, waving away the explanation as if it doesn't matter. "Anne Ashwood told us about the passages when she did the tour. There are tons of hidden hallways. That's how I knew about the library passage too.

"When I realized the key wasn't in the door, I went through the passage to Blaine's room. He was still in the bathroom. I decided I would be mature, salvage the week so I didn't ruin it for everyone else. I thought maybe if we had a good enough time and he saw how nonclingy I could be, he might not want to break up anymore. I went to the armoire so I could lay out his clothes for dinner."

"Oh no," I whisper.

"When I grabbed his pants, they were heavy. I reached into his pocket, and that's when I found your note and the knife."

Tears fall down my face. "I'm sorry I didn't tell you, Kass. I couldn't bear to tell you."

"I don't blame you," she says. "I knew something was wrong. You've been upset for weeks. But I had no idea you were carrying around a secret this terrible. When I read what he'd done to you—"

"To me?"

"He'd risked your future! Caye's future! Your mom would go to jail if anyone found out she and Blaine were sleeping together."

I suck in air as Kassidy's mouth twists with the pain of saying the truth aloud. Even when I'd called the anonymous tip line to report my mom, some part of me still felt like maybe none of it was real. There's no chance of that now.

Kassidy continues. "Blaine left his burner phone under his pillow. When I scrolled through his texts, I found out they were still messaging each other. There's no way it would have stayed secret."

I hold my head in my hands. "This is all my fault."

"I'd never felt rage like that," she says, her eyes wide and wild, bright against the jagged branches behind her. "I barely remember what happened. I just know that everything went hazy, and when he came out of the bathroom in his towel, I banged him on the head with the washbowl. He fell to the ground, and I kept banging, but his arms were still twitching, so I took the gold knife you'd put in his pants pocket and stabbed him. Then I burned the note in his fireplace, went back into the hidden passage, stuffed my gloves and the knife into a trash bag, and changed out of my bloody dress. I hadn't gone in there to kill him, so I hadn't prepared properly. I picked a new dress closest in color and design to the one I'd been wearing and hoped you wouldn't notice. Then I lay on the bed and pretended to nap."

Now I knew why she'd looked so much thinner in her dress after I came out of the bath.

"I just wanted to scare him," I whisper, the knot under my rib cage burning so fiercely it feels like I might combust from the inside. "If I hadn't put the knife and the threatening note in his pants, he'd still be alive."

"You're my best friend, Izzy," she says. "You're more important to me than Blaine could ever be. I couldn't let him get away with destroying your life."

"It was my mom's fault, Kass. She was the adult."

"Blaine was eighteen," says Kassidy. "He knew what he was doing."

"He turned eighteen two weeks ago, and this has been going on for months," I say. "Why do you think he's been acting weird all semester? She was tutoring him, and he probably didn't want his grades to suffer. What she did is horrible."

Kassidy looks thoughtful for a minute, but then she shakes her head. "No. I know your mom. She's been so lonely all these years, taking care of you and Caye. I know how convincing Blaine can be. In her texts, she talked about feeling guilty, but he kept pushing her forward. Even this week, when he had no grades to worry about. It's his fault."

She's wrong, but she probably can't justify what she did without making him the villain.

I take a few steps toward her. "I begged him to stop seeing her," I say. "He told me if I got in their way or told you about the affair, he would make their relationship public. I thought if he believed I might really kill him, maybe he'd keep his mouth shut and I wouldn't lose everything."

"I would have found out eventually," says Kassidy. "Blaine doesn't keep a tight enough hold on his phone to keep a secret this big."

"The police haven't found his burner cell," I say.

"They won't," she says. "I crushed it and threw it off the cliff into the ocean days ago."

I'd been worried for no reason. Kassidy had taken care of everything.

Thunder rumbles over the angry waves below the bluff. The

wind howls and drives the rain hard into my skin, like needles. I'm shivering so violently my teeth are chattering.

"I'm so sorry, Kass," I say. "I've ruined everything."

"None of this is your fault, Izzy," she says. "I want you to remember that when I'm gone. You've been nothing but the best friend a person could have."

The hairs on the back of my neck stand up. "When you're gone?"

"It's like in the movie," she says. "When Marla Nevercross discovers Cara Ashwood is the killer. She watches Cara walk toward these cliffs, and a single tear rolls down her cheek, because she knows she'll never see her sister again." Kassidy waves her hand toward the water. "It's my turn to walk away, Izzy."

Now I understand why she fled the library. She has no intention of letting the detectives arrest her.

"Kass, no! You had a mental breakdown caused by extreme emotional distress. They'll understand that. They'll go easy on you. Your life isn't over because you made a mistake." My thoughts are wild, desperate. "It's my fault too! I hid the knife. I kept my mom's secret. And your parents can hire the best team of lawyers. They'll get you the help you need."

"I called home," she says. "My dad's going to be arrested. He's been selling supplies off the books to foreign governments and keeping the money. That's what my parents were arguing about when you were at my house." She shakes her head. "I can't put my mom through two trials and visiting both me and my dad in prison. And I can't look Blaine's parents in the eyes. I'll always be a murderer, no matter what my sentence is."

Far from shedding only a single tear, I'm sobbing. "Please don't do this, Kass. I need you."

"No, you don't," she says. "You're the strongest person I know. And I want you to do one last thing for me. I want you to say goodbye, and then I want you to walk back to the house. You don't have to be Marla—you don't have to watch. But I've already made my decision." She smiles her perfect, beautiful smile. "And you know I never change my mind."

I can't let this happen. I shuffle forward, trying to make it look natural, like the ferocious wind is blowing me toward her. Maybe if I can get close enough, I can grab her and drag her away from the cliff.

She sees exactly what I'm doing and steps all the way to the edge. "I'd be gone before you could get to me," she warns.

"We can get rid of the evidence," I plead, not daring to get any closer. "The detectives might not even know for sure who did it. Maybe they were bluffing in there, trying to get one of us to confess."

Kassidy shakes her head. "Pilar de León knows. They found my diamond embedded in Blaine's wound. And I'm sure some-one's told her about the secret passages by now. Once we leave, they'll get a warrant to search the empty rooms, and they'll find blood and probably fingerprints and who knows what else. The only other person with access to the passage and the knife is you, and I'd never let you take the blame for Blaine's death. This is over, Izzy. You need to let me go."

I can see the determination in her eyes. Kassidy is doing what she's always done: making a decision, then following through at any cost. I can scream and beg, but she'll remain as hard as stone. And she's too close to the edge for me to stop her.

All that's left to do is what she asked.

"I'm going to miss you so much," I cry. "I don't know what I'll do without you."

"You'll be brilliant," she says fervently. "The best of us."

I hold out my hand, wishing I could touch hers one last time. But Kassidy does what Cara Ashwood does in the film: She blows me a final kiss. "Don't forget me, Izzy."

"I'll love you forever, Kass."

She wipes away her tears and stands tall, her graceful head held high, as if steeling herself for what she's about to do. "Don't tell anyone what happened," she says. "Let it be a mystery."

It takes everything I have to give her one last loving smile and then to turn and walk back to Ashwood Manor, my tears mixing with the rain pouring endlessly from the sky. I walk until I reach the terrace outside the drawing room. Then I look back at the sea.

She's gone.

sit alone on the deck of the ferry the next day, staring out over the calm waves as we return to the mainland. Seabirds, with wings stretched out to the sun, float like feathers on the same breeze playing with my limp curls. The others are inside, behind the glass, as far away from me as possible.

I keep replaying the night before in my head on a loop: Detective Cates rushing onto the terrace just minutes after Kassidy disappeared, tearing his hair out and asking if I knew where she'd gone. Me shaking my head and saying nothing.

Kassidy had wanted it to be a mystery. Keeping her secret was the only thing I had left to give her.

Detective Cates had spent all night searching the house and the grounds, insisting the rest of us stay in the drawing room under the supervision of Pilar de León. She'd squinted hard at me once or twice, as if she were trying to read my mind, but even if she had, all she would have found there was empty, heart-wrenching horror.

Everyone else avoided my eyes, except for Marlowe, who held my hand on the couch while I stared unblinkingly into the fire. Maybe the others thought I'd killed Blaine and pushed Kassidy off a cliff; no part of me cared anymore. Kassidy was gone, and nothing else mattered.

A wet and shivering Detective Cates tried to question me after his search, but I pressed my lips into a firm line and refused to open them. Eventually, Pilar de León told him I needed sleep, that he wasn't going to get answers by yelling, and that she would keep watch over the hallway to make sure no one else disappeared.

But of course I didn't sleep. I lay in my cold bed, without Kassidy's warmth beside me, and cried. All I could see was her face, smiling at me one last time, looking like a lost, rain-soaked angel in her silver gown. Maybe she hadn't jumped at all; maybe she'd flown away.

THE FERRY DOORS slide open, and Pilar de León sits next to me on the bench.

"Have they found her—" I almost say *body*, but I catch myself.

"No. The police boat has been out all morning, but there's no trace of her."

I nod.

"I'm not going to ask you about Kassidy," she says. "But I would like to finish the film in my head about Blaine's murder."

I'm done lying about Blaine. Whatever happens to me, I deserve it. "What do you want to know?" I ask.

"Why did you bring the knife to Ashwood Manor?"

I stare at the sky, which is so blue no one would ever know a tropical storm had devastated the area the night before. The library windows had been shattered by an oak tree that was uprooted by hurricane-force winds. Ellison's arms got scraped up, and Pilar de León is nursing a cut over her eyebrow, but everyone had been remarkably lucky to avoid serious injury.

"I brought the knife so I could threaten Blaine," I say. "He and my mom have been having an affair, and I wanted him to swear he would never tell anyone. I thought the knife would scare him and make him realize I was dead serious."

"Did you want to kill him?"

"I just wanted it all to stop," I say. "I knew that if anyone found out about them, my mom would be arrested, and I wouldn't be able to go to Brown, because I'd have to take care of Caye.

"I snuck into Blaine's room while he was in the shower. I thought he'd be terrified I was some kind of secret psycho, and he'd ditch my mom and never talk about their relationship. But when I walked into the bathroom with the knife, I imagined his blood mixing with the water and swirling down the drain." I sigh. "Picturing the worst made me lose my nerve. I left the bathroom, wrote a note telling him he was dead if he said anything about my mom, instructed him to delete the texts on his burner phone, and left the knife and the note in his dinner pants.

"It never occurred to me someone might stumble on the knife and use it to murder him. All this week I've felt so guilty. Even though I didn't plunge the knife into his back, I was the reason he was dead. Or at least I thought I was until you said the washbowl was the real murder weapon."

"A piece of luck for you," says Pilar de León.

"Do you think they'll put me in jail?"

She raises an eyebrow above her flowery eyeglass frames. "According to the note we found in Blaine's room this morning, Kassidy brought the knife to the island."

I gasp. "She wrote a confession?"

"She did," confirms Pilar de León. "Explaining how she

snuck into Blaine's room, hit him with the washbowl, and then stabbed him with the knife she'd brought, and telling us where to find her bloodied gloves and dress."

"My prints will be on the knife," I say. "They'll know she was lying."

"I have a feeling there will be no prints on the knife," says Pilar de León thoughtfully. "Kassidy was a thorough young woman, a quality I admire. Either way, there are plenty of reasons your prints might be on Kassidy's knife."

I throw a sharp glance at her. "You know it's not hers. What if they ask you to testify in court?"

"In what court?" she says. "Kassidy is missing. If she stays missing, she will be presumed dead. There's no reason to try a dead person in a criminal court. And besides, you couldn't bring yourself to harm Blaine. Violent threats are not ideal, but sometimes we must do what we'd rather not to protect our families. We have plenty of evidence against your friend—the confession just confirms what we already know. This case will be closed, and there will be no reason to investigate further."

I can't even bring myself to be relieved. Kassidy is dead because she knew me. Because in the first week of high school she decided we would be best friends and so we were. Because she always tried to save and protect the weak. Because she was good.

But even good people can snap when they're pushed too far into misery.

"Did you always know it was Kassidy?" I ask.

"I thought it was likely," says Pilar de León. "The only thing that stumped me was how she could have exited a locked door.

I thought perhaps she had taken the key while you were in the bath and you'd underestimated how deeply you slept in the tub. But then the staff told me about the secret servants' passages.

"The timeline was cleanest if she did it—it would mean Blaine was killed when he was recently out of the shower. Fergus and Ellison had alibis for that time period, and it seemed unlikely the girl who wanted to hurt Blaine with itching powder would upgrade to murder. And Marlowe—if you'll excuse the slight to Kassidy—would have been much cleverer. Like you said yesterday, this was a crime of passion, and Marlowe is a thoughtful, measured young man, more disposed to premeditated action."

"Why didn't you think it was me?"

"You were the second-best suspect," she admits. "I hate to say that my connection to your family probably swayed me against you more than I desired. But your devotion to Kassidy was clear from the first moment I saw you together. I thought it was unlikely you'd murdered her boyfriend at a celebration she'd planned based on your love of the 1920s. I knew you'd done something—guilt was written on your face in every interview, and then there was the fact that your fingerprints were found inside Blaine's armoire." She stops. "I assume *you* were the noise Marlowe heard the night he searched for his cuff link?"

I nod. "I wanted to sneak my knife out of Blaine's pants, but it was gone. Marlowe surprised me coming out of the room, and I hid in the armoire."

"Detective Cates thought the prints were strong evidence against you," says Pilar de León. "I thought you were hiding an affair or another indiscretion. But once we found the diamond from Kassidy's bracelet in Blaine's wound, you became a less likely suspect. Kassidy told us none of the period clothes or accessories she'd brought for everyone had diamonds."

"Did you know Kassidy would . . . disappear?"

Pilar de León sighs heavily. "I was very concerned about her mental state. One reason I placed Detective Cates in front of the library door was so no one could leave, even after I'd announced the resolution of the investigation. I didn't want Kassidy to have the chance to do what I think she did. I couldn't predict, of course, that the storm would crash through the house."

A flock of birds soars low over the water. "In old books, the detectives let the murderers kill themselves as an act of mercy," I say.

"That's because the death penalty hangs over their heads," she says gently. "Your friend's life would have been tainted, but it still had value."

We're silent for a while, until Pilar de León clears her throat. "I'm afraid I have some other unpleasant news. An anonymous tip has been received by the Harker Police Department hotline, alleging an affair between a teacher and student at Marian Academy. Your mother has been named as the teacher."

"I see," I say. I'd been wondering when that particular shoe would drop.

"It was brave of you to make the report," she says. "Especially knowing what it means for you and Caye."

"Marlowe helped me realize I couldn't let my mom escape the consequences of her crime," I say. "What if she did it again with other students in the future? I couldn't have that on my conscience." Tears well in the corners of my eyes. "Besides, I owed it to Blaine. If I'd reported my mom earlier and told

Kassidy the truth, he would be alive right now. I'll have to live with that guilt forever." I chew the inside of my cheek. "What will happen to my mom?"

"A warrant will be issued and served this week. Blaine was seventeen when the affair started, and his family is wealthy and connected, so she'll almost certainly go to prison. She may receive a light sentence, though, since she's the primary caretaker of a disabled child."

"I'll be applying for guardianship," I say. "My mom doesn't deserve to parent Caye. She kidnapped us away from our dad. It's going to be hard, but I can take care of Caye without her."

Pilar de León watches the seabirds following the ferry. "I talked to Noemí this morning," she says. "Your father had a small life insurance policy that named you and Caye as beneficiaries. It could help you get by for a few years. Noemí said she'd be thrilled to host you and Caye for as long as you'd like. There's a university in the next city over, and I know many doctors who would handle Caye's care as a personal favor to me." She shakes her head. "It's the least I can do after failing to find my friend's family for so long."

The tears begin to fall down my face. It's funny: After four years of holding them back, now I can't seem to stop them.

Pilar de León pats my hand. "Think about it."

Soon after she leaves, the ferry doors slide open again. Marlowe stands there, hovering in the doorway.

"I wasn't sure you wanted to see anyone," he says when I wave him over.

"I want to see you."

He sits close to me, his body warm and heavy against mine.

"I can't imagine what you must be feeling," he says.

There's a question I've been wanting to ask him since the first night at Ashwood Manor. "How did you know about Blaine and my mom?"

He frowns. "I was studying one night and realized I'd forgotten a book in my locker. I went to Marian and saw them together in her classroom. They thought the school was deserted that late. You changed too. You stopped speaking in class and acted cold to your mom in the halls. So I assumed you knew as well."

"I found a stash of letters and pictures hidden in her pillowcase when I was cleaning," I say. "I've never been so disgusted. They met up at my apartment during editorial staff meetings."

"I'm so sorry all this is happening to you," he says, folding my hand into his. "It's more than anyone should have to bear."

Then I tell him the whole story—about Pilar de León and my aunt and my dad. "Pilar de León told me they're going to arrest my mom this week," I say. "I don't know how I'm going to face her."

"Do you want me to go back to your apartment with you?"

I stare at Marlowe. "You'd do that?"

"Of course." He squeezes my hand. "This summer is going to be hard, but I'll be here. Whatever you need."

"Noemí told Pilar de León that Caye and I can move to Mexico and live with her." A thrill runs through me saying it aloud.

"That's amazing, Isadora. Do you think you'll do it?"

"I don't know," I say. "I've spent so much time trying to leave my upbringing behind and be like the rest of you I'm not sure I've ever considered what *I* really want." I shiver. "The idea of starting classes in September, so soon after losing Kass, is impossible. Maybe if I get away from these nightmares, I can start to dream again. I know that's what Kass would have wanted."

"I think a fresh start is a wonderful idea," says Marlowe.

"Any interest in visiting Mexico?"

He grins. "Have I mentioned I qualified for my pilot's license last month?"

I roll my eyes. "And of course your family has a private plane."

"Tell me when you want me there, and I'll fly down," he says, nuzzling my cheek.

"If I even go."

"I think you will."

For the first time since I walked away from Kassidy on the bluff, I feel light. "I think I will too."

ACKNOWLEDGMENTS

———◆———

One cold night in Chicago, I trudged through ice and snow to buy *Breaking Dawn* at a bookstore on the Magnificent Mile. I'd spent the previous week devouring the first three Twilight books instead of studying for finals, and I wasn't about to let weather or my grim pile of legal textbooks stand in the way of finishing the series. Over the next decade, I would read many books when I was supposed to be doing other things. And time after time, one name appeared at the end of the young adult novels I loved most: Jodi Reamer. When I say she was my dream agent, I really mean she was my daydream agent—the person I thought of in those starry-eyed moments when I imagined strangers reading my words.

Jodi, I feel nothing but "pinch me" luck that you loved my manuscript, and I can't thank you enough for expertly guiding me through the many steps of publication.

A special thanks to Rey Lalaoui, who pulled my query from slush—your work changes lives, and you certainly changed mine.

If I'd known editors like Polo Orozco existed, he would have gotten his own daydream. Saying he has a keen eye doesn't begin to convey how essential he was to shaping these pages.

Polo, your hard work and gracious optimism made the editing process a joy.

There are so many other talented people I have the privilege to thank. Alessandra Birch and Cecilia de la Campa, whose foreign rights savvy means this story will travel farther than I ever will. Cindy Howle, Misha Kydd, Jennifer Baker, and Elizabeth Johnson, who polished the manuscript until it shone. Artist Vasya Kolotusha and designer Kaitlin Yang, who created such a striking and vibrant cover. Eileen Savage, who designed the interior. Managing editor Natalie Vielkind and production manager Amanda Cranney at Penguin Young Readers. And everyone else in the Penguin universe, including the teams of Jen Loja, Jen Klonsky, Shanta Newlin, Elyse Marshall, Emily Romero, Christina Colangelo, Alex Garber, Carmela Iaria, Helen Boomer, and Kim Ryan.

Thanks to my parents, Jeff and Susan Muñoz, for filling my childhood with books and for encouraging me to wander off the path of a traditional career. To Erin Muñoz, for reading endless first chapters of stories that will never be published and entire books that will. And to Adrienne Muñoz, for being sunshine in a sea of clouds.

Thanks to my early readers: Megan Sibley, Michele Strohfus, and Nikki Freyre and family. Thanks to MCB for believing in me so wholeheartedly all those years ago. Infinite thanks to Kevin Beverage, from Pyramus to present, for your thoughtful guidance on all things writing (and all things not).

And to Kevin Rix, who gave me the best gift of all: time. Te amo.

HOT KEY BOOKS

Thank you for choosing a Hot Key book.

If you want to know more about our authors
and what we publish, you can find us online.

You can start at our website

www.hotkeybooks.com

And you can also find us on:

We hope to see you soon!